SURRENDER

D1475556

Books by Tawny Taylor

"Stark Pleasure" in *Yes, Master*

Darkest Desire

Dangerous Master

Darkest Fire

Decadent Master

Wicked Beast

Dark Master

Real Vamps Don't Drink O-Neg

Sex and the Single Ghost

SURRENDER

TAWNY TAYLOR

APHRODISIA
KENSINGTON PUBLISHING CORP.
www.kensingtonbooks.com

APHRODISIA BOOKS are published by

Kensington Publishing Corp.
119 West 40th Street
New York, NY 10018

All Kensington titles, imprints, and distributed lines are available at special quantity discounts for bulk purchases for sales promotion, premiums, fund-raising, educational, or institutional use.

Special book excerpts or customized printings can also be created to fit specific needs. For details, write or phone the office of the Kensington Special Sales Manager: Kensington Publishing Corp., 119 West 40th Street, New York, NY 10018. Attn. Special Sales Department. Phone: 1-800-221-2647.

Aphrodisia and the A logo Reg. U.S. Pat. & TM Off.

ISBN-13: 978-0-7582-9030-4
ISBN-10: 0-7582-9030-6
First Kensington Trade Paperback Printing: June 2014

eISBN-13: 978-0-7582-9031-1
eISBN-10: 0-7582-9031-4
First Kensington Electronic Edition: June 2014

10 9 8 7 6 5 4 3 2 1

Printed in the United States of America

For David

Acknowledgments

A special thank you to my awesome editor, Martin Biro. Martin, you're the best!

1

I closed my eyes. I pulled in a long, deep breath. I exhaled. My mind was racing, images flashing behind my eyelids.

Those eyes.

The sharp blade of a nose.

The chiseled jaw.

Those lips.

Those lips.

My heart was pounding. Hard. I felt a little dizzy.

I hadn't even talked to him yet. How would I ever convince him not to throw my baby brother in jail?

Pull it together, girl.

Twenty-three. Twenty. Three. That was how many times I'd heard Joss say, "Abby, I'm in trouble. Big trouble," since our father died. Twenty-freaking-three times too many.

I knew Joss could pull through his crap and get himself together, so I shouldn't have bothered stepping in to drag him out of one scrape after another. But I did. Because, despite his long, difficult struggle with addiction, Joss was a good person. He didn't go out of his way looking for trouble. Trouble seemed to always come looking for him.

And this time there might not be anything I could do about it.

Breathe.

If Kameron Maldonado, owner of MalTech Corporation, decided to report my brother's alleged crime to the police, he could end up in jail. For years.

My brother. A felon.

Breathe.

My brother. In prison.

Breathe.

The only family I had left, gone.

Breathe.

My sweating palms were sticking to the leather couch. I dragged them down my thighs. My scratchy polyester skirt wasn't going to dry them. But I wiped my hands on it anyway. When I heard the door to my right rattle a little, my heart skipped a beat. I jerked my head, glancing at it, then at the young woman sitting behind the reception desk directly in front of me. She was staring at a computer screen.

I glanced at my watch. Twelve twenty-five. I'd been sitting here for almost a half hour. My appointment had been at twelve.

God, this was torture.

The doorknob rattled again, and once more panic charged through my body. My head spun. The door swung open, and my breath caught in my throat.

Kameron Maldonado stepped out, moving out of the doorway. He was smiling over his shoulder at the man behind him. "We'll get together later this week to talk about the details. Thanks." Kameron extended a hand, and the man shook it.

The visitor returned Kameron's thank you and then, as he passed me, gave me a fleeting look before waving good-bye to the receptionist.

I turned my attention back to Kameron. He was standing next to the door, looking at me.

"Abigail Barnes?" he asked.

I nodded, stood on wobbly legs that felt boneless and heavy. Not expecting a handshake, but preparing for one anyway, I dragged my palms down my legs again as I shuffled toward his office.

After a quick, formal introduction and a brief handshake, Kameron closed his door behind me, circled his desk, and stood, waiting for me to sit in the chair facing him.

My stomach twisted.

Of all the situations Joss had put himself in, this was by far the worst. He had put not only his job in jeopardy, but mine too. Somehow I had to convince this man not to fire us both.

I sat, back straight, body stiff, heart thumping so hard I could hear it.

"How can I help you, Mrs. Barnes?"

"Miss," I corrected. My mouth was dry. I licked my lips, but that did nothing to help. My tongue was as dry as the Sahara.

He nodded. "Miss Barnes."

"I'm here on the behalf of Joss Barnes. My brother." A huge lump of something coagulated in my throat. I tried to swallow it. It didn't budge. I tried again.

Kameron's brows lifted. "Are you all right, Miss Barnes?"

Swallowing a third time, I nodded.

He stood, strolled to the cabinet recessed into the wall behind me, and opened a door. Within a second, he was standing over me, a cold bottle of water in his hand.

I accepted with a weak "Thank you," unscrewed the cap, and sipped.

"Better?" he asked as he leaned back against his desk.

I nodded.

Looming over me, he crossed his thick arms. God, he was big. Intimidating. Extremely intimidating.

"Your brother is in serious trouble, Miss Barnes. If what I heard is true, he not only violated more than one clause of his employment contract, but also broke the law. I was told he stole company property and sold it. I can't let that go with a warning."

We were so screwed.

Feeling utterly defeated, I nodded. "I understand." My nose was starting to burn. Dammit. This was just too much. It was all too much. Our father's death. Mom's disappearance. And my brother's rebellion and addiction. I was a fighter. I was a survivor. If I hadn't been, my brother and I wouldn't be where we were today. But I was too young to deal with this much crap. Every time things started to turn around, something new would come up and drag me right back down into the gutter.

When would life stop kicking me around? When?

My hands were shaking as I lifted them to drag my thumbs under my eyelashes. My eyes were burning now too. A sob was sitting in the pit of my stomach, but I was holding it in. Holding my breath.

I needed to get out of there. I couldn't cry in front of this man. No. *No-no-no.* I stood too fast and felt myself stumble. He caught me, hands clamped around my upper arms. Our gazes locked.

Something really strange happened. A crazy, unexpected bolt of electricity charged through my body. I heard myself gasp.

His eyes widened slightly. "Don't go." He gently forced me back into the chair. "I haven't finished yet."

What was there left to say? Was there any chance he was going to help me?

Afraid to hope anything decent could come out of this mess, I nodded and waited.

He released me, stared down, arms crossed over his chest once again. "Your brother has put me in a hell of a position."

"Is there anything I can do?" I asked, my voice cracking.

His eyes narrowed slightly. He tipped his head to the right. "Why? Why are you so willing to put your neck on the line for him?"

What kind of silly question was that? "He's my brother."

"But he just about got you thrown out of here. You understand that, don't you?"

Just about?

Just about!

I wasn't fired yet.

"Yes, sir. I do," I said, screwing and unscrewing the cap on the water bottle I clasped in my hand. "If my brother was a complete lost cause, I wouldn't have bothered trying to help him. I would've let you fire him. Hell, I would have stood by and watched him be arrested, too. But I can't. Because I know there's more to this situation than you and I know. He's not a bad guy. Sure, he's hit a bump or two lately. He'll get it figured out."

"Maybe you're right. Maybe there is more to this situation than we know. But, say he is guilty. What do I do with him until I figure out what really happened?"

"Good question."

"If he did do it, how could I risk keeping him on, knowing he might steal something else?"

"Another good question."

Leaning closer, he placed one hand on each arm of my chair, trapping me. I felt myself pushing back into the chair. I could smell his cologne, could see the flecks of silver-blue in dark, dark gray-brown eyes—the color of my favorite chocolates. I could feel the warm caress of his breath on my face.

My heart jerked again. But this time it wasn't because I was afraid. No, I was . . . warm. I was breathless. I was staring at his lips and wondering what they might taste like.

What was going on?

"How long have you been working for us, Miss Barnes?"

"T-two years," I stuttered, my gaze locked on his mouth. What was he getting at? What was he thinking?

"Hmmm."

My gaze inched up, following the line of his aristocratic nose to those dark eyes again. I saw something there, the flicker of something obscure, something wicked. My heart rate tripled, quadrupled, maybe. "Sir? Please don't fire me. My job is our primary source of income. Our father died. It's been really hard on us both, but especially Joss. He was only thirteen and a boy with no father—"

He leaned closer. "I'm sorry about your father." I was trapped, his body like a big wall hovering over me. Why was he standing so close? Why was he looking at me like *that?*

"Sir?" I murmured when he inched even closer. I'd never had a boss act this way with me before. If I didn't know better, I would swear he was . . . he was . . .

His head dipped down. Now, his mouth was hovering over mine. Not inches. No. It was a tiny fraction of an inch from mine. His breath softly caressed my lips. Warm. Sweet.

Was he going to kiss me?

Was he expecting some kind of bribe? A payment in return for my job?

I was frozen. Shocked. Unable to move. Unwilling to move. It was wrong for him to use his position to try something like this. Wrong. Illegal. Unethical. Immoral.

But, wow, was he a beautiful man. Sexy. Intelligent. Mysterious. I wanted him to kiss me. My lips were tingling already, and he hadn't even touched them yet. My blood was pounding hard through my body, too. My heart was slamming against my breastbone. I let my eyelids fall shut, enclosing myself in darkness and swirls of red.

"Miss Barnes?"

"Sir?" Something soft brushed against my lips. And again. Little sparks of electricity sizzled and zapped under my skin.

Heat whooshed through my body, up to my face, down between my legs.

The intensity of my body's reaction took my breath away. And still I couldn't move. A crazy impulse popped into my head. I wanted to throw my arms around his neck, tangle my fingers in his silky hair, and pull him to me.

I can't do that. I can't.

"I'm not going to fire you," he whispered. As he spoke, his lips grazed mine. The touches were minute, almost imperceptible. And yet the effect was mind-blowing. I wanted more. I needed more. A real kiss. Lips. Tongue. Teeth. Full body contact.

"Thank you." I shuddered. My fingers wrapped around the seat of the chair.

"Before you thank me, you need to know one thing."

"Yes?"

His mouth claimed mine. At last. And ohmygod, what a kiss it was. It started out smooth and gentle, a slow, patient seduction. But within seconds, his tongue traced the seam of my mouth. And once I opened to him, I was swept up into a wild, thrashing world of carnal need. His tongue stroked and stabbed, possessed. His hands cupped my face, holding me captive. I couldn't escape. I didn't want to escape. I craved more.

A moan swept up my throat, echoing in our joined mouths. Finally able to move, I lifted my hands, sliding them up his arms. I could feel the bulge of thick muscles under his crisp, starched dress shirt. They moved over his wide shoulders. My fingertips brushed silky curls at his nape.

Ohmygod, what was I doing? Kameron Maldonado was kissing me. The owner of the company! His tongue was stroking mine. One of his hands gliding down the column of my neck. The other slid to the back of my head. My scalp stung as he fisted a handful of my hair and pulled, forcing my head to one side.

He growled.

I groaned and licked my lips. They tasted like him. Sweet. Delicious. The swirls behind my eyelids were spinning now, and my heart was doing leaps in my chest.

His tongue flicked along the pounding pulse beating beneath my skin, down my neck to the ticklish spot at the crook. There he nipped me, and a shock wave of heat blazed down my body. Goose bumps coated my right arm. My nipples hardened.

Inside my head, I just kept saying, *Ohmygod, ohmygod, ohmygod.* I was lost in sensation, overcome with need. Eager to feel his weight and heat pressing against me, I pulled. But he didn't budge. The hand that had been at my neck inched lower, the palm sliding down to cover my breast. I whimpered, arched my back, pushing into his touch.

"Miss Barnes, you don't have to do this to keep your job," he murmured against my neck.

"I . . . I know." I didn't really know anything. I had no clue what this meant. I had no idea what would happen after it ended. But I did know I wanted what was happening and wished it would never end.

He kneaded my breast through my clothes, and I bit my lip, stifling a cry. "I want you," he said.

"I . . . I want you, too."

"No." He palmed my face. "Open your eyes."

I did as he asked, and my breath left my lungs in a soft huff. Wow, was he sexy. His hair was slightly messy, the curls a little unruly and wild. I'd never spoken to this man before. I'd only seen pictures of him down in the company cafeteria. In the pictures he looked good, but not anywhere as amazing as he did right now.

"I want you to be my assistant."

Was he offering me a promotion? And if he was, what kinds of strings were attached? There had to be strings.

"I . . . don't understand," I admitted.

"I'm offering you a job. You'll be my assistant. You'll be paid a salary that should meet your needs, and you'll have access to a company car, expense account, and business phone. But there is one condition, a fairly significant one."

I could imagine what that condition would be, considering where his hand was.

I felt the heat draining from my body as my brain started functioning. Reality was like a cold, hard slap to my face. It stung.

I would have to sleep with Kameron Maldonado. Not because I found him incredibly sexy. Not because I wanted to. But because I had to. I would be one of *those* women, the kind that fucked their bosses to get a job.

Me. Pretty-but-not-beautiful me.

I'd never, ever thought I would even consider such a proposition. For one thing, I'd never expected to have something like this come up. I wasn't a perfect ten. With a chest that was a little too small and hips a little too wide, eyes a little too big and wide-set and a jaw a little too narrow, I wasn't exactly Playboy Playmate material.

But it seemed Kameron Maldonado didn't care. . . .

"What about my brother?" I asked.

"He's going to be let go. But I won't report what he did to the police or to my associates. It'll be kept between you and me. This is why I need you working as my assistant. Depending upon the fallout, I may need your help."

"I'll do anything I can to help."

"Good. I expected you to say that. And, as far as that condition I mentioned . . ." His hand inched down my stomach, stopping just above my pubic bone. "I'm accustomed to getting exactly what I want, when I want."

Despite the fact that I was so aroused, my panties were sodden, I whispered, somewhat coolly, "In other words, to keep my job, I have to sleep with you?"

"No, you'll sleep with me because you want to. I won't ask you to do that. I'll only ask you to allow me the liberty to touch you whenever, however, and wherever I want."

That was some "condition." But it wasn't exactly what I'd expected. By having pulled the actual act of intercourse off the table, Kameron had made it a little more palatable to me. I wouldn't be forced to have sex with him. Though I could almost believe he was telling the truth when he said I would want to. The way he touched me made me melt. What girl could resist?

After a few moments I nodded. "You have yourself a new assistant."

"Very good." The hand that had been resting, hot but softly, above my mound wandered down my thigh. It found the hem of my skirt. "Open your legs for me."

The way he'd said that made me melt, his voice husky. So, so sexy.

My face burning, I parted my knees slightly and watched as his gaze inched down my body. He placed one hand on each of my knees.

"Wider, Abigail."

Oh God.

I moved them wider apart.

He shook his head. "Lift your hips." He slid his hands under my butt and raised it off the chair. Then he pushed my skirt up and forced me back onto the chair. Now I was sitting there with my skirt wadded up around my waist and only a pair of cotton panties between his eyes and my most private parts.

What would he do next?

Hands on my knees, he pushed so they were opened in a wide vee. He visibly inhaled. "You smell so good, Abigail."

My insides clenched. I felt a gush of liquid heat saturate the crotch of my panties. Already I was aching for him to touch me there, to slip a finger into my aching center and stroke. I couldn't believe it. A throbbing need was building deep inside. With every second that passed it was getting worse.

I reached down, but he knocked my hand away. "A couple of ground rules. First, I can touch you. How I want. When I want. Where I want. You may not touch me without express permission to do so. Do you understand?"

That was a strange rule.

"Yes," I said.

"Good. Hands down. Where they were."

I curled my fingers around the edge of the chair's seat.

He placed a single index finger on my thigh. One little fingertip, and oh so slowly it wandered up, up, up. My insides did triple flips when it reached the crease between my inner thigh and pussy lips.

Every cell in my body wanted that finger to keep going, to dip into my center. Instead, it circled around the places that ached the most for his touch, skimming over my skin, leaving a trail of tingling need.

"Are you a virgin?" he asked.

My face burned. "No. I've . . . I've had sex."

"How many partners?"

I was mortified by his question. What did that matter, how many? Did I really have to admit that I was almost as inexperienced as a virgin? I started to pull my knees together, but he stopped me, holding me wide open. "No, you won't hide from me. Not your body. Not your past. I want to know everything about you. Every secret."

A frigid chill raced up my spine. "That wasn't part of our deal," I snapped.

He laughed. It was a deep, throaty guffaw, accompanied by sparkles in his eyes that made him look young and alive. The sound reverberated through my body, amplifying my agony.

"Tell me what I want and you'll receive a reward. A very nice one." His gaze flicked to the part of me that burned for his touch. "There is a valid reason why I asked."

"I . . ."

The finger that had been tormenting me started wandering again. "You . . . ?"

Embarrassed, I glanced away, focusing on the wall directly behind his desk. "I've had two partners. Two."

"Only two?"

"Only two," I repeated.

Did he have to make this more mortifying? Wasn't it bad enough that I'd had to admit I was practically a virgin at my age? I had a very good reason for my lack of experience. And it had nothing to do with a lack of opportunity. Men did want me. Well . . . okay, so they weren't beating down my door. But I'd always considered that a blessing. Trusting men didn't come naturally to me.

This situation wasn't exactly helping matters.

And yet, here I was, letting a man I barely knew blackmail me into letting him touch me, toy with me, seduce me. Why?

That fingertip pushed against my pussy, easing between my swollen tissues. The cotton between his skin and mine pulled against me as he pushed harder. The pressure felt so good against my hard clit. Fresh waves of heat rippled through me.

I could swear I was going to combust.

I shouldn't be so hot, so needy.

I whimpered, legs spreading wider, thighs burning. A part of me wanted to tear those panties away and beg him to take me. Another wanted to clamp my legs closed and go hide somewhere until my brain started working again. This was crazy. This was insanity. I was playing with fire. I'd been burned before. I had a feeling that was nothing compared to what would happen if I let this . . . whatever this was with Kameron Maldonado . . . happen. I was making a mistake. A big one.

But, oh God, I couldn't seem to stop myself.

His phone rang, and I jerked hard. He smiled, brushed his lips against mine, trailed his finger over my sodden panties, and straightened up. "I'll leave you to go pack up your desk. You'll be moving into your new office tomorrow."

"I . . ."

"That'll be all for now. Thank you, Miss Barnes."

My brain was spinning as I stood and pulled my skirt down over my soggy panties. Barely able to walk, I shuffled to the door and let myself out.

I swore I saw the girl at the reception desk smile ever so slightly as I pretended not to stagger toward the elevator.

How many flush-faced women had she watched stumble out of Kameron Maldonado's office before me?

How many women would she see stumble out of his office after me?

Was I making the mistake of a lifetime?

2

The next morning I was a nervous wreck as I drove to work. Before the thing with my brother, I'd loved my job at MalTech. As an administrator in the purchasing department, I knew what I'd be facing every day. I had a routine. I liked routines. With what happened yesterday, I had no idea what to expect today. The unexpected made me nauseous.

I parked in my usual spot. That gave me a tiny measure of comfort. Very small. Minuscule. Just like I had every weekday for the past year, I walked into the building, waved at the receptionist at the desk in the lobby and went to the elevators. But this time, instead of hitting the button for the third floor, I hit the one for the tenth.

I tugged on the hem of my skirt as I waited.

When the bell rang, I had a mini panic attack. I stepped into the car, moved to the back to let in the other five people who'd been waiting with me, and tried to pretend I didn't feel as if I was going to be sick at any moment. Up we went, stopping at each floor, picking up riders, losing others. Once we cleared the eighth level, I was alone.

As the elevator rumbled upward, my heart started pounding hard in my chest, and I felt a little lightheaded. When the car eased to a stop, I held on to the handgrip behind me and counted to ten. The door whooshed open, and within seconds I was in the reception area. The young, attractive brunette at the desk glanced up, saw me, and said, "Miss Barnes. I'm Stephanie. Congratulations on the new position."

"Thanks." I returned her smile. "Abby."

"Abby." Stephanie nodded toward the door. "Mr. Maldonado's expecting you. Go on in."

Oh God.

I sucked in a deep breath and started walking. My knees felt soft, like they were made of gelatin. I pushed open the door.

He was sitting at his desk, talking on the phone. He motioned for me to close the door, which I did. Then I shuffled up to stand in front of his desk.

"That's fine," he said to the person on the phone. He was looking at me, his gaze assessing. Up and down. "Good. We'll nail down the details in the next couple of days." As he paused to listen, he licked his lips. I'd never seen a man lick his lips like that, so sexy. "Nope. That's it. Thank you. I'll talk to you tomorrow." He ended the call, stood, smiled. "Good morning, Miss Barnes."

"Good morning."

"Sir," he enunciated. His hands were clasped behind his back. For some reason, this made me feel a little less threatened. "You'll call me *sir*. I appreciate formality. There's a time and place for it."

Ah, so the man had a thing for power. "Yes, sir," I repeated.

Yesterday, I'd been desperate, shaken, scared. I had agreed to his ridiculous terms because I had felt trapped. But after I had left, I started to think about it, and the more I thought about it, the more this whole thing irritated me.

How dare this man, who had probably never known what it felt like to be at another man's mercy, use his position to manipulate me. I was a human being. With some self-respect. And morals. I was not a hooker. I was not a whore.

He circled me. I felt his gaze on me. Despite my growing ire, my skin warmed. On my nape, my arms, my back, and, once he'd made it back around to my front, my face. "This outfit is acceptable, though it's a little old-fashioned."

His words grated. So now he was going to tell me what to wear? Really? "Sir, it's what I can afford—"

"You can afford better now. This will get you started. Buy quality pieces." He reached into his pocket, pulled out a money clip full of bills, and peeled off a few. He handed them to me. I didn't look to see what denomination they were. I didn't care. Because I wasn't going to take his damn money. What a jerk. I wasn't a charity case. And I wasn't a dumb floozy who would swoon at the sight of a couple of hundred dollar bills. Though that money could come in mighty handy right now. But not for stupid clothes.

Clothes! Sheesh.

I jerked up my chin and thrust the hand holding the money back at him. "I will decide when I need to buy some new clothes, thank you."

He waved his hands, stepping out of my reach. "Fine. Do what you want with the money. Consider it a signing bonus."

I didn't like this, and I let my new stubborn boss know it by giving him a squinty glare.

He chuckled, and his eyes sparkled. "You'll earn every penny. And it won't be doing what you think. I can be a real pain in the ass to work for. Literally." He motioned for me to follow him across the room. He stopped at the door positioned directly across from his desk and opened it. "This is your office. It is only accessible through my office. And only you and

I will be permitted to enter it. Everything you need should be here. If not, let me know. You can get settled later."

The room was pretty big, with all the essentials—a sleek desk, file cabinets, a comfy-looking chair, and a wide window that brought in plenty of light, even with the shades drawn. But it lacked warmth, personality. The walls were pristine white. No art. Nothing personal anywhere. It felt institutional. I would need to change that. For the time being, I set my purse on the desk and shoved the *signing bonus* in the front pocket.

"Now . . ." He circled back around to his desk, sat, motioned to the chair in front of him. As I was taking a seat, he pulled a small bound notebook out of a drawer and set it, and a pen, on the desktop in front of me. "Enough of that. Let's get to work." After waiting for me to flip to a blank page, he began, "This morning, I have a ten o'clock appointment. . . ."

By noon, I did feel slightly justified in accepting the so-called signing bonus. Slightly. As it turned out, it had been roughly the equivalent of a month's salary at my old pay scale. A whole freaking month. I'd been living on that much money all this time, and now my new boss expected me to spend that sum, every penny—he'd made that crystal clear—on clothes, shoes, a new haircut, and makeup.

But there was a valid reason for his request. In his words, he needed me looking polished, chic, and professional since I would sometimes be accompanying him on business trips or to charity functions. It would seem that I would be hobnobbing with the rich on a regular basis, and he didn't want me to be embarrassed or humiliated.

While I had prided myself in dressing well for what I could afford, even I had to admit my clothes were second rate when compared to the luxurious designer garments his business associates would be wearing. If I wore my perfectly respectable

Jaclyn Smith suit to an event, I would get all kinds of attention, for all the wrong reasons.

Thus, I was ready to head to the mall during my lunch hour and spend some of that cash. Conveniently, the mall where I used to window shop was a five-minute walk away. In an hour I could spend at least a thousand or so. On a mission, and thinking I'd do myself a favor not eating anything during my lunch break, I grabbed my purse from my shiny new desk, and opened the connecting door to his office.

I was stopped dead in my tracks by one very big man. He was blocking my exit with his hulking body.

A shiver raced through me. It was followed by a little blaze of anger.

"Where are you going?" he asked.

"I was heading out to do some shopping on my lunch hour, like you suggested, *sir.*"

"That's a fine idea. Unfortunately, I made other plans for you." He forced me back into my space and shut the door behind him.

From the dark glitter in his eyes, I had a feeling he wasn't thinking about splitting a submarine sandwich.

Fuming a little, and confused, and conflicted, I stood frozen in place, my purse hugged to my chest as he sauntered over, cupped my chin, and lifted it. "I've been thinking about those lips all morning."

A little tremor quaked through me at the heat in his eyes.

"I . . . I . . ."

"Shhh." He leaned down, brushed his lips across mine. It was hardly a kiss at all, a soft touch, fleeting. A tease. He took my purse out of my hands, set it on my desk. "Come here." He led me to my chair and, hands on my shoulders, forced me into it. Now he was looming over me once again, looking bigger and more powerful than ever. I felt small and vulnerable, unsure what he expected. Unsure what would happen next.

This was so wrong, him manipulating me like this, forcing me to do things. Treating me like a toy that he could play with whenever he pleased.

"Open your legs, Abigail." He eased to his knees, which put us on more equal levels.

My knee-jerk response was to grit my teeth and refuse. What would he do? Would he really fire me? If he did, what would be the reason he would give? He certainly couldn't put "failure to allow me to sexually harass her" in my file.

His brows drew together. "I thought we had an agreement."

"Yes, well. We did. But I thought about it last night, and I have some issues—"

"Part your legs. Now."

Jerk!

His tone raked along my nerves, making my inner rebel dig in her heels. "You said you wouldn't force me."

"I said I would be permitted to touch you when and wherever I wanted."

Glaring now, I snapped, "What kind of man does that to his employees? What kind of man has to blackmail women into being his sex slave?"

"You are not my sex slave." He grabbed my chin. "Though I think you'd love that, being my sex slave."

"Don't you wish."

He laughed again. Yesterday, my body had responded to the low rumble of his laugh, warming, softening. And I liked the way his eyes glittered. Not today. Today the sound made my blood turn to ice. "You have more spirit than I thought. I like a challenge."

"You're in for one hell of a challenge, sir."

"Good." Standing upright again, he stared down at me,

silent, eyes calculating. "I will give you two choices. Open your legs or leave."

"Fine. I'll leave." I started to push out of my chair.

But before I got my butt completely off the seat, he added, "For good. You're out. Do you understand?"

Asshole! I hated him. Even though he made my body burn and quake. Even though I had dreamed about him all night long. Even though the thought of him touching me again made me breathless.

"What kind of game is this?" I smacked the arms of the chair.

"It's a good game. A fun one. You'll like it. You'll see. Before you know it, I won't have to threaten you. You'll want to do what I ask."

"Like the others?" I had heard the rumors. Plenty of them. About him sleeping with employees. Oddly, I'd dismissed them all, thinking no business owner would risk a sexual harassment lawsuit in this day and age. Silly, stupid me.

His lips curled. "Perhaps."

So he had done this to his other assistants. This was his thing. Bastard. Asshole.

Dammit, I was so stuck.

How I wanted to leave! I wanted to tell him to go to hell, get my purse, and head to the nearest police station to report him for sexual harassment.

But I couldn't.

I couldn't report him, because he'd report Joss, and at this point, I didn't know exactly what Joss had, and had not, done.

I couldn't walk out because our rent was due and I didn't have the money to pay it. It had taken me so long to find the job at MalTech. And since then, the economy hadn't gotten any better. In fact, around here, it had gotten worse. If I walked out today, I would be unemployed, with nothing to fall back on.

Not even unemployment.

I couldn't even tell the bastard to go to hell. And, judging by the curve of his lips, he knew it.

His gaze flicked to my knees.

Vowing to start hunting for a new job ASAP, I parted them a tiny bit.

"More."

Dammit.

Face burning, I inched them open a little more.

He bent at the waist and used his hands on my knees to push them wider. As my thighs parted, my pencil skirt strained. He jammed it up, lifting my ass off the seat to clear it out from under me. "Now, that's better." His gaze meandered down my body, stopping at the juncture of my thighs where my black satin panties were getting damp, despite my conflicting emotions. "I like these." Just as he had yesterday, he teased my tissues through the material with his finger. But this time he found the hard little nub pulsing with heat and rubbed it. His lips softly caressed mine.

Oh, this was so wrong. Wrong, wrong, wrong! But suddenly I didn't care. It felt so good being touched by such a gorgeous man, such a powerful man.

A wave of need swept through me, and I felt my thighs tensing, my legs pulling wider apart.

"Hmmm. You're so responsive. Wet." He hooked his finger in the sodden material and pulled, and it tore away.

Shocked, angry, I jumped. He'd just ripped my panties. My panties. Mine! Those hadn't been cheap. I almost said something, then remembered the money sitting in my purse. He'd paid for plenty of pairs of panties. No doubt he figured he could rip them off all he wanted.

His finger eased into me, and a moan slipped from my lips.

All thought fled from my mind. And hot anger was instantly displaced by another kind of burning.

"Shhh." He added a second finger, slowly pushed them in, then pulled them out. In and out. In and out.

It was decadent pleasure, being stroked so intimately. God help me, I didn't want him to stop.

I closed my eyes, content to focus on all the other sensations charging through my body. As he leaned closer to nip my earlobe, the scent of his cologne filled my nose. I inhaled deeply, drinking in the tangy scent. When I licked my lips, trembling as my need grew, my mouth filled with the taste that was uniquely him. Sweet with a hint of mint. My skin burned where his lips touched me. My earlobe, the sensitive spot just below it. Even though he hadn't touched my breasts yet, my nipples were tingling, hardening into sharp little points.

I reached for him, laying my flattened hands on his chest. My fingertips traced the lines of his defined muscles through his cotton dress shirt. He was so hard and strong.

"I didn't tell you to touch me." He took my arms at the wrists and placed them on the chair's arms. Then, taking me by surprise, he pulled off his necktie and used it to tie one of them to the armrest.

"Hmmm," he said, glancing around the room. His gaze snapped to my open crotch, and he smiled. Leaning over me and slipping his hands under my buttocks, he eased my ass off the chair again. I felt him grab my panties at the waist. Down they went. Off my feet. And then he tore them again, creating a long strip of black satin. He used it to tie my other wrist.

He'd tied me up. I'd never been tied before.

His smile made my heart thump heavily, and simmering heat pooled between my legs.

He'd tied me up.

"Do you like this, Abigail? Do you like feeling powerless?"

I did.

I shook my head. His lips twitched, but he didn't smile. "I think we're going to get along just fine." A little rougher than before, he pushed my legs even wider apart. Using both hands, he pulled my wet flesh apart too, bent down, and dragged his tongue over my clit.

My spine arched and I thrust my hips up. Oh God, that felt so good.

He pushed me back down, then shoved two fingers inside me, thrusting them in and out roughly while his tongue flicked back and forth over my tingling nub. With every plunge of those fingers, my body burned hotter. My stomach tensed. My legs. My chest. Oh God, I was going to come.

A flare of heat blazed through me.

Yes, yes, yes!

He stopped, just as I was about to tumble over the precipice.

My heart was thumping, I was gasping, writhing. My eyes snapped open.

Why did he stop?

He was smiling. It was an evil expression, taunting. But in a playful way. "Frustrated a little?"

"No."

"Good. That's just a hint of what's to come. Now, let's get back to work. Your lunch break's over."

Cruel bastard!

I gritted my teeth as I watched him untie my wrists. My tissues were still burning, twitching, and wet. Now I had no panties. And I was still a little lightheaded from breathing so hard and from the endorphins that had been charging through my system like a mad rhino.

Not to mention, I was starving.

How would I concentrate?

Grumbling under my breath, I shuffled after my demanding

tease of a boss back out to his office. As he circled around his desk, I noticed there were cartons sitting on it. Foam ones. Restaurant carryout containers.

Oh God, someone had come into his office and placed those on his desk while he'd been tying me to my chair!

I was mortified at the thought that everyone would be whispering about the boss and me in my office, moaning and whimpering.

I slid a glance at the closed door. How much had they heard?

Kameron cleared his throat. "My receptionist is extremely trustworthy. She would never talk about anything she saw or heard. Never."

Why didn't that make me feel better? Was it because she would know I was doing something with the boss, something besides taking dictation or setting up appointments?

God, she would think I was one of *those* girls, whores who did their bosses to get ahead.

Suddenly, I wasn't so hungry anymore.

Oblivious to my guilt trip, Kameron was unwrapping the cartons. He placed one in front of me.

I thanked him, knowing I needed to act like this whole thing was okay for now. I had agreed to his terms. There was no backing out until I had another job lined up. I hadn't been 100 percent okay with the situation when it had been just the two of us in my office. And now that I was aware of at least one other person knowing, suddenly I felt even worse—dirty and ashamed.

The sooner I found another job, the better.

He was holding a fork in his hand, looking at me. "Eat. We need to get back to work."

I poked at a potato, popped it in my mouth. Chewed. Swallowed without tasting it.

"You've become quiet," he said as he studied me with those sharp, piercing eyes.

"I'm fine."

His gaze didn't leave my face. Not once as he ate, which made it that much harder for me to eat. "Is it Stephanie you're worried about?"

I shrugged.

"She's in no position to judge you."

"Meaning . . . you've tied her to her chair too?"

His lips quirked. "No. I've never done that with an employee before."

Now, that statement surprised me. Since he'd seemed so casual about our arrangement, and since he hadn't denied my earlier accusation that there had been others, I'd assumed he had done the same thing with at least one other assistant.

He tipped his head. "You're surprised."

"A little. You didn't—"

"I didn't deny having played these games with others," he finished for me.

"Why?" I asked, trying to understand. This man was odd. He did and said things that didn't make sense.

"I didn't deny it because I have played these kinds of games with others. But I didn't mean other employees." He leaned forward slightly. His eyes narrowed. "You don't like me very much, do you."

"Well . . ." I was treading in dangerous territory here. What Kameron had proposed wasn't respectable. In fact, it was grounds for a hefty lawsuit. He'd taken advantage of me, my dependency on my job, and my situation with my brother.

Angling back, he smiled. "You don't have to say it. Point taken."

I didn't want to hope that confession might spark a little

guilt, leading to him cutting me free of our deal, or at least certain elements of it.

"Why, then? Why'd you do it?" I asked. "If you haven't done this before, haven't crossed that line. Why did you do it to me?"

He studied me for a long moment. "I don't know. If someone had told me a few months ago that I would basically blackmail a woman into being my submissive, I would've—"

"Submissive?" I cut him off. "That word was never mentioned. What does that mean, your submissive?"

"I'm using the term loosely here, to mean you are being made to do whatever I ask, whenever I ask it, including performing certain sexual acts."

Submissive.

For some reason that term didn't bother me so much. It was better than office slut or prostitute for some reason.

Submissive.

"Is that what you truly expect from me? Am I your submissive?" I asked.

Once again, he didn't answer right away. "Yes. I'll draft a contract. We'll put it all in writing. Then you'll know exactly what you're agreeing to. I'll get it to you by the end of the day." He flipped the top over the remaining food in his lunch container and handed it to me. "Please put this in the refrigerator. I have a lot to finish up before five o'clock."

Taking his actions as a command to leave, I closed up my lunch, put both in the small refrigerator built into the wall unit opposite his desk, and closed myself in my office.

I was alone now. Safe in my little office. Away from those piercing eyes of his and his deft hands and wicked mouth.

Alone with the memory of what he'd done to me.

Here.

In this very chair, just a short time ago.

My insides pulsed.

I was (maybe) about to sign a contract, becoming Kameron Maldonado's submissive.

What if it was more than I could handle?

What if he put things in there I couldn't do? What if he expected too much? What would I do?

I needed to find a new job today!

My cell phone rang, and I glanced at it.

My brother.

What was it now?

3

"Abby? Where are you?" It was my brother. He never called me with good news. Never.

"I'm at work. Why?"

"It's no big deal. I just need some money."

It's no big deal. How many times had I heard that line? My insides twisted. Already he'd caused me hell this week. What was next? "What's going on? Why do you need money?" I asked, afraid I wouldn't like the answer.

"Well . . . I'm sorta in jail."

"Jail?" My gaze jerked to the door between my office and Kameron's. Had he lied about going to the police? "The bastard!" How could he? I shot out of my chair.

"It's no big deal, Abby. I was caught driving with a suspended license."

"Oh." I stopped in my tracks, circled back around to my chair, and flopped into it. God, the crazy ups and downs this kid was taking me on. "Joss. Dammit. There's going to come a day when I can't help you. You've got to stop—"

"I'm sorry," he said, interrupting my tirade. "I swear it won't happen again. I gotta go. My time's up. Will you come?"

I wanted to pull my hair out. Dammit, what was it going to take to get my brother to straighten up? What was it freaking going to take? I was so tired of it all—the drinking, the fights, the arrests. It had been going on for so long. Too long.

"Please. This time was different," he said. "And that other stuff. I didn't do that."

It was always different. It was never his fault. "I'll see what I can do." I shoved my fingers through my hair. It would probably look like hell, but I didn't give a damn right now. It felt like I had the weight of a semi truck on my shoulders. For one small bit of time, I wished I could shove that weight off and just breathe.

"Thanks. Sis?"

"Yeah," I said on a sigh.

"I'm sorry I've made your life a living hell these past few years. I swear I'm trying to get my shit together."

"I hope that's true. I hope you're trying. Because if you don't straighten up quickly . . . I don't know if I can live like this anymore." I blinked. My eyes were burning. Dammit.

Dammit.

"I hear you. Love you."

"Love you too." I clicked off and tossed my phone into my purse.

Dammit, dammit, dammit. Why did loving someone have to be so damned destructive? Why?

A couple of hours later my office door swung open. Kameron strolled in. He was halfway between the doorway and my desk when he stopped. His brows scrunched together. "What's wrong?"

"Nothing." I blinked a couple of times. Sniffled. Even after so much time had passed, both my nose and eyes were still burning.

He was holding a manila envelope in his hands. The contract, I assumed.

I extended an arm. "I'm guessing that's for me?"

He looked down at his hands, then up at my face. "It can wait—"

"I'll take it now, thank you. I want some time to read it over."

Some expression I couldn't quite name flashed across his face. He placed the envelope into my hand. "You've done enough for today. Go home."

That was one command I didn't mind following. "Thank you, sir." Tucking the envelope under my arm, I collected my purse. He headed back to his office. As I hurried through it to the lobby, he watched me.

"Good-bye, Abigail," he said as I pulled open the door.

"I'll see you tomorrow, sir," I said before I scurried out.

Two thousand dollars. Two freaking thousand dollars. That was what it had cost me to bail Joss out of jail this time. If it hadn't been for Kameron's generosity, I wouldn't have had the money.

"This is the last time," I warned Joss as we walked out to my car. "If I hadn't just gotten a big bonus, your ass would still be in jail. I can't afford to help you anymore."

"I hear you." He slumped into the passenger side and clicked himself in.

I flung myself into my seat and rammed the key into the ignition. "What the hell was so important—forget that. I don't want to hear the excuses. You don't have a driver's license. Don't drive!" I yelled.

"I promise I won't."

Seething, I drove him home. I stomped to my room to change my clothes. He slinked away, heading to his room to hide until he found some more trouble to get himself into.

Why? Why did he insist on destroying his life?

I banged open my closet door and hung up my work clothes. Then I stomped into the bathroom, cranked on the water, and scalded myself into a (slightly) better mood. I came out drippy and clean and a little less furious. Then, my stomach reminding me I hadn't eaten since lunch, I headed to the kitchen to find something to eat.

I was digging in the freezer, checking out my options, when someone knocked on my door. The knock was loud and insistent.

Great, now what? Police, maybe?

I peered through the peephole.

I didn't recognize the woman standing outside. I cracked open the door.

"Hello," she said with a heavy accent of some kind. "Is Joss at home? I thought I saw him."

"Yes, he is." Who was this woman? Was she trouble? A drug addict, maybe, looking for some drugs? These days, anyone who banged on my door looking for my brother was suspect.

"May I speak with him?" the woman asked.

"One moment. Let me see if he's gone to bed." I shut and locked the door before heading back to my brother's room.

I knocked, and he responded with a "Yeah?" shouted through his door.

"Some woman is outside, wanting to speak with you."

His door inched open. "What woman?"

"I don't know. Youngish with an accent, dark hair."

"Okay. Let me put on a shirt." While he dressed, I headed back to the kitchen, which was open to the living room and within sight of the front door.

My brother loped through the living room to the front door and opened it. "Hi."

The woman scurried into our apartment. "Joss, I just wanted to say how sorry I am for what happened today. If I'd known you would get into trouble, I wouldn't have asked—"

"It's okay," Joss interrupted. "I knew I shouldn't be driving, but I did it anyway. That was my choice."

Okay, I was curious. What had happened?

I inched around the end of the counter, listening, pulling on a corner of the frozen dinner box in my hands.

"But you wouldn't have if—"

Again, Joss interrupted. "It's okay." My brother set a hand on the woman's shoulder, but he didn't appear to be overly intimate with her. "How is Eduardo?"

"He's better. He had to get over thirty stitches and some shots, but the doctors said he'll be okay." The woman was wringing her hands, looking guilty, emotionally torn.

Okay, this wasn't what I had been thinking. Not at all. For once, Joss had been trying to help someone?

"Good. Any word on the dog?" my brother asked.

"No. If they don't find it, Eduardo will have to get more shots."

Dog. Shots. The picture was getting clearer.

Joss said, "I'll keep my eyes open, see if I can catch him."

"Be careful. Please." The woman back-stepped toward the door.

"I will."

At the doorway, she hesitated. "Thank you again. I'm sorry you got into trouble. I tried to tell the officer, but he wouldn't listen."

"Don't worry about it. The only thing that matters is Eduardo. We got him to the hospital and he's going to be okay."

"Yes."

"Keep me posted, okay?"

"I will." The woman patted my brother's shoulder. "You're a good man."

"Thanks." He closed the door. Our gazes met as he headed back toward his room.

I stopped him with a question. "Why didn't you tell me?"

"Because it doesn't matter, right? I was breaking the law. You told me you didn't want to hear any excuses."

Shit.

His words struck me harder than a physical blow.

"I was expecting something else. Another kind of excuse."

"Yeah, I know. The way I've been lately, who could blame you?" He visibly sighed.

"What about the thing at MalTech?" I asked. "You haven't told me what happened. Is it different from what I might think too?"

"I didn't take anything, if that's what you're asking." His shoulders slumped a little. "I'm sorry, Abby. Really sorry. About what happened at work. And this. You got me the job at MalTech. And I blew that. I want you to be able to trust me. I want you to respect me again, like you used to."

God, his words were like daggers in my heart. He'd nailed it when he said I didn't respect him anymore. "I want that too," I said, thumbing away the tears leaking from my eyes.

My brother yanked me into a big bear hung. "I swear I'm going to get everything straightened out. Whatever it takes, I'll do it. I'll make it happen."

Stepping out of his embrace, I gave him a weak smile. "I hope so. But it's going to be rough. Now, after this latest arrest, you have a court date to make, probably fines to pay. You don't have a job, don't have a reference to get a new one."

"At least driving with a suspended license is only a misdemeanor. Won't hurt me too bad. Once I pay the fines, my record should clean up. But if someone from MalTech goes to the police . . ."

"That isn't going to happen," I told him.

"How do you know?"

"I talked to Kameron Maldonado. We've . . . worked out an understanding."

"You . . . ?" My brother's eyes widened, then narrowed to little squints. "What kind of understanding?" His voice was low, practically a growl.

"Not the kind you think," I lied. In all likelihood, he was probably thinking something very close to the truth. "I'm working directly under him now, as his administrative assistant."

His squinty eyes got even more squinty. "Why?"

"I guess so I can help him clear up the mess you allegedly made," I said, feeling my face warming. The last thing I needed was my brother running back to MalTech and causing more trouble. Somehow I had to convince him the situation was perfectly legit. "Part of it I think was he felt bad for me, since I told him we relied upon your income to supplement mine. With the new job comes a pay raise. I'm making more now than you and I had combined."

"But—"

"Don't. Don't wreck this for me, Joss," I snapped, letting my tone tell him I didn't want or need his interference.

"Is he . . . doing anything inappropriate? Or making you do anything you don't want to do?"

I knew why he'd asked that. He'd heard the same rumors about Maldonado that I had.

"No, though I'm not crazy about filing," I added, hoping the joke would lighten things up. "Never have been."

Finally, my brother's expression changed a little. He was still suspicious. I could see it in the tightness in his jaw. But at least now he wasn't ready to rip off anyone's head. "If he does anything, tries anything, you'd better tell me."

"I will." A lie. But, whatever.

Joss took a step toward his room, pausing next to me to give me the side eye. "Something about this sounds fishy."

"So far, everything's good. I swear." If he knew I had come home from work with my torn underpants in my purse, he might disagree. I was going to have to dispose of them carefully.

"O-okay. I've sent my resume out to a few companies and I'm meeting with an employment agency tomorrow. I'm going to find another job. I'm the man of the house. That's my responsibility."

If he had done what he just said, that was encouraging. "That's good."

Outside of the third degree I was given about my new job, I was very happy about the way this conversation had gone. With the news about the employment agency appointment, Joss was sounding more like the Joss I'd hoped he would someday become. If it wasn't all an act, we might be turning the corner.

Maybe my prayers had finally been answered.

The next morning, my phone started ringing the instant I stepped into the shower. And it didn't stop. Not while I washed up, or while I shaved my legs, or while I finally got annoyed, cut off the water, and wrapped myself in a towel.

I answered with a grouchy sounding, "Yes, sir?"

"Pack an overnight bag."

Click.

I glared at the phone, then tossed it on the bed. "Good

morning to you too," I grumbled as I stomped into some clean panties.

I dressed in something work appropriate and travel friendly, then went down to the kitchen for some coffee. Caffeine. I needed caffeine. Lots of it.

After getting the coffeemaker going, I went down to our storage cage in the building's basement, dug out a small carry-on suitcase, and hauled it upstairs to pack. On the way up, I filled a cup of steaming hot happiness and slurped my way back to my room.

Assuming I was supposed to be packing for one day, I packed enough clothes for two, just in case. Work clothes, underwear, makeup and hair stuff, shoes . . . and one sexy something, just in case he was expecting it. And the contract, which I hadn't read yet. After the drama of last night, I hadn't been in the right frame of mind to tackle it. I was rolling the packed suitcase down the hall and finishing up cup number one of coffee when Joss poked his head out, took one look at my suitcase, and growled, "What the hell?"

"Business trip."

Joss rolled his bloodshot eyes. "Yeah, right."

"A business owner does go out of town on business trips, you know. Especially ones who have branches in other states. And they usually take their administrative assistants with them."

"The bastard knows what he's doing," my brother seethed through gritted teeth. "Don't let him treat you like a whore."

Rage pulsed through me at the sound of that word. "Oh, he won't. I won't let that happen. I'm no man's whore."

That seemed to take a little fire out of Joss's eyes. "Demand separate rooms."

"I will."

His gaze zoomed up and down my body. I was wearing a pretty conservative outfit. Slacks, a blouse, and cardigan sweater. Two-inch pumps. My hair was neat but also fairly conservative, smoothed back into a low ponytail. "I hope this is all legit. But something tells me it's not. We've both heard the rumors about Maldonado, that he's a sick bastard who sleeps with his employees and then fires them."

"No, I haven't heard that rumor," I lied. "Do you have any proof?"

"No, but—"

"When you have some proof, then bring it to me and I'll decide whether I want to keep this position or not. In the meantime, he's paying me good, the work isn't bad, and neither are the hours. We need the money." I didn't add the part about how a lot of my money had been going to lawyers to keep his butt out of jail.

His lips thinned. "Fine."

I gave him a hug. "I promise, Kameron Maldonado isn't going to treat me like his slut. I wouldn't put up with that." I glanced at my watch. "Now, I need to get going. I'm assuming we leave sometime this morning. I wouldn't want to cause a delay by being late."

"Fine. Call me later. When you get wherever you're going." He grabbed me and hugged me hard. "I would feel like absolute shit if something happened to you because of me."

"Nothing's going to happen." I squeezed back, then stepped away. "Gotta go."

"Be careful," he shouted after me as I race-walked to the door.

"I will!"

I had to break a few speed limits to get to work on time, but I made it with not a minute to spare. Leaving my suitcase in my car, I hurried inside, poked the elevator button at least five times, and counted the seconds before the bell chimed. The door rolled open, and my heart jumped.

My new boss was standing there, giving me mean eyes.

"You're late," he said.

"Technically, I'm on time. The elevator—"

"We have to leave now." Stepping out of the car, he steered me toward the exit with a hand on my back. "Where's your suitcase?"

"My car. I didn't know if I should—"

"We'll pick it up on the way out."

As we stepped out of the building, a black limo rolled to a stop directly in front of us. The driver scurried out and opened the door. I sat. Kameron sat next to me.

His jaw tensed. "You haven't gone shopping yet."

"I haven't had time." I felt my face warming as I recalled yesterday's lunch hour. "I tried going during my lunch—"

"And I let you leave early yesterday."

"Yes, okay. You did. But something urgent came up."

"What?" he barked. "What came up?"

"That's none of your business. You're my boss. Not my husband. Or my father."

Much to my surprise, he chuckled. "Point taken. Again."

A little amused by his reaction, I glanced at him. His lips were curved into a lopsided semismile. It was a sexy expression.

"We'll get some shopping in later today," he said. "New York has a few decent places to shop."

"New York?" I echoed. I'd always wanted to go to New York. Correction, I'd always dreamed of going to New York. The Statue of Liberty, Times Square, the art galleries, Coney Island and, of course, the Museum of Modern Art.

"We'll be there for at least three days. If you didn't pack enough, we'll take care of it after we land."

Without thinking, I volleyed back, "Yeah, well, if you'd

been a little more forthcoming when you called, I would've known how much to pack."

That earned me a full belly laugh. And a scowl. "Touché, Miss Barnes. Though I should punish you for being so outspoken. . . ." His expression once more turned wicked, and my skin started burning.

Punish me? What exactly did he mean by that?

4

During the entire one-hour flight on the company's private jet (I didn't know the company owned a private jet!), Kameron worked on his laptop, leaving me to amuse myself. Fortunately, I'd downloaded a book onto my phone. It wasn't a gripping page turner, but it was better than staring out the window and counting the minutes. Or staring at Kam like a goon while he worked.

For some reason, despite the fact that he'd basically blackmailed me into some sort of sexual arrangement I didn't understand (because I hadn't yet read the contract he'd given me), I just loved to look at him. And every time I did, I discovered some small thing that made him that much sexier.

After we landed, Kameron spent the limo ride to our destination on the phone while I gawked out the window. I read the signs as we crawled through clogged streets. Water Street, Broadway, West Street. Lots of cars and taxis and people and signs. It was almost too much to take in.

"Your first time?" he asked.

"Yes," I said, shifting to look his way. "It's so . . . busy."

"That, it is." He tucked his laptop into his briefcase. "We're stopping at the condo first, to freshen up. My first appointment is in a couple of hours, so you'll have a little time to relax and orientate yourself."

"Sounds good."

The limo pulled up to one of the many towering buildings I'd admired. This one had a gray stone façade on the first floor and red brick on the many floors above. The driver opened our doors, and out I stepped. Before following Kameron to the glass entry, I craned my head to look up. One, two, three . . . ten, eleven, twelve, thirteen, or was it fourteen? Fourteen floors. We stepped inside. Wow. Glossy wood paneling, a gorgeous chandelier overhead, an information desk to the right, and sleek, white leather couches on the left. We angled through a wide opening just beyond the information desk, to the elevators.

This was New York luxury.

In the elevator, I watched the numbers illuminate as we zoomed up, up, up. We stopped on the fourteenth floor. Together, I carrying my purse and he his laptop case, we stepped out into a neutrally decorated hallway. And within minutes I was standing in a spacious living room, looking out across blue water and the Statue of Liberty. "Wow."

"This place was a steal for the location. And it has a pretty decent view." Kameron stepped up beside me. "Let me show you your room." He took my hand, weaving his fingers between mine, and pulled. Reluctantly, I followed. We traveled through the living room and down a hallway. He opened the first door. "Your room." Pulling me in, he motioned to another door set off the side. "Your bathroom."

My gaze swept across the luxurious space. The bed was huge, neatly made with crisp white bedding. The walls were painted a soft gray. Darker gray curtains flanked the window to the right of the bed. And directly across from the bed stood a sleek, white dresser with a flat-screen television hanging on the wall.

I felt like I was in a five-star hotel. "This place is . . . insane."

"It's really quite simple. I've toured some condos that would take your breath away."

"I can't even imagine."

"I didn't want to spend a great deal of money on a place here. I don't spend a lot of time in the city. I just needed some-place to sleep."

"Just someplace to sleep." I chuckled as my gaze hopped around the room again. "You and I live in such different worlds."

"Do we?" He placed his hands on my shoulders and turned me toward him. "Are our worlds really so different?"

"Of course they are. Look at this place. I live in squalor compared to this."

"And I was raised in a trailer park," he said, his thumbs dragging over my collarbones. "We had a single-wide mobile home. We lived there until I was twelve, then moved up to a bungalow in Redford."

This shocked me. I'd always assumed he had come from money. As that old saying went, it took money to make money. So he'd somehow gotten his hands on capital to build his fa-ther's business into the huge conglomerate it was today. "I'm sorry if I made an unfair assumption."

"No need to apologize. It's a common misconception. One I usually don't bother to correct. But . . ." His brows pulled. His lips twisted. "Hmmm."

"What?"

"Nothing." He looked into my eyes for a moment, and I felt like the world had stopped spinning. His head started dipping down. He was going to kiss me. Ohmygod, he was going to kiss me.

I closed my eyes and held my breath and silently waited for

his lips to find mine. When they did, I sucked in a little gasp. His mouth pressed against mine, possessing it, claiming it. It wasn't a soft kiss. It wasn't a tease. Not at all. And when I parted my lips to pull in some much needed air, his tongue slid inside, filling my mouth with his sweet, intoxicating flavor. Our tongues met, tangled. And with each stab and stroke, more of my body warmed. My chest, my face, my stomach, and farther down. Between my legs. One of his hands skimmed down to my breast, cupping it through my clothes.

My spine tightened, arching forward, pressing my burning flesh harder into his hand. A soft moan bubbled up my throat, echoing in our joined mouths.

I could hardly believe this was happening. I was in a beautiful apartment in New York City. With a man who threw away more money than I made in a year. And he was kissing me, touching me, like he couldn't get enough. Like I made him burn as hot as he made me.

I let my hands wander over his clothed form, imagining the muscular body that lay hidden beneath the soft wool jacket and smooth cotton shirt. But as my hands inched down to his stomach, he grabbed my wrists and jerked them behind my back.

Startled, I tried to pull away, but he yanked me roughly, forcing me against him. His eyes were dark, his eyelids heavy, as he looked down at me.

"Do you remember what I said earlier?" he asked, his voice a low growl.

"When?"

"You take far too many liberties with me," he murmured, looking as if he might gobble me up at any moment. "I didn't say you could touch me."

"Oh." My face flushed. "I'm sorry, sir. I thought you'd—"

"I didn't say you could touch me," he repeated.

A little quiver buzzed up my spine.

Walking, he forced me backward until I was trapped between the wall and his scrumptious body. I didn't mind that so much. No, it was actually quite nice. He was warm too, and the heat radiating off him only amplified the burn sizzling in my blood. A wet, pounding need was thrumming between my legs, and I longed for him to rub it away.

Still holding my wrists behind my back, he kicked my feet apart. "I can't wait to punish you," he murmured as he nibbled and licked my earlobe.

Instantly, my left side was covered in goose bumps. I tipped my head to the side and closed my eyes. Ahhh, he did things with his teeth and tongue that no man had ever done to me before. He nipped just hard enough for me to suck in a little gasp and tighten all over. Then he gently laved that same spot, soothing the burn. Within seconds, I was hot and cold, shivering, breathless, and dizzy.

My hips were rocking back and forth, my wet tissues rubbing against his thigh. But the ache was only getting worse. I couldn't take any more.

"Please," I murmured.

"Please what?" Releasing my hands, he warned, "Keep them behind your back."

I nodded. "Please," I repeated, unable to articulate what I craved.

He unbuttoned the waistband of my pants. "I like skirts," he stated as he pulled the zipper down.

"Yes, sir." I wriggled while he pushed my pants down to my ankles. Then, at his unspoken prompt, I lifted one foot and then the other so he could remove my shoes and pants.

His hands skimmed up the outsides of my legs, coming to a rest on my hips. He pulled them, forcing them forward, and pushed his thigh against the damp crotch of my panties. It felt so good, and yet I craved more. So much more.

"You're wet."

"Yes, sir."

"You're warm." He pulled his leg out and replaced it with a hand, cupping my crotch. A fingertip teased my slit through my panties.

I shuddered. "Yes."

That fingertip pushed deeper, forcing the sodden material between my labia. "You want to come, don't you, precious?"

"Yes." I slid my feet wider apart, opening myself to him.

He hooked his fingers, sliding them between my panties and my simmering flesh. "You need to come."

So dizzy I could barely stand, I grabbed his shoulders as I fought to keep from falling over. Never had I wanted a man to touch me this much. Never had I been so desperate for relief. "Yes. Please."

"I didn't give you permission to touch me," he snapped. Moving too fast for me to process, he jerked away, leaving me stumbling and staggering.

"I'm sorry, sir." Unsure whether I should stay put or follow him, I took one faltering step forward.

"You must learn to obey," he said in a chilly voice that cooled my burning blood a little. If this stuff was a game, he took it very seriously. Maybe a smidgen too seriously. "Didn't you read the contract?"

"N-no."

"Why not? *You* insisted I give it to you last night."

"I intended to read it last night. But, like I said, something came up. I'll read it as soon as I get home." Dammit, didn't he expect his employees to have lives outside of work? He was expecting so much, maybe too much. But because my livelihood depended upon playing these games with him, I apologized without a second thought, "I'm very sorry, sir. I'll do better. I promise."

His cold expression softened a tiny bit. It was enough to allow me to take a deep breath. "On your knees."

I dropped to my knees, grateful for the plush carpet underneath them.

"Hands behind your back."

I clasped them behind my back, as commanded.

He pulled his tie from his collar as he circled me. Stopping behind me, he leaned over my shoulder. "That's more like it. I have no patience for disobedience. Do you understand?"

A shiver quaked my body. I was nervous and unsure, but also oddly aroused. "Yes, sir."

Smooth, cool silk circled my wrists, sliding across my skin. It felt nice. Not so nice, though, when it tightened, binding them together.

He'd tied my hands again.

A little pulse of unease zigged up my spine. As it reached the base of my neck, a wave of heat followed. Once again, my body was reacting to my apprehension in a way I hadn't expected. A second, stronger wave of heat burned through my center, pooling between my legs.

Crazy.

I had to be crazy to get turned on by this, by being scolded and tied.

Feeling guilty and conflicted, I let my head drop forward and closed my eyes. After everything my mother had gone through, how could I let this man treat me this way? Even worse, how could I enjoy it? Had my childhood scarred me somehow?

Had to be.

I felt tears burning my eyes as the shame of my response gripped me.

"Much better. Now, look up."

I lifted my head but kept my eyes closed. I wouldn't let him see my shame. That would only give him more power over me. I needed to hold on to something.

He cupped my chin in his hand and grazed my lips with his

thumb. "Does it hurt? Did I tie your wrists too tightly?" His voice was softer now.

"No, sir."

He released my chin. The tears were drying up, enough that I risked slitting my eyes open a little to see what he was doing.

He was standing before me, arms crossed over his chest. Staring. Assessing.

I opened my eyes a little more and focused on his face. His jaw was tight. His eyes were dark. His expression was serious. I wondered what he was thinking. Was he trying to decide what kind of cruel torture he'd do next?

Or was he trying to decide whether he'd fire me?

"Sir?" I whispered, opening my eyes fully and meeting his gaze. "This is all new for me—"

"No need to explain," he interrupted as he pulled up a chair. He set it directly in front of me, then eased into it. He sat, legs apart, leaning back, still studying me with an expression I didn't know how to read. "I can see you're willing to learn."

"Yes, sir." Willing for now. Willing until I found a new job and could walk away from all of this. It scared me as much as it intrigued me. And the fact that I was so intrigued frightened me more.

"And you're only doing this to keep your job?"

"And to keep you from going to the police," I added, making sure he didn't forget that part.

He leaned forward, resting his elbows on his knees. "Why are you willing to go to such measures to protect your brother?"

The answer seemed obvious to me. "Wouldn't anyone do the same?"

He shook his head. "No. If I had a brother, which I don't, I wouldn't protect him."

"Really?"

"Really. I wouldn't."

"You wouldn't protect your younger sibling?" I echoed, shocked and disappointed. Did this man care about anyone but himself?

"Not if he'd broken the law. Not if he'd risked my job. No. I'd let the law take care of him."

I didn't respond right away, fearful my initial reaction would make him angry.

"What do you think about that, Abigail?" His tone was cool.

I doubted he wanted to hear the truth. "I guess we see the situation very differently." My tone wasn't much warmer than his.

"That's all you're going to say?"

"It is."

"Hmmm." He stood, circled me, doing a full 360 before making a second lap. This time he stopped behind my back again. A fingertip traced my arm, from shoulder to the silk binding my wrist. Little tingles pricked my skin where he'd touched me. "You confuse me, Abigail."

I confused *him?* "I'm sorry," I apologized again. This time I wasn't sure exactly what I was apologizing for. At his soft touch, the muscles of my arm tensed slightly. My fingers curled into fists. And a tiny shiver wriggled up my spine.

"Are you different from the others?" he murmured. I didn't think he was speaking to me, so I didn't respond. I just held very still and let him do whatever it was he wanted, hoping it would be over soon and trusting what he'd said, that he wouldn't force me to have sex with him.

He continued around to my front again, pulled the chair closer, and sat, leaning forward. Our gazes met, and his lips parted slightly. His tongue slid out, swiping across his lower lip. I felt myself mirroring him.

Something passed across his face, and his jaw tightened once again. He reached between my legs, fingering my folds. His intimate touch, after having taken a break, startled me. I felt a little invaded. But within seconds, the tissues his fingers were exploring warmed. My insides clenched as a gently pulsing heat beat deep within me.

I closed my eyes, both in shame and in pleasure. The darkness swallowed me up, allowing me to just feel. His fingers grazed my skin, teasing me, tormenting me, never quite pushing hard enough or dipping deep enough. The longer the torture continued, the tighter my thighs became. I scooted my knees apart, surrendering to the demand of my burning tissues. They craved more. A lot more. I shoved the doubts and guilty thoughts out of my head and focused on the glorious sensations his touch was stirring.

I was his. To touch. Anywhere. Any time he wanted. That was our agreement. In essence, I was his toy. His plaything. It was all him.

His choice.

His demands.

Him.

For some reason, those thoughts eased my guilt. As if not having control made me less culpable, less slutty.

When he curled his hand and shoved two fingers inside me, I tumbled into a swirling world of heat and need. His strokes were slow, exactly what I needed. I felt my hips rocking back and forth, my greedy body working with his hand, my need building. My teeth sank into my lip. Within seconds, the burning between my legs was almost unbearable. Pulses of heat racing up and down my body. I was about to come. I was about to . . .

"Ahhh . . ." I groaned as the first spasm shook my body. My inner muscles rhythmically clenched around his invading digits as I shook and shivered through pure ecstasy. He stroked me deep and hard, the friction prolonging the pleasure, drawing it out until I was exhausted.

I felt my body slumping forward, strong hands catching me, scooping me up.

Then I was lying on my stomach, floating on a cloud of clean, white cotton. Tingling from head to toe, I turned my head to the side and watched Kameron kneel on the mattress beside me. The silk loosened, gliding off my wrists, across my back. Little aftershocks of pleasure shook me.

Warm, moist lips pressed against the inside of my right wrist.

"We need to get going," he murmured against my skin. "I'll leave you to get dressed."

And he was gone.

If I'd had any misconception about the purpose of our trip to New York, it was completely obliterated by that evening. This was, without any doubt, a working trip.

Riding in a slick, black BMW, we spent hours winding through congested New York City streets in between meetings. Kameron passed the time either working on his laptop or talking on the phone. When I wasn't taking orders to make phone calls on my new company-owned cell phone or typing his dictation into his computer, I was staring out the window, watching the scenery pass by.

By ten p.m., I was exhausted, my eyes blurry. I had a slight headache, and I was ready to eat and crash onto any horizontal surface that was stationary.

In contrast, Kameron seemed to have an endless supply of energy as he continued pecking at his laptop while jabbering into the wireless headset connecting him to his business associates via his cell phone. I rummaged in my handbag and found a couple of aspirins and a bottle of water in the car's minifridge. The water's cap was screwed on very tight, but Kameron was kind enough to open it for me. I popped the bitter pills into my mouth, added a big swig of water, and swallowed. Relief was on its way.

A little while later, I was struggling to keep my eyes open. With every moment that passed, it became harder and harder. My eyelids were drooping.

Wouldn't lift.

So heavy.

All of me felt heavy. Arms. Legs. Chest.

I felt myself falling, heard Kameron's voice. It sounded so far away. Low and husky and sexy. I felt the vibration of the vehicle as it crawled through the streets. I heard the hum of the motor and the sounds of traffic and people, a world that didn't stop.

Something was wrong.

No, maybe not.

Or possibly, yes.

I was hot. No, cold. Too hot and too cold. I turned my head, and the world swooped and spun. I laughed and let myself be carried away into a mist of swirling, warm bliss.

5

I was warm, lying on something that was soft and cozy. A leg brushed against mine, an arm flopped over my side.

A leg?

An arm?

What the hell?

I blinked open my eyes.

I was in the condo. In my room.

Okay. But . . . ?

I glared at the hand dangling from the arm that had decided it belonged draped over my body. It was a male hand. I had a pretty good notion who it belong to.

A leg swung across both of mine, pinning them to the mattress. I felt coarse hair scratching as it slowly dragged back again.

If I was feeling hair . . .

Moving carefully to avoid waking the man who had evidently invited himself into my bed, I wriggled to the opposite side of the bed. Then I lifted the sheets.

"Oh my God!" I blurted.

"What?" He was upright, hair mussed, eyes wild. "Is something wrong?"

"I'm naked." Semi reclined, I gathered as much of the covers as I could and heaped them on top of myself.

"Of course you're naked. Did you want me to put you to bed in your work clothes?"

He put me to bed? When?

What else did he do?

Why couldn't I remember?

"Well, yes," I said as I tried to slog through my hazy memories, to recall what happened last night. Had I really been that tired that I had fallen so deeply asleep I hadn't woken when we'd come upstairs?

"Why would you want to sleep in your clothes?" Kameron asked. "That couldn't be comfortable."

"Because . . ." My face was so hot I was afraid it might blister.

"Do you always sleep in your clothes?" Kameron's shoulders were bare. So was his chest. Clearly he didn't sleep in his work clothes either.

"No, but . . ."

His lips curled up a tiny bit. "Are you ashamed that I undressed you?"

"Yes!"

He grinned. "Now, we've gotten to the bottom of things. No pun intended." His gaze flicked to roughly my groin region.

I lifted the sheets just enough to peer beneath them again and glowered. "You couldn't have left my underwear on?"

He shrugged, stretched. "I was thinking of your comfort."

"R-r-right." I tried to keep the glower going while secretly marveling at how glorious his unclothed chest and stomach looked when he moved that way.

Wow.

Another question popped into my head, and a chill buzzed through me in its wake. "Did we. . . . ?"

"Have sex? No. But not for lack of trying." His grin amped up a notch. "On *your* part, not mine."

"What are you saying?"

"I'm saying you practically begged me."

"So, why didn't you?"

His shrug was very nonchalant. "Because you didn't say please."

Was he kidding? Really? Because I didn't say please?

What was I thinking? I wouldn't ask him to have sex with me! He was lying.

He let his head fall forward, rolling it from side to side. "I'm stiff. This bed isn't the best. I think I'll replace it."

Shaking my head, I tried to sort through what had really happened last night. Things just weren't adding up. "Speaking of that, don't you have a bed of your own?"

"Sure." He tipped his head to the right. Cracked his neck.

"Why didn't you sleep in it?" I challenged.

"Because you begged me to stay with you. And you *did* say please."

What a lie! "I did not."

"You most certainly did." He crossed his arms over his chest. The sheet was draped across his body, covering only part of him, from just below his belly button to his knees.

"How could I beg you to do anything? I was . . . wait a minute. Was I talking in my sleep?"

He shrugged. "I didn't ask. When we arrived here at the condo, I couldn't rouse you. So I carried you in and set you in the bed. While I was undressing you, you begged, pleaded, for me to stay with you." He paused for a moment. "Now that I think about it, you were mumbling. And maybe your eyes were closed. But I thought that was because the light was bothering you."

"I can't believe I slept through all of that," I mused, still unsure whether I believed that was what had really happened. "I've never slept that soundly before. Normally a tiny sound will wake me."

Once again, he shrugged. "You didn't have any alcohol to drink. Perhaps you were exhausted?"

"Yes, I was, but I've been that tired before and still remembered what I did the next day."

"How can you be sure you remembered, if you were sleeping?"

"Because I didn't wake up in bed with a man."

That argument didn't seem to convince him. "Did you take any medications?" he asked. "Maybe something to help you travel? I have a friend who takes medication for airsickness. That stuff knocks him on his ass for days."

"No, I don't get airsick." I tried to search the hazy memories of the previous night. The last thing I remembered was sitting in the car, feeling very sleepy. Unusually sleepy. Unnaturally sleepy.

Then, I remembered the aspirins. "I took aspirin. For a headache. But aspirin shouldn't knock me out."

"Are you sure it was aspirin?"

"Yes. I don't keep them in a bottle. I always carry a few in a baggy. Takes up less space in my purse." My head spun when I sat upright. I blinked, breathed slowly, fighting against the whirling motion. "Whoa."

"Are you okay?"

"I'm a little dizzy."

"I'm going to check your purse. Those couldn't have been aspirin." He climbed out of bed, giving me a full view of his nude backside.

"Whoa," I repeated. He had a perfect butt. Perfect back. Perfect shoulders.

He turned around, giving me a full frontal view of *everything,* and I wished I wasn't so freaking dizzy. Whoa didn't cut it. "You'd better lie down."

That wasn't why I'd said whoa, but I decided he was right, I did need to lie down. I went horizontal and the spinning stopped. Holding my head still, I listened to him pad around my room, to the soft *ziiiip* of my purse being opened, and the crackle of paper as he fished around in it for the plastic baggy with the medication.

"Found it." He circled around the bed, sitting next to me. The mattress sank under his weight, causing me to roll slightly toward him. "Are these the pills you took?" He dangled the baggy in front of my eyes.

It took me a moment to focus. "Yes."

He inspected them closer. "Hmmm." He stood, left the room. A few minutes later he was back with the bag of pills. And he was wearing a pair of black boxer briefs. Nothing else. It was a good look on him. Very good. "Okay, are you absolutely sure those were the pills you took?" he asked, shaking the baggy.

"Positive."

"They're aspirin. I looked them up." He dropped the bag in my purse.

"Okay. I guess I was just exhausted. And maybe getting sick. I'm not feeling so great this morning."

Sitting next to me again, he rested a hand on my leg. The slight mattress bounce made the spinning come back. I gripped the sheet under me in my fists. "You'll stay in bed today. I can handle things on my own."

This sucked! Here I was, in New York. And I was too sick to go outside. "I'm sorry."

"There's nothing to apologize for," he said. "Do you want something to eat before I go?"

"No. I don't think I could eat yet. I'm feeling a little

woozy." My bladder contracted, reminding me that it had been a while since I'd emptied it. "But I need to go to the bathroom," I said as I cautiously angled myself up again. I clutched the flat sheet to my chest as I sat upright.

"Easy," he said, placing his hands on my shoulders as I moved.

The spinning worsened as I stood, but then eased. The floor felt as if it were slanted rather than horizontal, which made it really hard for me to walk. Kameron followed me to the bathroom, his hands on my waist.

"Gosh, this is terrible," I said as I wobbled across the room.

"I'm going to call a doctor as soon as I get you back in bed." His voice was laced with concern.

I stopped at the bathroom door, hand gripping the frame. "I'll take it from here, thanks." I lurched in, my toe catching on the threshold. I felt myself falling, then felt myself being yanked upright again, a thick arm wrapped around my midsection.

"You're going to have to let me help you," my rescuer said.

"This is humiliating." My hold on the scrunched-up sheet tightened.

"Think I haven't seen a woman urinate before?" he asked as he walked me across the bathroom's slick stone floor.

"You have?"

"Sure."

I'd never seen a grown man urinate. At least, not since I was a child. I vaguely remembered seeing my father pee once.

Using his hands, he turned me around, holding me at the waist. Then he gently pulled the sheet away so it wouldn't end up in the toilet. "Okay, the toilet's directly behind you. Sit."

I slowly lowered myself down until the cool, hard seat was under me.

Kameron stepped back, presumably to give me some privacy.

My bladder said it wasn't far enough.

I gave him a little shooing motion. "Out."

He hesitated, then left, stepping outside the bathroom but leaving the door open.

My very full but somewhat finicky bladder decided that was good enough. He was back in the room, ready to lift me up within seconds.

"Not that I want to appear ungrateful, but I'm the kind of girl who likes her privacy in the bathroom."

"I understand. But I'm not going to risk you falling and cracking open your skull. Sorry." He hooked his arms under my armpits and lifted me, and within a heartbeat I was extremely grateful he was there holding me up. I probably would've fallen over if he hadn't been.

"Okay?" He asked, holding me tightly.

"Dizzy."

"I'll give you a minute."

As I held my head stationary, my forehead resting against his broad chest, the spinning eased. "Better now. I'd like to wash my hands and brush my teeth."

"Okay."

It took some fairly creative manipulations to get me to the sink without falling while he kept a tight hold on me, but we managed. Soon my hands were germ free, my mouth minty fresh, and I was being carried back to the bed.

The descent to the mattress was hell, but once I was horizontal, things settled down again.

"Wow," I said, closing my eyes. "That was . . . quite an ordeal."

He said, "I can't leave you alone for long."

"Surely this will ease up soon."

"I'm calling a doctor." He bent down, brushed his lips against mine, smoothed my hair back from my face. "Don't move from this bed."

"Yes, sir."

He gave me one last kiss on the forehead. "I'll be back as soon as I can."

And out he went.

I closed my eyes and let myself drift off.

"Miss Barnes?"

Someone was calling me? Was I dreaming?

I dragged open my heavy eyelids and had a mini heart attack.

There was a strange man standing over me. A strange man with thinning gray hair, a matching five o'clock shadow, and eyebrows in desperate need of grooming.

I jerked upright. "Who—"

"I'm Dr. Feigel. Mr. Maldonado called me," the doctor explained as he took my wrist in his hand, pressing two fingers to my pulse point.

"Oh."

He glanced down at his wristwatch for a few seconds, nodded, then reached for what I assumed was his bag, sitting on the nightstand. He pulled out a blood pressure cuff and strapped it on my arm. "What seems to be the problem?"

"I'm really dizzy."

"Dizzy as in faint? Or dizzy as in feeling a spinning sensation?" he asked.

"The second one."

"All right," he said as he squeezed the little rubber bulb, inflating the cuff. It tightened around my arm, cutting off the circulation. "Any other symptoms?" He released the pressure.

"I'm very sleepy. And I . . . don't remember part of last night. It might be I was sleeping, but I don't know."

"Hmmm." He removed the cuff. "Your blood pressure is a little low." He put it away, checked some other things—heart, throat, ears, temperature. "I think you should go to the hospital and have some blood tests run."

As he was working, I noticed I could move my head without the spinning being so bad. "Oh, I don't know. I think it's getting better."

"Are you sure?"

I shook my head, then nodded. "Yes. It is getting better."

His bushy gray brows scrunched together. "Did you have anything to drink last night? Any alcohol?"

"No. Only water."

He pulled a little light thing out of his bag and shined it in my eyes. "Did you take any medications?"

"A couple of aspirin."

"Are you sure that's the only medication you took?"

A little chill prickled my back. "Yes, I'm sure." Was he suggesting I was lying? Or I had taken some random pill without knowing what it was? Or did he see something suspicious that I should worry about?"

"I'm not finding anything wrong. You may have a slight infection of your inner ear." He started putting all his doctor tools back in his bag. "If your symptoms get worse or return, go to the hospital immediately."

"Will do."

"Okay. I'm going to leave now. I'll leave my card on your nightstand. If you have any questions, please call. My answering service can reach me at any time of the day or night."

"Thank you for coming." I waited for him to leave, then cautiously moved to the edge of the bed. I pushed myself upright. So far, so good. I eased to my feet. No spinning. I walked slowly, keeping a hand on the bed until I'd reached the end. No problems. I made it to the bathroom without falling, locked myself in, and cranked on the shower.

Ten minutes later, I was clean and feeling almost as good as new. As I pulled open the door, I tried to shove aside a troubling thought—that maybe Kameron had slipped me something for some reason. I hadn't mentioned the possibility to the doctor partly because it didn't make a lot of sense to me, and also because Kameron had hired him. Instead, I got myself cleaned up then, sitting on the edge of the bed, used my phone to do some checking on the Internet.

A listing of my symptoms landed me on a page about Rohypnol, also known as the date rape drug.

Dizziness.

Hot and cold sensation.

Nausea.

Difficulty moving.

Unconsciousness.

Memory loss.

Oh. My. God! I was drugged.

"You're up."

Who?

My heart leaped. My hands flew up. The phone sailed several feet through the air, hit the dresser, and landed with a thump on the carpeted floor.

I jerked around, looking over my shoulder.

Kameron.

"Are you all right?" he asked, hurrying to me.

"I'm fine." I tried to produce a convincing smile.

His brows scrunched. "Hmmm." Circling around the bed, he grabbed my phone and glanced at the screen before handing it to me.

I looked at it as my fingers curled around it. Thankfully, the impact had made it switch over to another screen. I was now on a web page about women's health. "You startled me."

"I see that." He sat next to me on the bed. The mattress sank, making my weight shift toward him. Trying not to be obvious, I scooted over a little to avoid rolling up against him. "Are you sure you're okay?"

"I'm not dizzy anymore. But I'm still tired."

"What did the doctor say?" he asked.

"He mentioned some kind of infection. Of the inner ear."

"You'd better rest, then."

"Yes."

Actually, what I needed was to get to the hospital and have a blood test run. I needed to know for sure whether I had been drugged.

Who would drug me, besides Kameron? And who would have had the opportunity?

Nobody.

If I had been drugged, it would have had to be him.

But then again, if it was Kameron, why would he do that? Why?

Swinging from confused to angry and back to confused again, I tried to decide how to handle the situation. If Kameron had drugged me, he wouldn't want me to have blood tests. He wouldn't want me to know. No, I needed to get to the hospital on my own somehow.

But there was another question weighing on my mind. How long could the drug be detected in my body? Was it already too late?

Hiding my phone under the covers, I lay back down. "I'm really sleepy."

"Okay." He leaned over me, eyes searching mine. Was he trying to determine whether I knew the truth? Or was he as worried about me as he appeared to be?

If that wasn't genuine concern I saw in his eyes, the man was one hell of an actor.

He angled down and rested his mouth against mine. It was a soft kiss that made me feel hot and cold at the same time.

Hot because my nerves were simmering.

Cold because I was scared too.

All this time, I'd assumed this man was trustworthy. Why?

Why would I make such an assumption? Because he was rich? Because he was really, really good looking? Because he was more or less blackmailing me into being his sexual plaything? Weren't those all reasons why I should have been wary?

He leaned back. "I have some more appointments this morning, won't be back until later this afternoon. I'll order you some lunch. What would you like?"

"Nothing too heavy, I guess. Thanks."

"Okay." He stood, stared at me some more, then, as if he'd decided I hadn't figured out what he'd done, nodded and left.

I went right back to that website and started skimming, looking for information on blood tests.

I didn't find a precise answer to my question, but I located an article suggesting I had as many as seventy-two hours. I grabbed the hotel's phone and called down to the lobby, asking for a cab. Then I hung up, threw on some clothes, and headed down. Within ten minutes I was sitting in the back of a grungy taxi, purse in my lap, heart in my throat.

If that man had drugged me . . .

God, what would I do? If I tried to sue him, he'd probably go to the police and report what he'd been told about my brother. Could I blackmail him into letting me free of our contract? What good would that do? At best, I'd be knocked back down to purchasing administrator, making a wage that didn't come close to paying our rent. At worst, I would be let go for some fictitious failing on my part.

Dammit.

The taxi jerked to a stop. "St. Joseph's Hospital," the cab driver said with a heavy accent.

Now conflicted, confused, I didn't move.

What the hell was I going to do?

6

"Miss? We're at the hospital," the cab driver repeated. A hospital security guard, pushing a wheelchair, approached the car. The driver said through the open window, "She's not moving. Maybe you need to help her?"

The guard opened the door and peered in at me. "Miss? Are you okay?"

I shook myself out of my stupor and nodded. "Yes, I'm fine." Still not sure if I wanted to know the results of the test, I sat in the wheelchair and let the guard wheel me inside. He parked me in front of a registration desk, wished me luck, and returned to his post.

That left me to try to explain to the woman at the registration desk why I was there.

"I . . . I think I may have been drugged," I said, feeling the backs of my eyes burning.

The woman's expression softened slightly. With a gentle but professional voice, she asked me all the pertinent questions, had me hand over my driver's license and insurance card, and then wheeled me into a waiting area.

I sat. And sat. And sat.

Over an hour later, my phone rang.

I checked it. Kameron.

Oh, damn.

I hit the button, answering, "H-hello?"

"Abigail? Where are you? I checked with the front desk, and they told me you left in a taxi?"

Should I lie? Tell the truth? "I'm . . . at the hospital."

"Why?"

"The dizziness came back. The doctor who saw me this morning told me to go to the hospital if it came back or worsened. So, here I am."

"Which hospital?" he asked, sounding anxious.

"St. Joseph's."

"I'll be up there in a few minutes."

"You don't—"

"Of course I do," he interrupted.

Click.

He was gone.

He was coming to the hospital.

I panicked for a moment. But then logic prevailed when I reminded myself that it wouldn't be a big deal if he came. After all, he wasn't my husband. The hospital would have to protect my privacy. They wouldn't be able to discuss any test results with him.

He'd have to wait out in the lobby.

Everything is going to be okay.

I sucked in a deep breath and let it out.

"Abigail Barnes," a nurse announced from an open doorway. I'd watched her call a few dozen names. The patients followed her and then were gone, probably escorted to a bed, diagnosed, treated, and sent home. Finally, it was my turn.

Moving carefully, I stood, smiled to let her know I was Abigail Barnes, and approached her.

"What are we here for today?" she asked as she led me back to a curtained-off area with a bed.

I waited until she'd closed the curtain before I explained, "I—I have reason to believe I was drugged. I want to know what it was."

"What makes you think you were drugged?" she asked as she wrapped a blood pressure cuff around my left arm.

I rattled off my symptoms while she checked my blood pressure, pulse, and temperature. Then she recorded everything on her clipboard and pulled open the curtain. "The doctor will be in soon."

And then I sat. And sat. And sat some more. Bored out of my mind, I lay back and closed my eyes. I wasn't dizzy anymore, but I still felt tired, hung over. I had almost drifted off when I heard the curtains gliding in the metal track overhead. I blinked open my eyes.

The nurse.

"There's a gentleman in the lobby asking to see you. Would you like me to bring him back?"

"Well . . ." I felt my face turning red. "I'm here because—"

"Got it. I'll tell him our policy is to only allow family members back."

"Thank you."

Off she went.

I tried to relax. But it was hard, knowing Kameron was out there waiting, probably frustrated he wasn't being allowed back to see me. Was he trying to get back here so he could keep track of what was going on? Was he trying to cover up what he'd done? Or attempting to keep me from finding out?

The more I thought about it, the more I began to suspect him. If he was low enough to use what my brother *allegedly* did to blackmail me into becoming his personal plaything, what more was he capable of?

My brother had been so right about this. So, so right. And of course, since he'd been such a train wreck lately, I didn't believe him. Instead, I believed what I wanted to about my new employer and his shady actions.

A young woman in a pair of scrubs strolled in, a clipboard in her hand. She extended an arm, introducing herself as a doctor, and I gave her hand a shake. She asked me some questions, then told me they were going to be collecting both blood and urine samples for testing.

"Will I know the results right away?" I asked.

"It'll take a while. Probably a few hours."

"Oh."

That meant I'd have to return to the condo with Kameron before the test results were in. That also meant it would give me some time to decide what I was going to do if the results came back positive.

It wasn't in my nature to hide my feelings, so I knew, in my gut, this was going to blow up in my face. If I learned I'd been drugged, I wouldn't be able to trust Kameron. And I wouldn't be able to pretend I did. He'd know.

A few minutes later, the nurse returned, took the blood, and left me with a little plastic cup with a lid. She directed me to the bathroom. Once I'd collected the specimen, I returned to my curtained safe zone and stayed put until I was discharged.

Kameron jumped up when he saw me in the lobby, charged up to me. "Are you okay? What did the doctor say?"

"She didn't have a diagnosis yet," I said. "They're running some tests."

"Okay. Let's get you back to the condo." He wrapped an arm around my waist as we walked toward the exit. "I've cancelled all my appointments for the rest of the day. I'm not going to leave your side until you're one hundred percent."

"I hate for you to miss—"

"Nothing is more important than you right now," he said, cutting me off. He sounded so sincere.

We stepped outside, and the black BMW, driven by someone else, crawled up, stopping directly in front of us. Kameron opened the door for me, and I ducked in and buckled myself up.

"You didn't eat the lunch I had sent up. Are you hungry?" he asked as he buckled his own belt.

My stomach rumbled. "A little, I guess."

"I'll order something right now. It'll be in the suite when we get there." He whipped out his phone and dialed.

I sat beside him, fighting the urge to cry.

Hours later, I'd eaten and was lying in my bed, staring at the television but not seeing it. My phone was set on vibrate so Kameron wouldn't hear it. He'd hovered around me for the first couple of hours, fussing over me like I was a sick toddler. I was extremely relieved when he finally gave up on the helicopter act. He didn't leave the suite, though. I heard him out there, moving around. Footsteps thumping on the carpeted floor. Talking on his phone.

He'd noticed I was acting differently—who wouldn't? But I'd been able to convince him that my change in attitude toward him had everything to do with my sickness.

I checked the time too often, frequently enough that time dragged. Three hours passed. Four. Five. Six. That doctor hadn't been lying. Sheesh. Just a little shy of seven hours after I'd been discharged, my phone finally buzzed.

"Miss Abigail Barnes?" I recognized the doctor's voice.

"Yes, it's me."

"We have the results back from your blood and urine tests. We got a positive on both for midazolam. Have you ever taken medication to treat seizures or insomnia?"

"No, I haven't."

"The concentration wasn't high enough to raise a concern of overdose. But it could produce the effects you described."

A chill swept through my body. "I was drugged."

I heard Kameron's footsteps approaching. He'd probably heard me talking on the phone. The door, which hadn't been shut all the way, swung open.

The doctor said, "If you'd like to—"

"Thank you." I hit the button, cutting off the call.

My blood was ice cold and yet my ears, face, and neck were burning hot.

He'd drugged me. It had to be him.

The water. I remembered drinking water in the car. That must have been it.

His gaze met mine. "What's wrong?"

He'd drugged me. God only knew what else he'd done when I was unconscious.

Bastard!

Tears burned my eyes. My nose. I sniffled.

A wave of rage surged through me, and I couldn't hold it back. "Why?" I screamed, the sound cutting through a sob. "That's all I want to know. Why?"

"What are you talking about?"

I shook my phone. "My blood tests came back. You still don't know what I'm talking about?"

"No. What?" He looked bewildered. He sounded bewildered. Wow, what an actor he was.

"Give it a break, Mr. Maldonado. I'm not buying the act."

"What act? What are you suggesting?"

"Why did you drug me? And why the hell aren't you admitting the truth?" I shrieked, unable to stop myself. He'd pushed me and pushed me with that innocent shit.

His mouth gaped, then snapped shut.

"Yeah. I know the truth. So there's no use lying anymore."

He stood. He paced.

"Trying to think up an excuse?" I sneered.

"No, I'm not."

"Good."

He stopped pacing. "It wasn't me."

I slapped my hands on my thighs. "Bullshit. Who else could it be? I haven't gone anywhere with anyone else. Only you."

"I don't know who else. What drug did they find?"

"I don't remember. And I didn't have a chance to write it down. It started with an M."

Kameron glanced around my room. His eyes locked on my computer. "May I?" He motioned to it.

"Sure. Whatever." Why was he keeping up the innocent act?

He flipped it open and, sitting on the bed, set it on his lap. "M, you say?"

"Yes. But you know what it was already. *You* gave it to me."

The keyboard went *tap-tap-tappity-tap.*

Then. "Midazolam?" he asked.

"Yes, I think that's it."

He was silent as he read the information on the screen. "What was the last thing you remember eating or drinking last night?"

"The water. In the car. On our way to the hotel. I used it to wash down the aspirin."

"I bet it was spiked."

"Sure. You spiked it. After you opened it for me, so I could take my aspirin."

"No, I didn't spike it. I swear to you." He closed the computer, set it on the bed, and focused on me. "Listen, I can understand how this looks, but it wasn't me."

I searched his face. I wasn't particularly good at catching people in lies. My own brother fooled me over and over and over. And I'd known him most of my life. So how would I ever discern whether a man I barely knew was speaking the truth?

Shaking his head, he shoved his hand into his pocket. He pulled it out, his fingers wrapped around his phone. And, dialing, he stomped out of my room.

My heart was thumping in my chest. I was breathing fast. Pumped up on adrenalin. I tried to slow my breathing and tiptoed closer to the door so I could eavesdrop.

"I need every bottle in the car tested immediately! Yes, right now. No. Make sure you don't tip off the driver. I don't want him to ditch the evidence." He paused. "Good. Call me when you get something." Another pause. "Yes. She's okay."

Was this whole thing a scheme to cover up what he'd done? Was he going to dump the blame on an innocent man?

Or was he really trying to get to the bottom of things? Was it unfair of me to jump to the conclusion that he would drug a woman after using my brother to force me into a shady contract with him so he could fondle me at will?

Dammit, this was driving me crazy!

When I heard him coming back, I dashed to the bed, pretending to be working on my laptop.

"I'll find out who did this," he said, teeth gritted. "Whoever it was, he'll pay." His fingers were curled into fists, his jaw so tight that the muscles of his neck were bulging. He was seething. He stared down at me, eyes searching. "Are you going to be okay?"

"I'll be fine."

He nodded, thumped back to the door, stopped, turned around. "I understand why you think it was me. Tying strings to your job offer was low. Illegal. Consider them severed. And the contract, wherever it is—"

I said, "My bag. I haven't read it—"

"Destroy it."

"But—"

"You'll keep the job, I hope." He shoved his hand in his pocket again. This time, he pulled out his money clip. I counted five bills he peeled from the stack. He set them on the dresser. "To compensate for your suffering last night and this morning. As for my inappropriate behavior . . . I wouldn't insult you by trying to pay you for that. I promise from this point forward, I will treat you with the respect you deserve. You were not at fault for what your brother did. I never should've taken advantage of that situation, or made you pay for his mistakes."

"Then why? Why did you do it? Why the contract? Why the strings?"

"I . . . I don't know. There was something about you. I . . . wanted you. No matter the cost. But that is no excuse." He closed the door behind him as he left.

I lay in bed, emotions churning, checking the clock every hour or so. I tried to sleep, thinking I'd be summoned the next morning to accompany him to his meetings. But dawn came, sunlight slicing like a blade between the curtain panels hanging over the window. No knock. No call. I showered and dressed and went out to the main living space. I found a tray of breakfast foods waiting for me in the kitchen. No Kameron.

I ate by myself and wandered around the suite, growing restless and bored. I even ventured into his room, saw the bed, neatly made up as if it hadn't been slept in. There wasn't a single scrap of clothing in sight. The man was a neat freak. I inhaled, catching the scent of his cologne lingering in the air. Whatever it was, it was really nice. It smelled expensive. Sexy. Wondering what it was, I tiptoed into his bathroom.

Again, nothing was out of place. His personal things were all stored out of sight. Worried he might catch me snooping, I abandoned my search for his cologne bottle, went back to the living space, and flopped down on the couch.

This trip had turned out so differently from what I'd expected.

Here I was, in New York City, a place I'd never been, a placed I'd dreamed of visiting, and I was alone, bored, and locked in a condo. I wasn't feeling sick anymore. Outside of the fact that I had been brought here by my employer and thus should remain where he could find me in case he needed me, there wasn't anything keeping me from doing a little exploring. From the look of it, the condo was in a safe part of town.

Then again, I didn't have a key.

I tried calling him.

No answer.

Surely he had an extra key somewhere. . . .

I started my search in all the usual spots, the drawers and shelves. I located some pictures in a drawer that captured my interest. Old photographs of Kameron with some other men. They all looked similar. The angle of their jaw. The shape of their eyes. The wavy texture of their hair. Brothers? No, he'd said he had no brothers. Cousins, maybe. Another photo showed an older couple. The man looked very much like Kameron. And the woman was very beautiful, with long hair and a body I envied at my age. The man was smiling playfully. His expression reminded me of Kameron.

Like father, like son.

I flipped through some of the other photos, smiling as I glimpsed a tiny slice of Kameron Maldonado's family life.

The front door clicked, and I jumped.

He walked in, stopped, frowned. "What are you doing?"

Feeling as if I'd been caught snooping in his underwear drawer, I dropped the photos and slammed the drawer shut. "I was looking for a spare key."

"Why?"

"I thought I'd go out for a little bit."

"Where?" He set his briefcase on the floor, next to the door. "Did you tell me you'd never been in New York before?"

"That's right, I haven't."

"You shouldn't leave the condo alone, then. It isn't safe."

"This area looks pretty—"

"It isn't safe," he repeated as he flipped up his collar and pulled his tie out. I watched as the silk slid along his neck, remembering how it felt gliding over my wrists. My insides warmed, and I swallowed. "I'm finished with my appointments today. I'll take you out."

"Thank you."

He unbuttoned his shirt while walking toward his room. "Give me a couple of minutes."

"Sure."

He closed himself in his room, presumably to change his clothes. I waited, excited to be finally seeing the city while being healthy enough to actually enjoy it. He emerged a few minutes later, dressed in jeans, a snug black pullover shirt, and a really sharp black leather jacket. "Ready to go shopping?"

"I . . . we're going shopping?"

"Didn't I promise you a shopping trip before we left?"

"Yes, but that was before—"

"Let's go." He motioned for me to take the lead. I went out into the hallway and, while he locked the condo, I poked the elevator button.

His phone rang just as he stepped up next to me. "Hello? Great. Okay. Thanks. Call me later when you get the report back." He smiled at me. "I have a car waiting downstairs. Where do you want to go first? Barneys? Bergdorf Goodman? SoHo?"

"I don't know." Really, how could I choose? I had heard of all of them but had never been to any.

"I think SoHo first," he said.

The door chimed, and in we stepped. The car was empty. Out of habit, I stood in the back. Kameron took a spot next to me. The door rolled closed, shutting us in the elevator together.

He glanced at me, and I felt my cheeks burning a little.

He was such a handsome man. Insanely handsome. And I

knew what his kisses tasted like—decadent. I knew what his caress felt like—intoxicating. I knew what his possession felt like—thorough perfection.

Never would I taste his kiss again, or shudder under his caress, or quiver as his body possessed mine.

Dammit.

I knew I shouldn't feel so disappointed, but I did.

"What's wrong?" he asked, sensing my wilting mood.

"Nothing. I'm just . . . a little worn out still."

"If you're not up to our excursion, we can go—"

"No, I'll be fine."

He looked askance at me as the elevator bounced to a stop. His eyes were dark with concern. Genuine worry. How could I have ever mistaken that worry for guilt?

He couldn't be that good of an actor.

Now, I felt guilty. For accusing him of doping me. For screaming at him. "Really. I'll be okay," I said.

"If you get too tired, tell me right away and I'll bring you back."

"Will do."

We stepped outside. The air, the sidewalk, the streets were damp, and the air was heavy with the scents of wet concrete and auto exhaust. I inhaled deeply as I was escorted to a waiting car.

As I buckled in, I turned to Kameron and smiled through my guilt. "I'm sorry I blamed you."

"Don't worry. I would've believed the same thing. Especially after the rough start we had." He set his hand on my knee and gave it a tiny squeeze. Little warm ripples of pleasure swept through my body at the touch. My gaze jerked to his hand, and in the next second, he snatched it away. "I promise you, I won't ever touch you inappropriately again. I was wrong to do that in the first place. I've never done anything like that before."

The rumors suggested otherwise.

So did his history with me.

There I go again, second-guessing him. Doubting him.

Unsure how I felt about his promise, I smiled and nodded and tried to ignore the waves of need pulsing through me.

It was going to be pure hell working so closely with this man now. Absolute torture.

7

Eleven thousand dollars. Eleven freaking thousand dollars. That's how much money Kameron had spent today. On me. Not by my choice, either. I'd given up a damn good fight, trying to dissuade him from spending so much. I'd begged, pleaded, demanded, threatened to quit. He ignored my begging, pleading, and demanding. As far as my threat to quit went, he warned me if I quit he'd hunt me down and drag me back to work.

There was absolutely no stopping him.

At the end of our shopping extravaganza, I had a mountain of new clothes and shoes. All of them gorgeous. A few of them terribly expensive. The bags were crammed in the trunk of the car, and exhausted, I flopped into the backseat with Kameron. My eyelids were heavy. My eyes were gritty, as if someone had dumped a bucket of sand in them.

I yawned.

"I shouldn't have kept you out so late," he said, lifting an arm to drape it across my seat back.

"I'm okay. Just sleepy."

He pulled me against him, cupping my head and forcing it to the side so it rested on his shoulder. Immediately, those waves of warmth started pulsing through me again.

Would they ever stop? And how would I ever be just his administrative assistant if he was going to continue to touch me, hold me, pull me closer to him?

Now that he'd promised not to hold me to our agreement, I didn't have a reason to find a new job . . . or did I?

"Rest," he ordered.

Fighting to ignore the desire building inside my body, I closed my eyes and concentrated on breathing. Slowly. Deep inhalation. Slow exhalation. In. Out.

I felt my body growing heavy.

He pulled me tighter against him, and I could feel the rise and fall of his chest as he breathed. His body heat warmed me, and a sleepy contentment spread through me.

This was so nice. I felt protected and safe. More than I'd ever felt in my life.

I'd always been the caregiver in our family. Me. I'd been the shoulder my brother had leaned on. It was so nice having someone for me to lean on for once. Really nice.

A tiny moan of contentment slipped from my lips.

"Are you okay?" he asked. The low rumble of his voice vibrated through my body.

"Yes. I'm fine. I'm good."

"Excellent."

The car pulled to a stop. Kameron gave my shoulder a little shake. "See there? It's the Empire State Building."

I turned toward him, following his motion as he pointed out his window.

"The architecture—" His head swiveled. He froze.

We were nose to nose.

Mere inches separated our mouths.

My gaze was locked to his.

It felt like someone had sucked all the air out of the car. I pulled in a little gasp. It wasn't enough.

His head tipped closer, closer.

Ohmygod. I held my breath. My heart started pounding. My eyelids fell over my sleepy eyes.

His lips found mine, lingered, barely touching. The contact was so light it tickled. I quivered.

"Abigail," he whispered, his breath a soft caress that made tiny, sharp blades of need pierce my body.

"Kameron?" I answered, unsure why he'd said my name.

"Stop me. Stop me now."

I didn't want to, dammit. I wasn't even sure if I could.

"That's an order," he said with a little more force.

I lifted a hand to his chest, flattened it. I could feel his heart pounding through his clothes, the swift rise and fall of his breaths. His shirt was soft under my touch, but beneath that lay tight sinew and firm muscle. My fingertip found something small and hard. I explored that sharp little thing, running my fingertip back and forth across it, and Kameron sucked in a gasp.

"That's not helping." It was a growl. Low and sexy and full of danger.

I couldn't help giggling. I felt powerful and powerless at the same time. With the mere flick of a fingertip I could make this large, strong, dangerous man quake. But at the same time, I was falling under the spell of the lust blossoming inside of me. In no time it would overpower me. I could feel it.

"Miss Barnes," he repeated. He hadn't moved. Neither had I. We were both frozen in place. I was warring with myself, trying to will my arm to move, trying to convince my muscles to contract so I could push him back. It wasn't working. "Abigail."

"Yes, sir?" Even to my own ears, my voice sounded heavy and laced with need.

His words echoed in my head. *There was something about you. I . . . wanted you.*

He groaned, jerked me toward him, and kissed me.

Instantly, my body flamed with need.

I whimpered, my lips parting, and his tongue slipped inside, filling my mouth with his sweet, intoxicating flavor. It caressed mine. His lips gliding smoothly. His hands exploring my back, fingers curling around the back of my jacket.

"Dammit," he whispered between thrusts of his tongue. The kiss was becoming more intense, as the ripples of heat spreading through me grew in strength. There was no way I could stop it now. Absolutely none. I surrendered to my weakness and grabbed two fists full of his hair, making sure he wouldn't stop either.

My tongue tangled with his. And his hands reached down, cupped my ass. In a single heartbeat, he unbuckled my belt, lifted me off the seat, and plunked me down on his lap, legs straddling his hips. I ground my throbbing center against the bulge in his pants, wishing there were no clothes between us. I ached for him to fill me, to stroke away the burning need deep inside.

Releasing his hair, I reached down and tried to pull his shirt off, but I couldn't. He wasn't letting me. His hands were busy too. Moving up my sides, fingertips grazing the outsides of my covered breasts before cupping my face, holding me in place so he could deepen the kiss.

Oh, how I loved the way he took control. I shuddered. I whimpered. I would have pleaded if I could speak. Responding to his kiss, my tissues swelled, clenching and unclenching. The scent of my desperation filled the air. I sucked in a deep breath, then let it out in a little huff when he fisted my hair and jerked my head back.

"Must stop," he grumbled against the base of my throat. His

tongue flicked over my skin, and my right side was instantly coated in goose bumps.

"No, please." I rocked my hips back and forth to the pounding of my blood through my body. My fingers curled around leather, grasping it, holding on. "Please don't stop. I want this. I want you."

One second I was on his lap, writhing, breathless, dizzy. And the next I was falling against the door. I was still breathless and dizzy, but he wasn't touching me anymore.

Angled over me, he said, "I meant what I said. You don't have to—"

"I want to."

"No." His lips were gleaming, his face flushed. "I won't do this to you. I won't." His voice softened as he added, "You deserve so much more, Abigail. A hell of a lot better than me." He helped me return to a seminormal sitting position. "Whether you realize it now or not, believe me, I'm doing you a favor by stopping this before it gets out of hand."

"O-okay." I blinked at him a few times, then turned away. He was probably right about that. He probably was doing me a huge favor by putting an end to all of this.

But at the moment, 99 percent of me didn't want to believe it.

He cleared his throat. "I think we need to put a little distance between us. Tomorrow I'll put you on a flight back home."

My heart sank to my toes. "Yes, sir."

"Dammit, I'm sorry." He sighed. "I'm really fucking with your head. I can't keep doing that. I won't keep doing it."

Staring out the window, so he couldn't see my face, I said, "Like you said, I'm hardly helping—"

"If I hadn't started it in the first place, it wouldn't be a problem now. Besides, it isn't fair to ask you to make up for my weakness. I'm the one who needs to get his shit together. I will. I'll do it for you."

Not sure what to say, I nodded and tried to concentrate on the lights and bustle of New York at night.

Roughly thirty-six hours later, I went to work, back at the office, to find an e-mail in my in-box. It was from Kameron. My heart started galloping in my chest as I clicked it.

I hadn't spoken with him since that night in the cab. He'd said good night when we had returned to the condo, and the next morning there was a driver and an airline ticket waiting for me. I was taken to the airport and flew home alone.

I missed him.

I missed him a lot.

And for several reasons, including how much I missed him, I decided to put my job hunt on hold.

> Good morning. Heard some news about
> your situation. I leased the car for the week. A
> previous passenger, affiliated with another com-
> pany, not MalTech, spiked the water. He's been
> arrested. I hope this news eases your concerns.
> Kam

Kam.

He'd called himself Kam. To me, that was a sign of intimacy. That right there lifted my mood. So did the rest of the e-mail. The truth had been confirmed. It hadn't been Kam. I'd been wrong. Was I ever glad of that!

Feeling a little lighter, I went about my day. Time dragged a bit, since Kam hadn't left me with much to do. I answered his phone and took messages, e-mailing them to him as they came in. Otherwise, I watched the hours tick by until lunchtime. For the first time since I'd taken the job as Kam's assistant, I went down to the employee cafeteria-slash-diner for lunch. The company had a pretty nice setup down there. There was a cook and a limited selection of entrées and side dishes along with a salad bar and made-to-order hot and cold sandwiches. Before my promotion, I'd go down and eat with Julie Pfeifer. A tiny blonde with big blue eyes and bigger black-framed glasses, and a cool, somewhat quirky personal style, Julie worked in the cubicle kitty-corner to mine. I hadn't spoken to her since I'd been promoted.

As I stepped into the room, the scent of the food made my stomach rumble. I glanced around and found Julie standing in line, waiting to place her order. Today she was wearing a funky jacket, high-waisted pencil skirt, and platform shoes. I went up to her and smiled. "Hi."

"Oh. Hi," she said, looking surprised. "I thought you'd left."

"Left?"

"Fired," she said, leaning closer. "That was the rumor."

"No. My brother was fired. Not me."

"Oh?" Her brows lifted.

"I changed departments," I added, avoiding what I knew she wanted to hear about—the reason for my brother's departure.

"Ah. Cool. Where are you at now?"

The cook placed her hands on the metal counter and looked askance at Julie.

To the cook, Julie said, "I'll take a Reuben please. Toasted."

The cook nodded, then turned to me.

"Nothing for me, thanks."

The cook started preparing Julie's sandwich, and we stepped aside to wait.

"Where are you working now?" she asked.

"Up on the tenth floor."

"Really? Tenth?" Her smile was a little strained. I sensed she wasn't just surprised by my news. She was surprised and a little irritated, or perhaps jealous. I decided not to disclose any more.

"How are things going in Purchasing?"

"You know, same old same old. I wish they'd fire Clarence. He's such a micromanager. Drives me insane."

"I feel for you." That was no lie. Clarence, a retired U.S. Air Force officer, nitpicked every minute detail of a job, even the most mundane. It was enough to drive anyone crazy.

Julie leaned closer to me and whispered, "Any way you could hook me up with a department change?"

"I don't know. I'll see what I can do."

"Thanks."

The cook slid a plate onto the steel counter, and Julie grabbed it, setting it on her tray. We moved down to the next section for the fries and preplated salads. I set a small chef's salad on her tray, and down we went to the cashier to pay. I paid for both our lunches, and together we filled our drink cups and took a seat at a table near a window.

"Thanks for buying my lunch," Julie said as she smoothed her napkin over her lap.

"After all the times you'd paid for mine, I owe you."

"I bought what, twice? And all you had was a piece of fruit and a drink."

"I still owe you," I said as I poked at my salad. "And I'll see what I can do about the transfer."

"Thank you."

We chatted while we ate. It was nice. I hadn't realized how isolated I was up in my fancy office. When I headed back up, I started to wish I was following Julie back to my old cubby. All it took was a small reminder about the piddly paycheck that went with that tiny workspace that changed my mind. Quickly.

At least I had something to do now. I composed an e-mail, asking Kam if he knew of anyone up on the tenth floor needing an administrative assistant. I wished to recommend someone. He responded within seconds saying he'd take her name and see what he could do.

Feeling like I'd accomplished something worthwhile, I concentrated on booking Kam's appointments for next week, then called it a day. Outside of lunch with Julie, the e-mail about her move, and the little bit of busy work I'd done, it had been a really boring day. I missed Kam as much when the day was over as I had when it first started. It was strange walking past his empty desk, through his empty office. Strange and lonely.

And he wouldn't be back until Monday. I hoped the rest of the week would pass faster.

But of course, it didn't.

Time crawled slower than a sleeping turtle.

The only highlights of those days were the brief and much too infrequent e-mails or texts I received from Kam. By Friday afternoon, I was literally counting down the minutes until the weekend. I was shutting down my computer when I received an e-mail from him.

> Hi Ab. Tell your friend to come and see me
> Monday morning at nine o'clock.
> Kam

Looked like he'd found something for her.

I sent off a response to him, then called her. She answered on the first ring.

"Great news!" I said. "You're to come up to Kam—to Mr. Maldonado's office on Monday morning. Nine o'clock."

"Why?" she asked.

"I think you're being transferred." I scooped up my purse and hooked the strap over my elbow.

"No way!"

"Don't quote me on that."

"Ohmygod!" she practically shrieked into my ear. "Thank you so much."

"No problem."

"What did he say? Do you know anything?"

"He didn't say anything. Just to have you come up and meet with him Monday."

"If I get the transfer—oh crap, gotta go."

The phone cut off.

If I had money to bet, and I am the betting type, I'd lay two-to-one odds on the fact that Clarence was standing in her cubicle.

At exactly five, I headed downstairs. On the way down I took a little detour through my old department to see if Julie was still in her cubby. No, she'd left.

I drove home. Nobody there. Joss was gone. I was alone. Hungry. I checked the refrigerator. Nothing to eat. I decided to splurge, called in a carryout order from Antonio's and asked for delivery. Then I changed into some comfortable clothes and flopped onto the couch to catch up on all my favorite shows. Two hours later I'd eaten way too much pasta, I was still alone, I'd watched a couple of shows, and I was bored, bored, bored.

I scrolled through my phone, looking for someone to go out with. I tried a couple of numbers, including Julie's. No answer.

My phone chimed. I had a text.

Hoping it might be Julie or my brother, I checked it. I hadn't heard a peep from Joss all night. That wasn't a good sign.

The text was from Kam.

Where are you right now? his message read.

I answered. **Home.**

I'm in town. Want to grab a drink somewhere?

A drink! Had he changed his mind about our relationship remaining purely professional?

Sure.

Pick you up in twenty, he texted.

See you then.

I jumped up from my couch and ran to my room. I tore through my closet, searching for something to wear. Kam had bought me all those gorgeous clothes in New York, over ten thousand dollars' worth. And I couldn't find anything that was quite right for going out for drinks. Most of the clothes I'd bought were for work. Suits and blouses. Blazers and pencil skirts. Trousers. The few evening pieces I'd bought were fairly formal, either very long or extremely dressy. I wavered between a pair of black pants and a blouse that was semisheer and one of the more casual evening dresses I'd bought. I tried the blouse and pants first, then changed my mind and went with the dress. It was charcoal gray and clingy, knee length, and made out of a smooth knit that hugged my curves and made me look ten pounds thinner. I opted for a pair of adorable, bright coral patent leather heels, a coral necklace, and gold bag.

I was stuffing my wallet into my purse when a knock on the door signaled Kam's arrival.

My heart hopped like a rabbit.

I took a deep breath before opening the door.

That breath left my lungs in a swift whoosh when our gazes met. His eyes were dark and full of emotion. He stepped in, pulled me into his arms, and crushed me to him.

"I missed you," he said in my ear.

"I . . . missed you too." I tipped my head back so I could look him in the eyes.

He stared into my eyes for a moment, then his gaze wandered down to my mouth.

My tongue slipped out, moistening my lips.

My heart started thumping against my breastbone.

Was he going to kiss me? Had he decided the whole I-won't-touch-you-again thing wasn't going to work?

His head dipped lower, lower. But just when I expected his mouth to meet mine, he pushed me back slightly and he took a step away. His face was the shade of a pomegranate. "You look great."

"Thanks."

"We'd better go."

"Okay." After I double-checked to make sure I had my house keys, I proceeded out the door. Kam steered me to the sleek black sports car parked outside my apartment building, his hand resting ever so softly on the small of my back. I sat in the passenger seat while he circled around the front and took his place behind the wheel.

Within seconds we were zooming down the road.

It was a gorgeous night. Not too warm. Not too cool. The vehicle's windows were open just enough to let in some fresh air without blowing my hair all over the place like a maelstrom. But inside the vehicle there was an odd tension. It seemed to pull at me, make me uneasy.

I was the one who broke the silence between us. "Thanks for helping Julie out with a transfer."

"Actually, I couldn't get her a transfer. Not yet."

"Oh." Julie was going to be very disappointed. I felt bad for her.

"I want to meet with her to find out why she is looking for a new job," he explained as he braked the car for a red light.

"Oh. I don't know if she'll tell you that."

"I hope she will. Do you know?" he asked.

"I have some idea."

He turned his head to look at me. "Tell me."

The light changed to green. I pointed. "I think I'd rather let her decide whether she wants to tell you."

"Fair enough."

We drove for another few moments without speaking. I switched back and forth from admiring Kam's profile—he was such a stunning man—to watching buildings and cars fly by. The tension between us was still as bad as it was when we'd first gotten in the car. I was the one, once again, who broke the silence. "How was the rest of your trip?"

"It was work. I don't like leaving town. It wasn't bad when you were with me. But once you left . . ."

Did my presence really mean that much to him? "It was pretty strange coming to work every day and not seeing you."

He smiled at me. It was the kind of smile that made a girl's heart literally skip a beat. "You say that now, but you'll probably wish I was gone again by Tuesday." He steered the car onto the freeway.

I didn't believe that for a minute. In fact, he had just returned and I was already dreading when he would have to leave next.

"We'll see about that," I said as the weight of my words sunk in. The truth was, I was falling for him.

Falling hard. Falling fast. Falling for my boss.

8

―――――――

"Thank you for accepting my spur-of-the-moment invitation." We were stopped at an intersection after having driven about twenty minutes on the freeway. While Kam waited for the light to change, he gave me a long, assessing once-over. "I was surprised to learn you were home alone on a Friday night."

I shrugged. "I was in the mood for a quiet night."

"Did I ruin your plans?"

"Nope. Not at all."

Neither of us said anything else until we were pulling into a dark parking area behind a towering brick and steel building. I just kept wondering what was going to happen tonight, after my rather awkward departure from New York. And he seemed to be in a very quiet, introspective mood. As strange as it was, I was okay with the quiet. I didn't feel like I had to fill the minutes with eager chatter.

"Have you ever been to the Cavern?" Kam asked as he shifted the vehicle out of gear, parking behind the building.

"No."

"I hope you like it. I'm not much for crowds, but this place is pretty nice." He unfolded his large frame as he got out of the car, then circled around to my side and opened my door. Seconds later, he escorted me to the club's back door and knocked.

"Isn't this a service entrance?" I asked.

"Like I said, I don't like crowds."

The door swung open, and a man greeted Kam with a handshake and a big, friendly smile, welcoming him inside. As Kam steered me through the open door, he introduced me to our host, Miron.

Miron gave me a quick up and down before extending a hand and offering one of those bright smiles. "Good to meet you."

"Miron owns the Cavern," Kam told me as we zigged and zagged around hustling cooks in the kitchen. The scents of food made my mouth water, and the deep throb of music pounded through my body.

"Only because Kam lent me the money to get the place up and running," Miron said over his shoulder.

"You had a great business plan." Kam was behind me. "It's been a solid investment."

"Yeah, well, you were the only one who saw the potential."

Kam smiled. "Which has paid off nicely."

The two friends shared a laugh. And Miron pushed open a door, leading out of the kitchen and into the dimly lit, sexy main space of the club. Two walls were brick, the black ceiling a soaring twenty feet or so up. Directly to my right was a stage for live performances, currently empty. And in front of the stage was a dance floor, also empty.

"Have a good time, you two." Miron motioned us out.

"Thanks." Kam gave Miron's hand another shake, then steered me through the door with gentle pressure on the small of my back. My skin prickled beneath my dress as my nerves responded to his touch. "It's a little early yet. This place will be packed in a couple of hours," Kam explained as he directed me toward the wall at the far end of the space. In front of the wall was an arched bar, unmanned. On either side of it were exits that led out to a smaller, more intimate lounge area with padded leather booths. Kam motioned me to the farthest booth. I sat.

Before I'd had a chance to say anything, a waiter approached us, smiling. "Mr. Maldonado. It's good to have you back, sir."

"Thank you. I'll take a bottle of Chardonnay."

"Very good. I'll be back shortly." Off the waiter went, to fetch our wine.

Kam's gaze locked on mine. "Are you sure I didn't ruin your evening, calling you last minute like this?"

Ruin? How could he think he had ruined my night? He had done nothing to wreck it . . . yet. "No, not at all."

His lips curled into a semismile. "I didn't feel like being alone."

It struck me then, for the first time, as I gazed into his dark eyes that he might be lonely. A man who looked like a model, who had enough money to buy anything he wanted, anytime, lonely. A man who spent hours upon hours talking to people, Lonely. A man who probably had women throwing themselves at his feet, lonely.

My heart jerked in my chest.

"I understand," I said. "Actually, when I said I was in the mood for a quiet evening, I lied. The truth is, I didn't have plans either. I ate dinner and had burned through all my TiVo shows already. If you hadn't called, I probably would've just gone to bed."

His expression softened. "Why a beautiful woman like you would be forced to spend Friday night alone . . ."

Beautiful. Kam Maldonado called me beautiful. My face warmed. "Thanks for the compliment. But it's not anyone's fault but my own. I don't try to get out and meet people."

"Neither do I."

The waiter made a show of bringing our wine and pouring some into a glass for Kam to sample. After taking a sip and giving a quick nod of approval, Kam waved him off with a pleasant thank you, then poured a glass for me.

I sipped. Delicious. Fruity but not too sweet.

In the distance, music started playing. Soft, sultry music.

Drinking his wine, Kam watched me over the rim of his glass. "Do you want to dance?"

"Oh, I don't know." I recalled the last time he'd held me, how confused and conflicted he'd acted. And how confused and conflicted his actions had made me.

"Friends dance, don't they?" he asked, tipping his head slightly.

"Friends?" I echoed. "Is that what we are?"

"I'd like that. Would you?"

I wasn't sure whether I wanted to be *friends* with him or not. A part of me liked the idea of having a safe, nonsexual, but personal relationship with this enigmatic man. But another was worried about how even a friendship might affect our working relationship. I also worried about the fact that I was so attracted to Kam. How I felt when he touched me. How I felt when he kissed me.

And how I felt when he didn't.

The truth was, my body craved his touch. It craved his kiss. When he wasn't touching me, I wanted to move closer, lean in, close the distance between us.

Friends. Friends? Could I be friends with a man I was so drawn to?

What if he started dating another woman?

How would I handle that?

My stomach twisted.

"Abigail?"

His voice yanked me out of my head, away from that awful what-if and back to the current moment. Our gazes met, and my insides flittered like little trapped butterflies.

I sputtered, "Yes, sure. Friends."

He chuckled. "You sound so enthusiastic. Am I that much of a bastard?"

"No, no!" I shook my head as I fingered the stem of my wineglass. My gaze dropped to the table, to my hand. His was resting on the table, not far from mine. Within reach. But I couldn't touch it, hold it. Just like the man himself. Within reach but forbidden. "That's not the issue."

"Abigail?" That hand, the one I had wished I could touch, reached for mine. His index finger stroked the back, ever so softly. "What is the issue?"

"Well . . ." My gaze lifted again, swept over his face. His brows were pinched. His lips turned down slightly at the corners.

He stood, took my hand in his. "Come, dance with me."

"But—"

He pressed an index finger to my lips. "Shhh. It's only a dance."

Only.

Dancing involved standing close. And touching.

Touching.

A quiver of need raced through my body.

He led me back through the doors and down to the dance floor. It was empty. The whole place was empty, except the two of us. The lights were low, red and blue colored beams casting a deep glow over us.

Kam pulled me to him, placed one hand on my back, and lifted my hand with the other. He swayed his hips. "Do you dance?" he asked, speaking softly in my ear.

"A little," I said.

He tightened his hold on me and started following a set of simple rumba steps. Slow, quick, quick. His hips were rolling as he moved. It was a seduction as much as a dance, and it made my heart thump heavily in my chest, my body warm.

The hand on my back slid down toward my butt, but his feet kept up that simple pattern. Slow, quick, quick. Slow, quick, quick. My heart was thumping out the beat. My body undulating to the rhythm. I was melting into him. We were moving as one. Our bodies writhing to the music, limbs entwined.

He snugged me tighter, until my entire body was flattened against him. The scent of his skin and cologne filled my nose. I breathed it deep, pulling it in, relishing it. My nipples hardened as they were gently grazed through the layers of our clothes. A steady throb pounded through my body, heat pooling in the deepest part of me.

How I longed for his touch. His kiss.

This was no dance. It was torture. Cruelty beyond words.

The bastard.

What the hell was he trying to do? Crush me? Destroy me?

"I can't." Surprising myself, I shoved him and hurried away.

Didn't he know what he was doing? How could he not realize how confusing this hot-and-cold act was?

"Abigail, wait." He ran to me, catching me by the waist and jerking me around. "The dance isn't over yet."

"Yes, it is." Breathless, I glared into his eyes. Even as I said those words, my hands skimmed up his body and he began swaying his hips to the music again.

We were dancing.

We were fighting.

We were living a strange, beautiful moment. It was magical.

His head tipped forward and his lips found mine. The kiss was as sensual and intoxicating as the battle-dance. I skimmed my hands up his body to his face, cupped his cheeks. I held him, refusing to let the kiss end. My lips parted as I sucked in a deep gasp, and his tongue slid into my mouth, filling me with the decadent flavor of man and wine.

My knees suddenly felt weak and soft.

No man had ever danced with me like this, kissed me like this, made me want him so much.

I whimpered. I shuddered. I grabbed fists full of hair and kissed him with all the emotion that was blasting through my body. And he possessed me. My mouth. My body.

His hands stroked. His tongue claimed. He took and took, and gave and gave.

When I couldn't take another second, I murmured, "Please, Kam. I'm begging."

He eased back, gently loosening his hold on me while keeping me steady. "Dammit, Abigail. Dammit."

"Don't!" My hands lifted to my lips. They were still tingling. And his flavor lingered. My tongue slipped out, dampening them, tasting him.

Looking conflicted once again, he reached for me, but I jerked away. "I didn't want to do this, Abigail. That's not why I called you tonight."

"Why did you call me tonight?"

"I . . ." He jammed his hands through his hair. "I wanted to make up for what happened in New York."

"The drugging?"

"Not just that. Everything."

"Everything?" Feeling slightly chilled, I wrapped my arms around myself.

Once again he reached for me, but this time he jerked his own hand back. I didn't have to move out of his reach. "I meant it when I said I didn't want to do this to you anymore. And here I go again, pawing at you like a horny high schooler. I'm an asshole."

"No. You're not—"

"Yes, I am. First, I take advantage of your situation, forcing you to agree to a ridiculous, illegal, and slightly immoral arrangement because of something your brother allegedly did. I still don't know what the hell really happened regarding him.

And then, when I try to make it right, I mess with you until you're so confused you think you want me to keep doing it."

Was that what was happening?

Yes, maybe.

No.

I wasn't confused. I wanted him to touch me, to hold me, to kiss me. I wanted him to want me as much as I wanted him. And maybe now it was time to let him know that. Maybe if he knew how I felt he would stop playing this game. "I'm not confused."

"Of course you are."

"No, I'm not." A hard knot of emotion twisted in my gut, and I felt my body tensing. "Don't tell me what I am or am not feeling," I snapped.

"But—"

"No, listen to me." Adrenaline was flowing through me now, making me feel high, making me feel powerful. I grabbed the front of his shirt and yanked. The fabric gave way, revealing a slice of muscled chest and tight stomach. "I want you."

Something dark flashed across his face, but he didn't move. Not for one, two, three seconds. Then he lunged at me, hauled me against him, and kissed me. This kiss was nothing like the last one. That one had been a seduction. This one was feral and raw. A plundering. As his mouth possessed mine, he half carried, half dragged me to the nearest table in a dark corner, lifted me up on it, and pushed his hips between my thighs.

"Yes," I said on a sigh as he ground the hard lump in his pants against my burning tissues. "Yes." I wrapped my legs around his waist, holding him against me.

He shoved his hands into my dress, pulled the cups of my bra down, allowing my breasts to spill out, and pinched my nipples so hard I shivered. I was burning up, melting, losing my mind. Everything in the world had narrowed down to this one small space, where one sensation after another pummeled my system.

The sound of our labored breathing, the scent of my need blending with his cologne, the sight of his beautiful face as he angled back just enough to pull my panties down and unzip his pants.

His cock sprang out, thick and erect and glistening with pre-come.

"Tell me you have a condom." He was breathless.

So was I. "I don't. But I have an IUD."

He found my entrance and, hands cupped under my ass, slammed his hips forward, surging into me.

The sensation literally made my head spin. I shut my eyes and clung to him as he took me hard and fast. The thrusts were powerful, urgent, exactly what my body craved. And with each one, my muscles tensed harder, heat swirling round and round within me, pushing me closer, closer to the pinnacle.

He literally lifted my bottom off the table, deepening his possession. His cock pushed deep inside, teasing the entry of my womb. Filled me to utter perfection.

"Touch yourself," he demanded. "Do it now."

I licked my finger, dampening it, and placed it on my clit. Matching my strokes with his, I circled over the sensitive bud. Within seconds, colors exploded behind my closed eyes as the first convulsion of a powerful orgasm gripped my body. My inner muscles clenched around his girth.

"Oh, yes. I'm going to come." He gave me two long, slow thrusts and then froze, groaned, and slammed deep inside one last time.

It took us at least fifteen minutes to catch our breath. He didn't move. He didn't withdraw from me. He leaned his head forward, resting his forehead against my uncovered breasts.

It wasn't until my heart had slowed to a somewhat normal pace that I realized I'd just had sex in public. In a bar. Hoping nobody had caught us, I slitted my eyes open and glanced around.

I didn't see anyone.

The music was still playing. A different song, but just as sexy as the one we'd danced to. I reached out, running my hands up his chest. My fingertips teased his nipples, and they hardened to little peaks.

He groaned and opened his mouth, but I put my index finger on his lips.

"Shhh," I said.

He nodded, took my hand in his, flipped it over, and sweetly kissed my palm. Then he murmured as he pulled the bodice of my dress back in place, "We should . . . we'd better get going. Miron will be opening the doors any minute now." He glanced down at his torn shirt. "I don't want to have to explain this."

I tugged the ripped pieces toward the center of his body, making a failing attempt at covering him. "You mean you don't have women regularly ripping your clothes off?"

"No. If there's any ripping, it's generally me doing it and the woman being on the receiving end."

"Well, then, I'm glad it's different with me."

"It's most definitely different with you. Very different."

Those words made me smile.

After giving me a little kiss on the forehead, he fixed the skirt of my dress as he withdrew from me. And before he zipped himself up, he helped me off the table and retrieved my discarded panties.

We left the bar, my hand in his.

He didn't take me home. Instead, he took me back to his house. He didn't ask me. He just assumed I would be okay with it.

I was, but that was beside the point.

After he parked, he said, "Stay here," got out of the car, ran around to my side, and opened the door for me.

I thanked him as I straightened up. We were standing close.

It was dark outside. We'd just had sex. I slid my arms around his waist and cozied up to his warm bulk.

This felt so good, so right. Especially when he wrapped his arms around me and gave the top of my head a sweet kiss.

My gaze swept across the front of the building. It was huge. Brick. Stately.

"Let's go inside," he said.

Leaving one arm wrapped around his waist, I fell into step beside him, our footsteps perfectly timed. We went inside, and he escorted me directly to his bedroom. "Stay with me tonight," he whispered as he skimmed his hands down my arms. "Please."

My heart melted at the husky tone of his voice. I didn't speak. But he had his answer when he reached down for the hem of my dress.

Yes, I would spend the night with him. Tonight. The next one. As many as he wanted.

As he slowly pulled my dress up my body and over my head, his dark gaze meandered over my form. "You're so beautiful."

I couldn't help smiling. "Thank you."

He gently tugged the cup of my bra, freeing my breast. Then he bent down to pull it into his warm mouth.

I froze for a moment, just luxuriating in the pleasure he was stirring in my body. With each hard suck, a trickle of warmth pulsed through me. My senses were becoming more alert as I focused. The soft sound of his breaths and my little whimpers and moans. The scent of sex that clung to my hands as I lifted them to curl my fingers into his hair and tug. The taste of his kiss, still lingering on my lips.

He moved to my other breast, pulling the fullness out from the shelter of my bra and caressing it with gentle fingers. It felt like my bones were melting, turning to formless goo. My legs began trembling.

Seeming to sense my struggle to remain upright, he scooped me into his arms. I squealed, surprised, and threw an arm around his neck. I giggled as he dropped me on the bed and stared at me like a hungry lion about to pounce on his prey.

"I wasn't going to do this," he rumbled as he crawled over top of me. "I thought we would just sleep." He bent his elbows, angling himself over me, dipped his head down, and nipped my lower lip.

Reacting to the heavy throb of need now pulsing through me, I wrapped my legs around his waist. Ah, the heat and friction were just what I needed.

No, I needed more. So much more.

"Kam," I said on a sigh as I tightened my legs around him.

One of his hands caressed my thigh. "You make me feel something I haven't felt in ages," he whispered as he nibbled on my neck. "Maybe never."

Little prickles tingled over my skin. I arched my back, wrapped my arms around his neck, and tried to pull him down on top of me.

"You're too impatient," he whispered against my burning skin.

"It's your fault."

"Mmmm." He bit me again, harder this time, and I squeaked, startled. Next, he gently laved the stinging away, and once again, I was desperate to feel his skin gliding over mine. His hand slid higher, cupping my ass. His fingertips dipped into the crease. "Have you ever taken a man here?" he asked, probing deeper.

"No." I clenched my bottom, wincing at the thought. Kam was well endowed *down there*. I couldn't imagine anything that large going into my anus.

"Mmmm."

"Won't it hurt?" I asked, sounding almost as doubtful as I felt.

"It may if you're not ready." He leaned back and looked me straight in the eyes. "Will you trust me?"

"I . . . I don't know."

"All right, then you tell me when you trust me, and I'll show you how good it can feel."

My whole body relaxed at his words, and I realized I'd tensed up from fear.

"I haven't forced you to do anything you haven't wanted to do yet. Not once. I won't start now."

"Okay."

He pushed himself upright and unbuckled his pants. "Will you help me?" he asked.

I sat up and went to work, unfastening his pants and pulling them down over his lean hips. My hands explored his smooth skin as I worked, satin stretched over hard muscle. Like the rest of him, his legs were perfect, the muscles well defined. And his ass . . . it was so cute I wanted to bite it.

After he'd disposed of his pants and shirt, he held the base of his erection in his fist and motioned to me. "Taste me."

My mouth watered.

I flicked my tongue over the tip, tasting salt and man. When he gave a little groan, I opened my mouth and took just the swollen head inside and swirled my tongue around the flared ridge.

A soft moan encouraged me to continue. I relaxed my throat, taking him deeper. My flattened tongue cushioned his thick rod as it inched into the back of my throat.

Kam grabbed my hair in his fists, holding me in place as he withdrew almost completely. Then, moving slowly, he pushed his hips forward again, forcing his cock deeper, deeper. I swallowed against the urge to gag and closed my eyes, focusing on giving him pleasure rather than taking for once.

"My sweet girl," he mumbled as he once again pulled back. Taking advantage of the opportunity, I licked the head of his cock like a lollipop, savoring the flavor of the precome that had gathered at the very tip.

For a third time, he pushed inside my mouth. Moving deeper than the last time, testing the limits of my throat. Out he glided, in and out, in and out, slowly, allowing me time to relax my throat. I rested my hands on his thighs, feeling their muscles tremble and tense with each inward thrust. His skin was warming beneath my fingers. His breath sounding more ragged.

Using my hair, he pulled me away suddenly.

"My god, you're going to make me lose control." He shoved me down onto my back and climbed over me again.

I threw my arms around his neck and pulled him toward me. This time he rested his weight on me. His erection poked at my slick opening as he kissed me with fierce, feral hunger.

His tongue swept into my mouth just as his cock slid inside. He curled his arms over the top of my head, cradling it, and began thrusting in and out in a lusciously slow rhythm. With each inward thrust, my body warmed. Pulses of pleasure thrummed through me. I felt so safe and cherished, especially when he kissed me tenderly.

Within minutes his skin was burning, our bodies slick and tense. I was on the brink of orgasm, teetering.

He pulled out abruptly and I cried out, "Nooo!"

"Trust me," he whispered against my lips. "Please."

My response was a whimper and a slight nod.

He angled up, reached into the nightstand drawer. When his hand withdrew, he was holding some condoms and some lube.

He handed the condoms to me. "Please."

I tore open a package and rolled the latex on, sheathing him while he squirted some lube on his fingers and began massaging my anus.

Oh my God, he really was going to try it.

He coaxed me to roll over and climb onto my knees, and he handed me a pillow. I angled down so I was hugging the pillow as I knelt, my chest resting on it. Once I was in position, he smoothed some cool gel on my anus and stroked the sensitive skin around it. With his other hand, he teased my clit. This I'd done myself, when I'd masturbated. My body responded immediately, warming up. My blood pounded hard and hot through my body, sensation amplifying *down there*. When he pierced my anus with his fingers, my inner muscles tensed, gripping his invading digits, and a rush of decadent pleasure pulsed through me.

"That's it, baby. You're going to take me, and you're going to love it."

I wasn't so sure about either statement, but I couldn't deny my body was loving what was happening so far. His fingers were slowly working in and out, stretching the tight ring of muscles at the very end, encouraging them to relax. Within minutes I was trembling, on the verge of orgasm, so close I could practically taste it.

He pulled my ass cheeks apart and placed the tip of his cock at my entrance. I was slick and prepared, and to my surprise he slid right in.

"Yesss," he hissed as he pushed deeper, deeper, filling me.

The sensation was different but oh so good. I was going to come, hard.

He withdrew slightly and surged forward again, driving deeper, stroking nerves I hadn't realized I had. "Baby," he muttered, reaching down and fingering my clit. "I can't last long," he warned. "Come for me." He increased the pressure on my clit, and a huge surge of pleasure slammed me.

My orgasm was like a tidal wave. It was powerful and overwhelming. I felt like I was tumbling head over heels in steaming, thrashing water. Every muscle in my body spasmed. The pleasure was beyond description. I trembled and shook and cried out. His voice joined mine as he found release too. And together we pulsed and throbbed until we were exhausted, spent, sated.

I heaved a heavy sigh as he pulled out. He threw away the rubber, rolled me over, and pulled me against him.

I was smiling as I tumbled into a deep sleep.

9

The next morning I woke up. Looked left. Looked right. No sign of Kam.

I closed my eyes and tried to fall back asleep. I was still exhausted. My eyes felt like they'd been plucked from my head and rolled around in a kid's sandbox, then shoved back in the sockets. I was sore from head to toe, but particularly between my legs. And my head was groggy.

But I couldn't fall asleep.

After lying there for what felt like hours, I got up, took care of some bathroom issues, got dressed, then stumbled and wobbled downstairs to find Kam and some caffeine. I wanted to wish him good morning. I wanted to kiss him, too. And feel his arms around me. But I also wanted to ask him about my brother, to find out if he had learned anything about the allegations. By now he had to have some information, at least what had happened and why my brother had been fingered as the culprit.

The caffeine, I found. A full pot. Steaming hot. But Kam, I

did not. I poured a cup of liquid energy and took it to the wide French doors in the nearby family room.

The sun had risen, but it was hanging low in the east yet. A quick check of the clock told me this was the earliest I'd roused on a Saturday in ages.

I would be taking a nap later, for sure.

But for now . . .

I wandered his huge house as I drank my coffee. In a small way, I felt like I was snooping as I checked out his photographs hanging on the walls, the treasures he kept hidden in his built-in cabinets and drawers. But in another way, I felt like this was a chance to get to know him a little better.

I discovered an office at the front of the house. It was decorated in very masculine décor. Two walls were a deep gray. Floor-to-ceiling wood bookcases loaded with volumes covered a third and the forth, behind the polished, old wooden desk, was mostly window, swathed in gray silk. I sat in the desk and stared straight ahead. The desk faced the room's entry. But next to it hung a black-and-white picture. Dragging my fingertips over the desk's glossy top, I wandered over to take a closer look at the photo.

The two men looked very much alike. One was older; one was younger. Father and son. Smiling. This was the second photograph I'd seen of him and his father. Funny, but he hadn't mentioned his father to me. Not once. Nor his mother. Nor any other family. I wondered if there was a reason why.

Staring at the picture, I downed the last of my coffee. Then I headed back to the kitchen for a refill. As I was pouring, someone opened the front door.

Thinking it was Kam, I set down the cup and scurried toward the sound.

I stopped in the center of the foyer. My skin prickled as a

chill swept up my spine. That was followed by a rush of heat blazing to my face.

"Mr. Maldonado sent me to pick you up and drive you home," the strange man said. He was older than me, probably by a couple of decades, lean and well groomed, dressed in a dark suit, white shirt, and tie.

That man surely knew what I was doing at Kam's house on a Saturday morning. I wondered if this was a normal thing, to be sent over to take Kam's latest plaything home.

Don't think about that. He said you were different.

Trying to hide my slight mortification behind a veil of nonchalance, I said, "Okay. I just need to get my purse."

"Take your time." The driver went to the kitchen. I heard the rattle of cups as I vaulted up the stairs.

When I came down, it looked like he was emptying the cup he'd just filled. He smiled. "Mr. Maldonado has the best coffee."

"It is good."

"Ready?" he asked.

"Sure."

We headed outside to a sleek black sedan parked in the driveway. The man opened the back door, but I shook my head and pointed to the front passenger door. "May I?"

"Sure."

We strapped ourselves in, and within minutes the big, black car was prowling down the quiet streets.

"Sorry you had to work on a weekend," I said.

"No problem. I work every weekend."

"You mean you don't get a day off? Ever?"

"I get a day off whenever I want. All I have to do is ask. Mr. Maldonado is a good man to work for. A very good man." As we rolled to a stop at a light, the driver looked at me. "I lost my wife last year. The kids are grown, gone. What else am I going to do?"

I heard the loneliness in his voice, the sorrow. "I'm very sorry about your wife."

The light changed, and he hit the gas. "She was a good woman. My best friend. My companion. My lover. It's taking some time to get used to living without her."

"I can understand that. How long were you married?"

"Forty-eight years. We had our good times and our bad times, but those were still the best years of my life."

Forty-eight. That was a lot of years. More than I had lived, up to this point.

Someday I hoped to have a husband who would say the same thing about me. Right now that dream felt so distant, out of reach. "How did you meet your wife?"

"She was dating my best buddy. We both were in the army. Deployed together to Vietnam. He went home before our tour was up . . . KIA."

I didn't know what to say.

"I was with him when . . . That day he made me promise to take care of her. So when I went home, I contacted her. We became friends first. Husband and wife much later."

It was only when he shifted the car into park that I realized we were at my apartment. He had known my address.

"Thank you for the ride," I said as I reached for the door handle to let myself out.

"It was my pleasure. Any time." He gave a little wave as I pushed open the door. "I'll see you again soon."

Soon.

That brought a smile to my face. And I wondered, as I strolled up the front walk, if he knew something I didn't.

A few minutes later, as I let myself into my apartment, I found my brother lying on the couch. At least twenty beer bottles lay scattered over the coffee table and floor, along with an open, half-full pizza box, napkins, and potato chip bags.

Dread wound through my body, like ropes tugging my insides into knots.

Dammit, not again.

I smacked his foot, which was protruding out from under the afghan he had draped over himself. "Go to bed," I snapped.

He groaned.

I heard a sound deeper in the apartment. A door shut. Nervous—I had no idea who it was—I tiptoed down the hall, hurrying toward the relative safety and privacy of my bedroom.

Over the past couple of years I'd become painfully aware of the fact that my brother didn't always associate with the nicest people. More to the point, some of his friends were downright scary. Felons. Thieves. Thugs. As I made my way down the hall, my eyes jerked left and right. My body tensed. My heart started pounding.

I breathed much easier the minute I had myself locked in my room. Shower first. I grabbed some fresh clothes and padded to my bathroom. The door was shut. I didn't usually keep the door closed. I knocked softly. No answer. Weird. But I decided I must have closed it yesterday when I was rushing around, getting ready to go out with Kam.

I pushed the door open.

My eyes jerked to the wild-eyed woman sitting on the toilet. I recognized her immediately. It was the woman who'd come to thank Joss for driving her kid to the hospital.

Mortified for her, I lunged backward, slamming the door shut again. What a shock that had been. When my brother had houseguests, they usually used his bathroom—the one in the hallway—never mine. It took a few seconds for me to catch my breath.

But a second later a loud thud in the living room had me gasping all over again.

What now?

I heard a low moan. And a familiar voice saying, "Fuuuck."

Then the sound of retching.

Praying my brother made it to the kitchen trash can, I flopped onto the bed, pulled up the covers, and buried my head under my pillow. He was an absolute bastard when he was loaded. A bastard and a pain in the ass. Mean and needy.

"Abby!" Joss slurred. "Abby!"

I heard my bathroom door open, soft footsteps cross the room, then my bedroom door open and close.

Furious and frustrated, both for the invasion of privacy and for having to deal with an intoxicated man-child, I stomped into my bathroom and slammed the door.

Let him clean up his own freaking mess this time.

In the bathroom, I cranked on the hot water, shucked my clothes, and steamed myself until I was feeling somewhat human again. Then I toweled off and put on some comfortable weekend cleaning-the-house clothes. Yoga pants and a T-shirt. When I padded barefoot out to the living room, my first instinct was to check on Joss.

He wasn't on the couch anymore. Or on the floor, where I expected him. Slightly concerned, I checked his room. He was in his bed. After checking the rest of the apartment, I concluded his houseguest had helped him get into bed and then left.

Getting a little payback in, I cranked on the TV, tuned it to a music channel, and started cleaning the living room. If he wasn't my brother, and it wasn't partially my fault for him being the way he was, I'd have thrown him out ages ago.

A few hours later the apartment was looking much better, and I was ready for a long nap. As I was dragging my weary body down the hall toward my bedroom, Joss's door opened. He blinked red, swollen eyes at me.

"You're home," he grumbled.

"I've been home for hours. Rough night?"

"Rough morning," he confessed.

"You do it to yourself."

"I know." He pushed off the wall, staggering toward the bathroom. A second later, before I'd reached my room, I heard more retching.

It was painful to hear. Not because I felt bad that he was sick, but because I knew why he was drinking so much.

A memory flashed through my head, powerful and painful. I shut my eyes and tried to shove it out

"You little bastard. I've told you over and over to clean up the dog shit. What do I have to do? Huh?"

I heard the thump, but I hadn't known what it was.

Then I saw him, my little brother, lying on the floor. Blood was oozing from his nose, and one side of his face was a deep scarlet. Later, his lip would swell and an ugly bruise would blossom across his cheekbone.

Our father had hit him. Hard. And, judging by the way he'd clenched his hand into a fist, he was about to do it again. He grabbed my brother by the shirt and hauled him to his feet. His arm pulled back.

Joss cried out, "Abby."

I ran.

I ran as fast and as hard as my legs would take me.

I ran down the street. I ran to the park. I ran until I couldn't move another inch. Then I collapsed on the ground, sitting on my butt, knees bent, face tucked down.

I shook. I cried. I tried to think of what to do. I needed to tell someone. I needed to protect Joss. But who could I trust? Who?

Grandma? Grandma was good to us. I would call her.

I made sure I'd wiped away my tears before I went home. I didn't want Dad to know I'd seen what he did. I was very quiet as I went into the house. I looked and listened. No sign of Dad. I grabbed the phone and dialed the number.

When Grandma answered, I had to swallow a sob. I told her everything, and she listened, not saying much. When I was finished, she told me she would take care of things. I thanked her and hung up.

A few hours later I learned a hard lesson.

You don't tell.

You don't tell anyone.

I also learned how hard my father could punch.

I hadn't realized I'd fallen asleep until my phone roused me from a dream. I blinked watery eyes, searching the semidark. I could hear the stupid phone, but I couldn't see it.

Grumbling, I shoved myself upright, then swung my legs over the side of the bed. Of course the phone stopped ringing the minute my feet hit the floor.

But it started ringing again a few seconds later, before I'd fallen back into bed.

Following the sound, I lumbered over to my dresser where my purse was sitting. It was still ringing when I dug it out of the deepest, darkest depths where it had settled.

Kam.

I poked the button. "Hello?"

"Hi."

"Hi to you, too."

"I . . . just wanted to make sure you got home safely."

Was that really why he had called? Wouldn't he know I had made it home okay after speaking with his driver? I had more than a sneaking suspicion Kam would have called him. "Yes, I did. Thank you."

"I'm sorry I had to leave this morning. I didn't want to wake you."

Ah, so there was the real reason for his call. He wished to apologize. Not a bad reason to call.

"It's fine," I said, smiling to myself. I plopped down on my bed and, sitting cross-legged, I hugged a pillow to my chest. "I'm a big girl. I don't need a babysitter."

"You found the coffee?"

"I did. It was delicious."

"Okay. Well, then. I'll see you tomorrow."

"Yes, tomorrow."

And with a click, the call was over.

That was strange. One of the oddest conversations I'd ever had.

Although I had spent a fair amount of time alone with Kameron Maldonado, I still felt like he was a mystery. He didn't ever talk about family or friends. He worked hard. He was generous. His employees had only good things to say about him. He made a mean cup of coffee. And he was amazing in bed. But that was about all I knew. I grabbed my laptop and powered it up, wondering what I might find about him on the Internet.

As it turned out, the Internet had all kinds of information about him. His father, Emile Maldonado, had immigrated to the United States when he was only eighteen years old. He'd been penniless when he'd arrived, but by the time he'd died, he had married, fathered one child, and built a solid, thriving manufacturing business. His son, Kam, had taken the reins when he died, and within a few short years Kam turned what had been a multimillion-dollar-a-year enterprise into a multibillion-dollar-a-year conglomerate, mostly by buying his competition or forcing them out of business and expanding into new industries.

Kameron Maldonado was a ruthless businessman.

I wasn't sure how I felt about that.

I powered down my computer and set out to do my regular Sunday thing. My brother was nowhere to be seen—not in his room, not in the apartment at all. That was okay. I didn't want to deal with his sorry-ass hangover today. While dancing to the tunes cranked on my stereo, I scrubbed the bathroom and kitchen, dusted and vacuumed and cleaned, stripped my bed and washed, dried, and folded the laundry. Then I headed out to do the grocery shopping for the week.

By eight o'clock I was ready to go horizontal for the rest of the night. After putting away the groceries, I flopped onto the couch and turned on the TV. I must have flipped through three hundred channels before concluding there was absolutely nothing to watch.

The front doorknob rattled as I was heading back to my room to grab my computer.

My brother, looking like he'd been run over by a truck, stumbled into the living room, took one steps, two, and collapsed on the floor.

I dashed over to him, rolled him over. His mouth was bleeding; his face was swollen and red. I grabbed the phone and called 9-1-1. And after I had more or less shouted for help in a panic, I dropped the phone and tried to wake him.

He didn't flutter an eyelash.

Was he . . . ? Breathing?

Was he . . . ? Not breathing?

A sob collected in my gut and I couldn't hold it down. It burst out of me, painfully. Tears streamed from my eyes. "Come on, Joss. Wake up, dammit."

Nothing.

"Joss!" I shouted. I bent my face over his, feeling for breath.

Nothing.

Nothing!

No!

I shook him. I screamed again. "You can't leave me! You can't! You're all I have!" I couldn't see. My eyes were full of tears, burning and blurred. "Joss!"

A loud knock on the door had me up on my feet. I dashed to open it. Unable to speak, I stuttered and pointed, "Th-th-there."

One of the techs went to my brother, stooping down and checking for a pulse. A second one, followed by a policeman, halted next to me and began firing questions at me that I couldn't answer.

"What happened?"

"When was the last time you saw him?"

"How long has he been unconscious?"

"How did he get home?"

"Was he in some kind of altercation?"

I kept repeating, "I don't know. I don't know. I don't know!" And crying. And asking if he was going to be okay.

A tech had given Joss an oxygen mask and started an IV. He wouldn't do that if my brother was dead, would he?

"Is he alive?" I asked, wiping tears from my eyes.

The tech nodded, then went to help his partner lift him onto the gurney.

The officer stepped aside to take a call.

I watched them roll my brother out, arms wrapped around myself to try to ease the trembling.

"We'll be taking him to County Hospital. Do you have anyone to drive you?" one tech asked me as they wheeled my brother toward the door.

"I don't know," I responded.

"I strongly suggest you not drive in your current state," the tech said.

"I won't," I said, automatically, without thinking.

"If you can't make it up there for a while, you can call and get updates," he suggested.

"Okay."

Minutes later I watched the red and white blinking lights disappear into the darkness.

The police officer stepped up to me then. "I was able to find out a little more about your brother's whereabouts tonight. He was in an altercation with another man. A witness called it in. I'm going to take her report now. She's one of your neighbors."

Sniffling and hiccupping, I dragged my hand across my face. "I think I know who she is. I haven't seen her tonight. She lives down the hall, I think."

"She's at the hospital too."

What had my brother gotten himself into now? My stomach twisted. "Oh."

"I'm heading there now to get more details." The officer pulled a card out of his pocket and handed it to me. "In case you need to reach me."

10

That night was one of the longest in my life.

I ended up waiting a while, until I wasn't feeling like I was going to pass out or throw up, before driving myself up to the hospital. I managed to get there and back without killing myself or anyone else. I did a lot of sitting and thinking at the hospital while my brother was put through one test after another. Brain scans and MRIs. He didn't regain consciousness, and was eventually admitted and moved up to a room on the third floor. I stood at his side whenever I could, my hand resting on top of his. But at the urging of his very kind nurse, I eventually left. I rolled into my parking spot at a little before six o'clock in the morning, went inside, and headed straight for the kitchen. I started up the coffeemaker first, then scalded myself in the shower, hoping that would wake me up a little.

As I dressed for work, I wondered if I should call in sick. I was so exhausted I could barely see. How would I make myself sound and look coherent?

A little desperate, I tried calling Kam. He didn't answer, so I left a message and hung up. Assuming I had no choice but to go in, I downed almost a full pot of coffee and drove to work.

My eyes were still a little bleary, but the caffeine was doing its job. I felt jittery but also awake. God help me when the effect wore off in about an hour.

Trying hard to quell the caffeine overdose shakes, I hurried inside. Adding to my jittery mood, I was anxious to see Kam. Would he kiss me like he did Friday night? Would he tie me to my chair and make me beg for release? Or would he try, once again, to just be "friends"? This ride with him was worse than any roller coaster, full of jerks and hairpin turns, wild plummets. Thrilling but also frustrating and confusing.

Waving at Stephanie at her post outside Kam's office, I hurried through the doors.

Empty.

Damn.

My mood sank.

I went into my office and plopped down at my desk, scanning the surface for notes from him.

Nothing.

Shoving my disappointment aside, I got to work, beginning with the most mundane task—filing. If Kam didn't come into the office today, it was going to take a lot of caffeine for me to keep motivated. A lot.

Nine hours later I powered down my computer.

There'd been no sign of Kam all day. Not a text. Not an e-mail. Not a phone call. Nothing.

A little bummed, and very tired, I drove back to the hospital to check on my brother. Because I hadn't had a lot of sleep the night before, I planned on making this a quick visit. I hoped Joss would be awake and I could talk to him. He'd put me through the wringer lately, but last night was by far the worst.

At one point I had been sure I'd lost him. And it terrified me how devastated I had been. All I wanted to do now was tell him how much I loved him. How much I needed him.

Reluctantly, I shut off my phone when I went inside, following hospital protocol. A part of me had hoped Kam would call me after I left work. Maybe I wouldn't see him at all today, but it would be nice to at least hear his voice.

I went up to Joss's room. He was sleeping. His face still looked awful. In fact, it looked worse. One eye was swollen and purple, and much of the rest of his face was deep scarlet and blue. I couldn't imagine what had happened, how he'd been battered so horribly. In truth, I didn't want to even try to imagine. It was too horrifying.

His nurse came in a few minutes later and gave me some good news. Joss had regained consciousness for a little while last night, but he had been in a lot of pain. He had several facial fractures as well as a broken rib. They had given him some medication to help him rest. She didn't expect him to wake any time soon, so I sat at his bedside for a while then, completely worn out, went outside to check my messages and head home, to my soft, comfy bed.

As I dragged my heavy body toward the exit, I saw that it was raining outside. Correction, it was pouring. The sky to the west was clear, so I decided to wait under the overhang for the rain to let up. I powered up my phone while I waited.

It chimed. I had a message.

I checked my phone log.

Kam had called, about an hour ago.

I was in the process of checking his message when another call came through. Kam again.

Suddenly not so exhausted and weary and crabby, I answered, "Hello?"

"Are you ready?" he asked, voice high and bouncy and full of excitement.

"Ready for what?"

"Didn't you receive my message?"

"Yes, but I . . . didn't have a chance to listen to it yet." I stuck my free hand out from under the shelter to see if it had stopped raining.

Good enough. Moving quickly, I headed for my car, stepping around puddles as I hurried along.

"Oh, I hope this doesn't mean I can't see you tonight."

He wanted to see me tonight!

My heart did a triple flip with a twist.

"I'm on my way," he said. "How soon can you be ready?"

"Oh. Um." I checked the clock on my phone. "I'm not at home." I picked up the pace, race-walking.

"Where are you?"

"The hospital."

"Why? Are you okay?"

"I'm fine. It's my brother. He was . . . attacked last night," I lied. In truth, I hadn't heard a word from the police yet. I didn't know if he had been the aggressor or the victim, whether he would go to jail when he was released or come home.

"Attacked? What hospital?"

"County."

"I'll be there in twenty minutes. I just need to turn around."

"It's okay. You don't need—"

"Tell me you don't want me there and I won't come. But otherwise I'm on my way." He didn't speak, not forcing the issue. Neither did I, not fighting him. "Like I said, I'll be there in twenty. Meet me in the lobby?"

"Thanks."

"It's no problem."

I clicked off and, instead of going to my car, made a beeline for the nearest bathroom in the hospital.

Despite having primped for work this morning, I looked like crap. The wind—I'd driven with the windows down to keep myself awake—had wreaked havoc on my hair, my makeup was pretty much gone, and I had dark, ugly, purple circles under my bloodshot eyes.

I dug into my purse, pulled out an arsenal to fix myself up, and did the best I could with what I had. In the end the improvement was small, but it was visible.

When I sensed it was getting close to that twenty-minute deadline, I headed outside to see if he'd called again. I couldn't get any reception inside. Not one bar. As I was waiting for my cell phone to connect to the network, I saw a black sports car zoom into the parking lot. It zipped into a parking spot.

I watched to see who got out.

Kam.

He literally sprinted across the parking lot, hauled me into his arms, and gave me a crushing hug. He smoothed my hair as he held me, a sweet, soothing gesture. When I tipped my head up to tell him I was okay, he caught my chin, dipped his head down, and brushed his mouth across mine.

"You look exhausted," he said.

"That bad?" I made an attempt at a joking tone. He saw right through it.

"You're always beautiful." He ran his hand down the side of my face.

I tipped my head, leaning into his touch. My heavy eyelids dropped. "I didn't get much sleep last night."

Something flashed in his eyes as his gaze met mine. "You came to work. Why didn't you call me? I would have told you to stay home, get some rest."

"I tried. You didn't answer."

His lips pursed. "If that ever happens again, just leave a message and stay home. You should go home and get some sleep."

"I will. I just wanted to check on him. See if he needed anything."

"Have you done that?"

"Yes."

"Good, I'll take you home," he said.

"I can drive myself—"

"No, you're too tired to drive. You shouldn't push yourself so hard. Going to work then coming here."

"But that's what I do," I explained. "I take care of my brother. I do my job for you."

"Yes, well, there's nobody looking after you." He hooked an arm around my waist.

"True, but—"

He started walking toward the parking lot, pulling me along with him. "You won't be any use to your brother, me, or anyone else if you let yourself get so run down you fall ill."

I'd heard that before. But as of today I had yet to fall ill from being overly tired. "I'm fine." Using every ounce of strength I could muster, I pulled away from him. As much as I kind of liked being protected, cared about, this was overdoing it a bit.

"No, you're not fine." He reached for me, but I jumped back again.

"Stop it. I don't need you telling me what to do. I've been doing just fine all this time, making my own decisions."

Kam froze. His mouth opened, then snapped shut. "I apologize. I was just trying to help."

"I know. Has anyone ever told you that you go a little overboard sometimes?"

He blinked. "No. Overboard?"

"Well, you do."

Looking introspective, he nodded. "It seems I do. With you."

His admission took the fight out of me. I even managed a smile. "I appreciate the fact that you seem to care—"

"I do."

"I can tell." Turning back toward the hospital, I waved for him to go with me. We fell into step, side by side, walking back to the hospital entrance. "I'm going up to check on my brother one last time. He's been unconscious since last night. I'll feel better if I can at least talk to him. Then I'll head home."

"Will you let me buy you some dinner?" he offered.

"Maybe. I'm not really in the mood to go out."

"That's okay. I have something in mind. Something I think you'll like." Surprising me, he said, as we approached the elevators, "I need to make a few calls. I'll wait for you down here. Unless you need me to go up with you?"

"I'm okay. Make your calls." The elevator bell chimed. As I turned to step into the car, Kam reached for my hand, caught it, and gave it a squeeze.

He said, "I'll be right here, waiting for you."

Our gazes met and locked, and my heart did a little jump in my chest. He looked so . . . sad. Or maybe it was worry. Because of me? Was I really that significant to him?

Really?

My insides warmed.

He cared about me.

My face flushed.

Cared.

Me.

The elevator stopped on the third floor, and I scurried out. Walking as fast as I could, I rushed to my brother's room. The door was open. I stepped inside.

Joss rolled his head, turning it toward me, and opened his one good eye.

He was awake! I dashed to his bed. "How are you feeling?"

He visibly swallowed. "Thirsty."

I checked his bedside tray. There was a pitcher of ice water and some cups and straws. I poured a little water into a cup, poked a straw in it, and held it for him so he could sip. His eye found mine. After he'd taken his fill, I set the cup on the tray.

"What time is it?" he croaked.

"A little after eight."

"Have you been here all day?" he asked, voice scratchy and hoarse.

"No. I went to work."

He lifted a hand. There were IV tubes taped to the back of it, and it shook as he reached for me. I placed mine in his. "Thank you for being here for me."

"That's what big sisters do."

"Not all big sisters. Am I in trouble?" he asked.

"I don't know. What do you remember?"

"Sue called me and asked me to go with her when she picked up Eduardo from her ex's house. When we got there, her ex-husband came outside and started shouting at her. She got out of the car, and they started fighting. The bastard punched her. In the fucking face. I couldn't just sit there and watch that. Not . . . no. I couldn't sit there and watch that shit. I had to help her."

"I'm sure the police will see that when they do their investigation."

"The police." He sighed. "They were called?"

"Yes."

"Damn."

"It's okay," I reassured him. "I don't think you have anything to worry about this time. Not if what you told me is true."

"It's true. I swear." He tightened his hold on my hand. "Do you know what happened to her? And Eduardo?"

"No." I didn't tell him what the police officer had said, about Sue being in the hospital. I didn't want him to worry about her or her son.

"Can you find out?" he asked, motioning to the cup again.

I lifted it to his mouth. "I can try."

His eye was pleading as he sucked on the straw.

Like I could deny him anything when he looked that pathetic. "I'll find out what I can. You need to rest. Heal."

"Thanks." He pushed the straw out of his mouth with his tongue, and I set the cup on the table.

"Have the doctors said anything about your condition?" I refilled his cup, in case he wanted more later.

"Yeah. They told me I have a few bruises, some fractures in my face, and a broken rib. I think they're keeping me one more day."

"Okay." Standing at his bedside, I felt my body getting a little limp. The caffeine was wearing off. Fast.

"Go home," he murmured, looking sleepy too.

"I hate to leave you here alone."

"I'm fine. They've got me pretty doped up. I'll probably sleep most of the night. You don't need to sit here and watch me." He released my hand, giving it a little push. "Go home."

"Okay." I bent down and kissed his forehead.

He gave me a little shove when I didn't get moving right away. "Go."

"Fine. I'm going." I grinned. "Call me if anything comes up. I love you, Joss."

"I love you, too." He waved me away. "Bye, sis."

"Bye."

I was hugely relieved after seeing him awake and talking, and after hearing his side of what happened last night. He was going to be okay. I wasn't going to lose him. Not today.

Just as he'd promised, Kam was waiting in the lobby when I returned downstairs. His gaze snapped to mine the instant the elevator door opened.

"How is he?" he asked.

"Recovering."

"Good. Are you ready to go home?" He tipped his head toward the exit.

"Yes." As I came closer to him, I asked, "Speaking of my brother, can you tell me what is happening with the investigation?"

"Later. We don't need to discuss that now." He placed a hand on my back as we walked outside. I started toward my car, but he gently steered me toward his. "I'll have someone get your car. I'd rather you not drive when you're so tired."

If I hadn't been as exhausted as I was, I probably would've fought him on that one. But the truth was, my eyelids were so heavy it was taking Herculean effort to keep them open. Acquiescing with a nod, I followed his lead to his car and plopped into the passenger seat.

My eyes stayed open for about five minutes. Then they fell shut. The next thing I knew, he was murmuring in my ear, and strong arms were lifting me. Without opening my eyes, I tossed an arm around his neck and let him carry me up to my apartment. But I had to open them when we stopped at the door.

Kam said, "Keys?"

I dug them out, shoved the key into the lock, and gave it a twist. Still holding me, Kam kicked the door shut behind us, then put me on the couch. "I ordered dinner. It should be here in about ten minutes. Are you too tired to eat?"

"I don't know." I blinked as I looked up at him. My eyelids were so heavy, the blink was in slow motion.

"Hmmm." He sat next to me, pulled me into his arms so I was semireclining against him. "Close your eyes. You can eat later." One of his hands smoothed down my arm. The touch was soothing. He was warm, and I was cozy.

And sleepy.

So sleepy.

It felt good being held as I relaxed into his embrace. Wonderful. I wanted to thank him for coming over and driving me home, but my body had given up. There was no energy left. Not even for speaking.

11

_____

What is that?

Where am I?

I jerked upright, blinking blurry eyes, struggling to focus them.

My room.

My bed.

I was in my bed.

Slowly, as I checked the clock, the memory of Kam holding me as I dozed on the couch returned. That had been around eight o'clock. Now it was . . . I squinted . . . six o'clock the next morning?

Tuesday morning.

Shit!

Noticing I was still wearing my clothes from the day before, I catapulted myself out of bed and raced to the bathroom to begin my morning routine. A half hour later I was tugging up a pencil skirt and stepping into heels. The entire time I wondered how long Kam had stuck around. A tiny part of me was disappointed he hadn't stayed the night.

He hadn't undressed me, either.

A little ache pulled in my chest. The twinge of pain made it hard to breathe for a moment. As I hurried into the kitchen, I focused on taking slow, deep breaths.

What was work going to be like today? Would Kam be kind? Would he be distant? Would he look at me with that dark hunger in his eyes?

In the kitchen I found a note from him, written in his neat but masculine hand.

> *Abigail, I put your dinner in the refrigerator.*
> *You needed sleep more than food. See you*
> *tomorrow.*
> *Kam*

The note seemed so . . . abrupt. And cold.

Is something wrong?

No, why should there be?

I read the note again. And again.

Maybe I was just reading too much into things.

Hoping it was just my overactive imagination, I grabbed my purse and *click-clacked* out to the car. It took me twenty minutes to get to work. As I rode the elevator up to the tenth floor, I concentrated on breathing again. And I kept running my sweaty palms down my thighs, drying them on my skirt.

I gave Stephanie a little wave as I hurried past.

I opened the door.

Kam was at his desk, on the phone, writing something as he talked. He didn't look up.

I made a beeline for my office, plopped into my chair, and scanned my desktop. It was covered with pieces of paper. Each one had a yellow sticky note glued to it. It looked like I had plenty to do today. Phone calls to return. Letters to type. Filing to complete. Appointments to change, reschedule, or cancel.

After making a quick call to my brother, I dug right in. I was grateful for all the work. I was anxious, on edge. Being busy helped me burn away some of the nervous energy buzzing through me. To my surprise Kam didn't come into my office. Not once. I didn't stop working until my stomach started rumbling loudly. I checked the clock. It was already after two in the afternoon.

Thinking I'd head down to the cafeteria to grab something I could munch on while I worked, I stood up, stretched, rolled my head from side to side. I'd been sitting too long. I was sore and stiff.

After getting the blood flowing a little better, I grabbed some cash out of my purse and headed toward the door connecting my office with Kam's. I yanked it open.

A man's white shirt.

I lifted my gaze.

Kam.

My insides twisted.

He looked so handsome today. Better than yesterday, though I didn't think that was possible.

"I was just coming to check on you," he said.

"I'm fine. Busy but fine." My stomach rumbled again.

He lifted a brow.

I patted my belly and grinned sheepishly. "Hungry."

"I'll get you something to eat."

I waved the ten-dollar bill in my hand. "I was going to grab something and bring it back up."

"I'm hungry too." Gently, he took my hand in his and moved it to my pocket. "We can go together. I'm buying."

Ah, so it had been my imagination. There was nothing wrong. He had just been busy. We stepped into the elevator. I moved to the back. Kam hit the button, forcing the door to shut before anyone else joined us. But instead of moving closer to me, he remained exactly where he stood, staring up at the illuminated numbers as the car started its downward descent. He didn't speak. He didn't look at me.

That was weird.

Which was it? Was something bothering him or not?

I wanted to know. Right now. But now was not the time to ask. This was not the place.

The car stopped at the second floor and again at the first. Other riders joined us. Every one of them acknowledged Kam with either a smile and nod or a "Good afternoon, Mr. Maldonado." Me, I was invisible in the back of the car.

When it finally stopped at the basement level for the cafeteria, the remaining passengers left the car. I was the last one. Kam paused as I stepped out, falling into step with me but not speaking to me. We walked into the cafeteria. The cook who usually stood behind the counter at noontime was gone. But there were premade sandwiches in a cooler. Bags of chips and cans of cola or bottles of water in vending machines. I was about to stuff my ten-dollar bill into one when Kam placed his hand over mine. The touch sent a quiver of aching need racing through me.

My gaze jerked to his.

I froze in place.

"I told you I was paying. What did you want?"

"The turkey and Swiss. Thanks." Feeling eyes on me, I stepped back and glanced over my shoulder. Who was staring? Was someone staring?

No?

I watched the machine's mechanical shelves spin as Kam pushed buttons. He fed several bills into the slot and pulled open the little door to get my sandwich. "This one?"

"Yes, thank you."

He handed it to me, and we moved down to the next machine. "Did you want anything from here?"

"A bag of chips. Thanks."

"Which ones?" he asked as he shoved more bills in the second machine.

"The whole grain ones."

The bag dropped down into a chute at the bottom, and Kam retrieved them for me, handing them over.

We moved down to the last machine. "Drink?"

Watching him, and still unsure whether he was acting more distant because something was wrong or because we were in public, I said, "Water's fine. Thanks."

Another few seconds later, I had a bottle of cold water, a sandwich, and a bag of chips in my hands. Kam had nothing.

"I thought you said you were hungry." I tipped my head toward his empty hands.

"Yes, yes, I did say that." He went back to the sandwich machine and studied the contents. "Any suggestions?"

"The turkey's very good."

"Then turkey it is." He bought himself a sandwich and water. He jerked his head toward a nearby table. "Did you want to sit down here and eat?"

Still feeling as if someone was watching, I glanced around. Several small groups of employees were loitering around the machines. That had to be the problem. He didn't want any rumors to spread. "No, thanks. I'd rather head back up."

Hands full, we went back upstairs, away from curious stares. When we stepped into Kam's office, he demanded, "Eat with me."

"Okay." I took my food to his desk as he circled around the back. As I unwrapped my sandwich, I asked, "How did you get used to it?"

"Get used to what?" he asked.

"The staring."

He shrugged as he tugged at the plastic wrap on his sandwich. "I'm not used to it."

"Yet you asked if I wanted to sit downstairs?" I tore open

my chips and popped one into my mouth. Salty good. I crunched quietly.

"Sure. Because if you'd wanted to, I would have joined you."

I swallowed the chip. "Even though you would be watched the whole time?"

"Yes."

"Why?" I asked, bewildered.

"Because it would have been what you wanted."

For some reason, that statement puzzled me. I didn't get the impression he regularly did what others wanted. No, more like he did what he wanted and everyone else followed along. I took a bite of my sandwich and chewed. "Do you always do what other people want?"

His jaw tightened. He didn't respond right away, and I wondered if I'd made a mistake by asking that question. While we weren't ripping each other's clothes off, or shoving our tongues down each other's throats, I felt this conversation was extremely intimate. "No," he said a little sharply. "No, I don't."

I really, really wanted to know then why he would have acquiesced to my wants, but I decided a topic change was needed to keep the conversation going. If the tight jaw and the clipped tone in his voice were any indication, I'd struck a raw nerve. "Thank you again for yesterday. For driving me home. And buying me dinner. And . . ." I felt my face warming. "Everything."

"You're welcome," he said. Even though I'd moved on to safer territory, his mien, his body language, everything was still somewhat distant.

"Is something wrong?" I asked.

"No. Why?"

"Well . . . you're acting a little . . . different today. And the note you left last night . . . I don't know. It felt different."

He didn't respond right away. His brows were furrowed, as if he was puzzled or confused. "I have a lot on my mind."

My stomach clenched a bit. "I didn't do anything wrong, did I?"

"No."

I wasn't sure if I believed him. But I didn't know what to say or do. Trying to pry whatever it was out of him probably wouldn't work.

His phone rang. He picked it up and said, "Maldonado." That was followed by a few seconds of silence, then, "Okay. Put him through." His gaze met mine. He poked a button. "Sorry, but I need you to go back to your office."

"Of course." I scooped up my half-eaten lunch and rushed to my desk. I set the food down, then went back to shut the door.

"Okay," I heard him say as I was pushing it closed. "What else did you find out?"

I wished I could have heard the rest of that conversation.

At six o'clock I decided it was time to call it a day. Kam hadn't poked his head into my office once since that phone call. He hadn't called me either. After the palpable tension during our brief lunch break, I had to conclude something was going on. Whether it had anything to do with me or not, something was wrong.

As I opened the door I checked his desk, expecting to find him there.

He wasn't.

He hadn't said good-bye?

I headed down to my car and swung by the hospital to check on Joss.

He was awake and looking a lot better.

I greeted him with a happy hug. "You look better."

"I'm getting released tomorrow."

"Good."

"A detective came by today," he informed me, looking unconcerned.

"What did he say?"

"He asked if I'd like to press charges against the asshole who did this. Sue backed out. She's too scared to follow through."

"Oh. What are you going to do?"

"The right thing. I'm going to protect her. I'm going to file charges."

"Good for you."

"Yeah, but I hope I don't regret it. Sue said she's been through this before, that even if he's convicted he probably won't spend much time in jail. She's afraid he'll be worse when he gets out."

"Considering what he's done to you, and her, I don't blame her for being afraid." I was the last person to judge the woman for being scared and keeping silent. After all, that was what I had done.

"I don't blame her either." He set his hand on mine. "And I don't blame you for . . . for being too scared to get help. You did what you could, sis. You were as strong as you could be."

My eyes started burning and watering. I blinked a few times, dragged my thumbs under my eyes. "Why are you jumping in the middle of this situation after everything you've been through?"

"Maybe because of what I've been through. Maybe I'm sick of assholes getting away with this shit while the victims suffer in silence." He sat upright, eyes full of anger. "I've finally found an outlet for all my frustration and anger. I've found a cause that I can focus all that pent-up energy on."

Feeling a shiver tingling along my spine, I wrapped my arms around myself. "But I'm scared—"

"I'm scared too, but that's not going to stop me. I need to do this. I need to help Sue."

"Okay."

"Will you pick me up tomorrow?" he asked.

"What time?"

"I'll be free to go sometime after the doctor makes his rounds."

"Okay. Call me."

"Will do." He swung an arm over my shoulder. "You don't have to worry about me anymore. I'm done doing stupid shit. I promise you."

Not believing him, but wishing I could, I nodded. "Call me tomorrow."

"I'm going to protect you, too. You've taken care of me all these years, but I'm a man now. It's my time to step up."

I couldn't help smiling. I'd always known there was a good man under there somewhere. A man with a big heart. It seemed he was starting to fight his way out.

My brother tipped his head and scrunched his brows. "What?"

I felt my lips curl into a smile, despite my worries about what he was doing. "I've been looking forward to this day for a long time."

"Thanks for being patient enough to wait for it, sis."

My eyes burned as tears collected. Was I finally going to see my brother's life turn around? Were the days of hell, where he went out of his way to try to destroy his life, behind us at last? One tear slipped out, dribbled along the side of my nose.

"Are you crying?" he asked.

"No. I'm just tired."

"Go home. Get some sleep. There's nothing you can do here."

"Okay. If you're sure—"

"I don't need to be entertained." He jerked his head toward the door. "Go home."

* * *

The knock on our apartment door at ten minutes to ten startled me. It was late. I wasn't expecting anyone.

Wearing a pair of shorts, a T-shirt, and a sloppy ponytail, I peered through the peephole.

Kam?

I opened the door, and he came stumbling in. A wave of alcohol fumes followed.

"I'm-fucked," he slurred. I hadn't realized someone could slur those two words. They were so short.

Having dealt a time or two . . . or more . . . with a drunk male, I blew out a heavy sigh and locked the door.

Why did I attract drunk men to my doorstep? Why?

"You've had too much to drink," I said as I reached for his arm to steady him a bit.

"No kidding?" He was semistanding. The wall was propping him up. His clothes were rumpled. His hair was a riot of sexy waves that needed combing, and unlike my brother when he was drunk, Kam looked absolutely adorable.

Adorable?

I needed to knock some sense into my head.

"What are you doing here?" I asked.

"Warning you."

"Warning me about what?"

He pushed away from the wall, took one wobbly step, two steps, three, threw his arms onto my shoulders and looked at me with bloodshot eyes. "You need to get your brother out of here now."

12

It seemed I was destined to be dealing with intoxicated men for the rest of my life. First, it had been my father. A decent man when he was sober. A monster when he wasn't. Then my brother had fallen under the spell of alcohol at a young age, first using it to self-medicate at the tender age of nine. By the time he'd reached the legal drinking age, he was a full-fledged alcoholic.

And now I had another man slurring and staggering around my living room. Unlike the first two, this one wasn't blood. But he held both my future and my brother's in the palms of his hands.

If it hadn't been for that fact, I would've escorted him down to the limo I hoped had brought him and instructed the driver to take him home.

Banking on the fact that so far he had been capable of semi-coherent speech, I asked, "What's going on?"

"Your brother needs to leave. Now. Tonight."

"He can't. He's still in the hospital. They haven't released him yet."

"Shit." Kam looked around my place, seeming confused, as if he didn't know where he was. He wobbled to the couch and flopped onto it. Sitting forward, elbows on his knees, he shoved his fingers through his hair. His head was tipped down. "What am I gonna do?"

I followed him to the couch but didn't sit. "What's going on, Kam?"

"I know," he said, but not to me. Looking up, he pointed at my chest. "You can go get him now."

"No, I can't."

"Sure. I'll go with you."

"No, you're definitely not going anywhere with me tonight."

"Why not?" He blinked in slow motion.

"You're not . . . exactly yourself at the moment."

He tossed a dismissive arm. "I'm fine." He smacked his knee and almost fell over.

"Sure you are."

His face scrunched. He blinked a couple more times. "You aren't making this easy. I'm trying to help you."

"That's very nice of you." I started toward the hallway, thinking Kam was going to need a pillow and blanket if he was going to be spending the night on my couch.

"Where are you going?" He tried to push himself up to his feet. He didn't quite make it. Instead, he fell forward, crashed into the coffee table. A loud "oof" accompanied the noise of splintering wood and breaking glass.

Another coffee table down. That was the third one this year. My brother had killed the other two.

That was it, I wasn't buying another one.

I hurried over to my intoxicated boss, now sprawled amid the rubble, hooked my arms under his, and pulled. It took every ounce of my strength to get him back up on the couch. But I did it, and, gauging from his exuberant hug, he was grateful.

"You're the best, Abigail. The fucking best. You deserve so much more than you have. From me. From everybody."

"Gee, thanks, Kam," I said, a giggle bubbling up from my belly. Some guys were real bastards when they were drunk. Not Kameron Maldonado. Evidently, he was a big pussycat.

Bent over him, caught in a crushing embrace, I wriggled a little, trying to extricate myself. He tightened his hold even more.

I sighed. "Kam, you need to let go."

"Someone should take care of you for a change," he mumbled as he stroked my hair. "You shouldn't have to worry about a damn thing. Nothing."

"That would be very nice, Kam. But I need to get up now."

"No. Relax."

As if I could.

"But didn't you just say I need to go get my brother?" I asked.

"What? Did I say that?" He jerked me, yanking me down on top of him. "That's better. Now rest." He stroked my back.

"But this isn't—"

"Shhh. Sleep. You need sleep."

Sleep I could use. But I was still a little confused about what he had said earlier. Was there really a reason for concern? Or had that just been a drunk man's rambling? Based on his sudden lack of concern, I was hoping it was the latter.

Even as I told myself there was no way I could sleep like this, lying on top of an intoxicated male, my body was relaxing. Whether it was the steady pounding of his heart that was doing the job or the gentle rise and fall of his chest as his breathing deepened, I couldn't say. Telling myself I would stay just long enough to allow him to fall asleep, I closed my eyes and let my thoughts drift. Memories of those insanely intense first moments with him flashed through my mind. His first touches. The command in his voice. The decadent heat that rippled through my body.

I squirmed a little, and he growled, slid a hand down to cup my ass.

My eyes flew open. A ripple of wanting washed through me.

Dammit, would I ever stop lusting after this man? Would the sight of his face ever stop stirring a deep longing in me?

Determined to get up and lock myself in my room, I pushed against his wide chest. Hard, defined muscle beneath smooth cotton. He was so strong, so beautifully built. My little finger touched something small and hard under his shirt. A nipple, most likely.

He growled, and the hand holding my ass slid over, fingertips sinking slightly into the dip between my ass cheeks.

Another wild wave of lust flowed through me.

My pussy tightened, dampness slicking my folds and my panties. I needed to get up. Now. I shoved against him, drew one leg up, and tried to use it to lever myself off him.

"If you don't lie still," he grumbled as he kicked a leg over one of mine, trapping it, "I'll tie you down."

I gave up. Even drunk, he would probably have no problems restraining me. I wasn't about to find out for sure.

A few seconds later he inhaled slowly. "That's better. Good girl. You'll get your reward later. After you've had some sleep."

Every cell in my body burned at that promise.

Sleep. Maybe I'd be better off if I just fell asleep.

I closed my eyes and tried to focus my thoughts on happy things, peaceful things. His warmth soothed me. The deep *thump-thump* of his heart lulled me.

Finally, I drifted.

* * *

It was still dark when I woke. I was a little confused at first, not sure where I was. I was lying on something soft now. Definitely not on top of Kam. Blinking in the darkness, I ran my hand across the surface. Smooth, cool sheets. I was in bed. My fingertip bumped into something big and hard and warm.

Kam?

He growled.

Yes, Kam.

Somehow he'd managed to get us both into my bed. Considering he'd been having trouble just standing not so long ago, that was one hell of an accomplishment.

He rolled over and flopped one leg over mine and an arm across my stomach, pinning me in place. He grumbled something unintelligible. Talking in his sleep.

I felt myself smiling, even though I realized I could have been hurt when he'd carried me. The fact was I hadn't been hurt. I hadn't even woken. And now, lying in bed with him, I felt safe, warm, and cherished.

His words echoed through my head. *Someone should take care of you for a change.*

Wouldn't that be nice? Wouldn't it be nice never having to worry about anything? About paying the bills. About keeping my brother out of jail.

Then again, would I know how to live like that? I'd been taking care of people for as long as I could remember.

He stirred in his sleep, mumbled something I couldn't quite make out. Then he pulled me closer. I smiled and snuggled against him. Maybe I wouldn't like being coddled long term, but this was nice. I could let myself enjoy this.

Eyes closed, I started drifting off to sleep again. But just as I was sinking deeper into a dream, Kam jerked upright.

"Fuck!" he said.

Groggy, I blinked up at him. "It's okay. It's still early."

He turned to check the clock on my nightstand. "No, I need to go. I have a lot to do." He swung his legs over the edge of the bed. "What time is your brother being released?"

"I don't know. Sometime after the doctors make their rounds." Cold dread curled through me. So last night hadn't been nothing after all? There had been a reason for worry?

"Don't come into the office. Go to the hospital and get him out of there as soon as you can. Is there anywhere you can take him to stay? With a friend? A relative?"

My heart was pounding hard in my chest now. Panic was setting in. Why hadn't I pushed him last night? Why hadn't I tried to get him to tell me what was wrong? Was it too late to protect Joss? "No. Why? What's going on?"

"There's still time. I'm just trying to play it safe," he said, not seeming to say it to me.

"Kam, what's happening?"

"One of our biggest investors found out about the little problem, and he's hiring someone to look into what happened. I did what I could to cover up your brother's connection to it, but all it'll take is a phone call or two before he'll find out the truth, and they'll be looking into pressing criminal charges."

"Oh." I swallowed hard. I had thought, since Kam hadn't mentioned it in a while, that that situation had died down. Clearly that was a mistake.

Would this be the one time I couldn't do anything to help my brother? Would this be the one mistake he would pay the consequences for? What exactly did Kam know?

"Kam? What have you found out?"

He stood. To my surprise there wasn't a single wobble in his step as he left my bedroom. I was pushing myself out of bed when he returned and shoved a piece of paper into my hands. "Take him here. He'll be safe for now, until we can figure something else out."

"Is it that bad?" I asked as I fingered the piece of paper with an address written in Kam's neat handwriting.

"Yes, it is. Worst-case scenario, your brother will be brought up on larceny charges. Considering the value of what he has stolen, he'd be looking at a felony conviction and a fair amount of jail time."

What he has stolen.

"Have you found proof that it was him?" My hand shook as I set the paper on the bed and pushed to my feet. "I mean, I'm assuming if he had stolen something valuable, as you imply, he would have turned around and sold it to someone right away. He doesn't have any money. I would know if he did."

Facing me, he cupped my shoulders. "You have no idea how hard it was for me to come here and tell you this. I didn't want to hurt you. I see how much you love your brother."

He had proof.

I curled my fingers around his wrists, holding on to steady myself. Suddenly my knees were feeling a little soft. Clearly he was convinced my brother had stolen whatever was missing. "Kam, what proof do you have that it was Joss?"

"Technically, I don't have any proof yet—"

"Then you could be wrong."

"I could. But it looks bad for him. Very bad. There's a lot of circumstantial evidence against him. You need to talk to him. Get him to tell you exactly what happened. If he's innocent, I'll be the first one to step up and defend him."

"Okay."

His hands smoothed up my neck. He pushed my hair behind my ears. "He hasn't spoken to you about it?"

"Not once."

"Even though he was fired?" Scowling, he released me, rubbed his stubbled chin, and sat on the edge of the bed.

"Don't you think that's strange? Wouldn't you think he'd defend himself if he was wrongfully blamed?"

"Not necessarily." Not sure what to think, what to do, I sat next to him.

He leaned closer, brushed another strand of hair back from my face. "I'm sorry about coming over here last night in such a state."

"It's okay."

"No, it's not," he said. "I shouldn't have lost control like that. There's no excuse."

"You didn't hurt anyone. Just tell me you didn't drive."

"No. I had someone bring me over."

"Then no harm, no foul."

He shook his head. "I let it win."

Let what win?

Once again, feeling like Kam was about to open up and let me see a side of him few people saw, I asked, softly, "What do you mean?"

"I let the shit that had happened earlier get the better of me." He shoved his fingers through his hair again. "That doesn't happen very often, but I get really irritated with myself when it does. I should be stronger than that."

I set my right hand on his knee. "Everyone has a breaking point."

"Everyone but me." His gaze locked on mine. "I can't have a breaking point. I can't afford to be weak. Not ever." Cold determination glittered in his eyes.

"I think you're expecting far too much of yourself. You're not a machine. You're a human—"

"No, I'm not. Not when so many people are counting on me. People like you." He cupped my cheek and stared into my eyes. "I never wanted you to see me like that."

I curled my fingers around his wrist again. I wanted to say I was charmed by his drunken honesty, but I didn't. I knew that confession would have blown up in my face. I was also really scared and disturbed by the fact that I had responded so strongly to him when he was drunk and vulnerable. Instead, I said, "All you can do, Kam, is try your best. That's all anyone can do."

"That sounds more like the rah-rah quote from a motivational poster. This is the real world." He released me, heading toward the door.

"You're so calloused," I called out to his back.

Pivoting, he looked at me. "You have no idea, Abigail." He gave a little wave. "Get your brother to that address as soon as you can, and then come to work. I have a lot of things for you to do. I'll see you later."

He left. No good-bye.

At exactly eleven o'clock, I was escorting my brother from County Hospital. I didn't say much to him until we were locked in my car, safe from being overheard. Not knowing where to start, I silently rehearsed the conversation in my head while I drove.

He was the one who provided the in. "You missed the exit."

"Yes, I know."

"Where are you taking me?" he asked.

"Somewhere safe."

"From Sue? Are you trying to keep me away from her?" he snapped, becoming visibly angry. "Because it won't work—"

"This has nothing to do with that. Absolutely nothing."

"Then what's going on?"

I took a deep breath. "Kam—Mr. Maldonado—came to visit me last night. I guess he has some investors involved with the company. One of them got wind of your alleged extracurricular activities and is hiring a detective to dig into the matter. I'm taking you somewhere safe, to keep you out of prison."

"Oh." He shifted positions in his seat.

I glanced at him.

He was looking pretty pale.

"Are you okay?" I asked.

"Yeah, I'm fine."

He didn't sound fine at all. "Will I have access to a phone?"

"No. Speaking of which, I need you to hand over your cell phone." I extended a hand, expecting him to place his phone in it.

He didn't.

"It's for your own protection," I told him.

He still didn't give it to me.

"You won't do anyone any good if you're in prison."

He didn't speak, but he finally took his phone out of his pocket and gave it to me.

"Will you please tell me what happened?" I dropped his phone in my purse. "I know you don't have any money. I know you didn't do anything. Kam and I are going to try to find out who is really guilty."

Nothing.

I asked, "Do you know what was stolen? Do you know who did it?"

Silence.

Dammit. He had to be protecting someone. Who?

"Please, Joss. You need to give me something. Because if I can't find out who really did it, you're going to be arrested."

We stopped at a traffic light, and I took that opportunity to turn pleading eyes his way.

Finally he sighed. "The truth is, I don't know."

"What don't you know?"

"I don't know anything."

I'd never been so grateful to hear those words.

Able to breathe a little easier, I asked, "Did you tell anyone that before they fired you?"

"I told *everyone* that."

"But me."

"But you." He jammed his fingers through his hair and sighed again. "After all the shit I'd pulled, I didn't expect you to believe me, so I didn't bother."

"I do. I believe you."

"You probably shouldn't. I mean, I've lied to you more than I've told the truth."

The light turned green. "That's reassuring to hear," I said, not trying to hide the sarcasm, as I depressed the accelerator.

"I'm talking about the past though. Not the present."

"Well, everyone has to start somewhere."

"You really believe me?" he asked softly.

"Yes."

He made a little sobbing chuckle sound. "I don't deserve to have a sister like you."

"Sure you do."

"No, really, I don't."

We pulled up to another red light. "When we get to the safe house, I want you to tell me everything you can think of. Everything that happened the days before you were fired. Whether you think it's significant or not. I probably don't have a lot of time. Thanks to your record, the investigator's going to get plenty on you within the first few hours of work. You're the perfect person to blame a crime on. We need something to fight him with."

Joss looked defeated. He shook his head and tossed his hands in the air. "I can't give you anything. I swear I don't know a damn thing." He sounded as defeated as he looked.

That sad expression kick-started my mothering instinct.

"Don't worry, little brother," I said. Whether it was the

knowledge that I had Kam behind me, or something else, something deeper inside me, I felt empowered and determined. "I'm not going to let them arrest you without putting up a hell of a fight. My days of cowering in the corner while you're beaten are over."

13

I made it into the office just before one o'clock. I'd scribbled down several pages of notes during my conversation with my brother. But, being honest with myself, he had been telling the truth when he said he couldn't give me anything helpful. Nothing stood out. There was absolutely nothing to go on.

I was the world's worst detective.

As I exited the elevator, I waved at Stephanie and hurried into Kam's office. As usual, he was on the phone. Head down, fingers raking through his hair, voice low. I went to my office and checked my desk, expecting a bunch of sticky notes with tasks glued to my computer screen.

Nothing.

That was quite a surprise. He'd told me early this morning he had a lot for me to do.

I headed back out to his office. This time he looked up, raised an index finger, indicating I should give him a minute or two. Within a few seconds, he ended the call.

I started toward him, but he waved me back to my office. I

got there before he did but hadn't made it to my desk yet. He stepped inside and closed us in.

"Did you take care of that situation this morning?" he whispered.

"Yes."

"Okay." His gaze wandered up and down my body. The timing was ridiculous, but it seemed certain parts of my anatomy didn't care. They warmed. "I've been on the phone with the investigator on and off all morning. He's gathering a hell of a lot on your brother already. Did you get anything from him this morning?"

I pulled my legal pad out of my tote and handed it to him. "That's all I got."

He chewed his lower lip as he skimmed my notes. His brows furrowed. I hoped that meant he had caught something I'd missed. He handed it back to me. "We're going to need a lot more than this if we're going to keep your brother out of prison."

My insides twisted. How horrible would it be for him to end up in prison for something he hadn't done? After everything that he had done in the past, that would be cruel irony.

I toyed with the edge of the pad. "I had a feeling you were going to say that. But he swears that's all he knows."

Pushing himself off the wall he had been leaning against, Kam crossed his arms over his chest and began pacing the floor. "Let's talk this through. We have the theft of something that was in your brother's possession immediately prior to being stolen."

"Is there a reason why you aren't telling me what that item is?" Mirroring him, I wrapped my arms around my body.

He halted, stopping directly in front of me. His gaze met mine. "There is."

"Which is?"

"You're going to have to trust me on that." Returning to

pacing, he said, "The item was then sold to our competitor for an unknown figure. Your brother's whereabouts were unknown at the suspected time of the sale, and he is not able to adequately prove where he was. He had called in sick, missing three days of work. Maybe we should start there? I want you to call everyone he knows and find out if anyone can testify to his whereabouts during the days immediately leading up to his dismissal."

"I can do that, but wouldn't it make more sense for you to hire your own investigator to find out the truth? I'm no Nancy Drew."

"I'm looking into that as we speak." His expression softened. Once again, he stopped pacing. He stepped closer, wrapped his big hands around my arms, holding me gently. His thumbs skimmed back and forth over the cotton of my blouse. The nerves underneath fired hot. "But it isn't easy finding someone trustworthy. You care about your brother. You love him. You don't want to see him going to prison. That makes you far more likely to work hard to protect him."

"True, but don't private investigators have access to computer databases and stuff like that?"

"I doubt it. And even if they did, do you think that's going to help at this point?"

"I don't know."

To me, Kam's argument for not having hired a private investigator seemed a little weak. Surely a professional would do a far better job getting to the truth than little ole me.

"Can you get the phone numbers of your brother's friends?" he asked.

"I have his cell phone."

"Good. Call them. Call them all. Find out where he was every minute of every day, especially the three days he missed work." Releasing me, he reached past me, grabbing the doorknob to leave.

I caught his arm. "Thank you for believing he's innocent."

"I didn't say I believed he's innocent. I don't. But I'm giving you the opportunity to prove I'm wrong." After that stinger, he left.

Now I was more determined than ever to help my brother. It was Joss and me against everyone.

Once again.

As always.

I wondered if that would ever change.

That afternoon I started at the top of his contacts list and worked my way down. I talked to two people and left a lot of messages. The two I talked to hadn't seen him during those days.

Things were not looking good.

By six o'clock I was getting frustrated. And yes, I was feeling defeated too. I shut down my computer and headed out. Kam's desk was empty. So was Stephanie's. I stopped at a grocery store to pick up some of my brother's favorite foods before taking the long drive out to the safe house.

Once there, I parked, loaded my arms up with the bags of food, and headed up to the front door. I knocked. No answer. I tried the door. Unlocked. I called my brother's name as I let myself in.

He didn't respond.

Please tell me he didn't do something stupid!

After setting the bags on the kitchen table, I ran from room to room, calling his name. He wasn't in a bedroom or bathroom. I dashed outside and checked the yard. There was a path that cut through the tall trees lining the far end of the property. I ran down the path, hoping he'd just gotten a little stir crazy and needed some fresh air. The path, I soon learned, opened to a narrow, private beach on a small lake. I looked left and right. I checked the water. No sign of my brother.

"Dammit!" I yelled into the still quiet. "Damn you!"

Furious, tears gathering in my eyes, I stomped back up the path. When I was hidden under the cover of the band of trees, I plopped down on a fallen tree and dropped my face into my hands.

Was I the only one who cared whether he went to jail?

Maybe that was my problem. Maybe I needed to distance myself, allow him to pay the consequences for his mistakes.

But he didn't steal anything. This time he would be paying the consequences for something he hadn't done.

But he wasn't exactly cooperating with my efforts to clear him either.

"I should let them haul you off to prison," I grumbled. "If you aren't going to accept my help, then why should I keep fighting you? Why?"

Now more angry than upset, I shot to my feet, a plan worked out in my head. As long as I was able, I would try to prove his innocence. But I was through protecting him. *Done. Finis.*

As I emerged from the woods, I caught sight of a shadow passing across the wide glass doors leading onto the deck.

Oh, thank God!

I ran toward the house, let myself in. I called his name as I rushed through the living room, turned the corner, and nearly ran smack-dab into Kam.

"What the hell?" I shouted, stunned. I wobbled, arms wheeling.

He caught me by the waist. "He's gone."

"He's gone?" The air left my lungs in a rush, and I staggered. "Do you know where?"

"He's safe."

It took several seconds for what Kam said to sink in. When

it did, I practically collapsed against him. "Oh, thank God. What's going on?"

"It wasn't safe for him to stay here, so I gave him enough cash to keep him for a while and told him to disappear."

"Where did he go?"

"I don't know. That was the point. I didn't want either of us to know where he is. I didn't want you or me connected with him until we get this mess straightened out."

I was relieved but at the same time shocked and angry. How could he do something like this? Slap a couple of dollars in my brother's hands and shove him out the door? "But he might need—"

"Please don't worry. He has enough money to take care of anything he might need and then some." He ran his hands down my arms. "I'm sorry, but I couldn't let him stay here any longer. The investigator is hot on his heels now. He would've been found."

I felt tears burning my eyes. This was the first time in a long while that I felt powerless to help him. I didn't know where he was, didn't know what he was doing or whether he needed me. I laughed and sobbed at the same time. "I must look silly, crying like this. He's an adult, after all."

Kam dried my tears with his hand. "No, baby. Not silly at all. You love him. You're his surrogate mother. Of course you're worried."

"We need to find out who really stole whatever it was."

"You still believe it wasn't him?" Kam asked.

"I do."

Gently, he smoothed my hair back. His gaze was locked on mine. "What did you find out from his friends?"

"Not much. He talked to one of them last week. He told her he was in Toledo, taking care of a problem for a friend. That was it."

"Okay, so if we can find out who that friend was or where he went, that might help us out."

"Maybe. But I don't know where to start looking. Are you sure it wouldn't be a good idea to hire our own investigator?"

"I'd rather keep up the appearance that neither one of us is involved, especially you. One of the reasons why I had to send your brother away was you. The investigator is looking at you too. If he started tailing you, you'd lead him right to your brother."

"I understand now." I walked to the closest chair and sat. I was feeling weak. Worn out. "What a mess this is."

"It *is* a mess. You've got to hang on, be strong."

Be strong. I had been. For so long. Longer than he realized.

"I hope I can do that. I've always been able to before." I curled my legs, tucking my knees under my chin and wrapping my arms around my shins. "But it's getting harder and harder to be strong. Do you know what I mean?"

"I sure do." He sat on the couch next to me and pulled me onto his lap. I cuddled up to him, once again relishing how safe I felt in his arms.

I felt our breaths matching. I felt my heart beat slowing. I felt my muscles relaxing and the awful knot in my belly unraveling. I tipped my head up and met his gaze. His eyes were dark. His face, except for a tiny muscle along his jaw, was relaxed. My gaze inched down to his mouth. The memory of our last kiss flashed in my head, and my heart started beating hard again.

Kam palmed the side of my head. His tongue dampened his lips. My blood warmed.

"I can't," he murmured.

"You can't what?" I whispered.

"Kiss you."

I felt myself leaning toward him. "Did I ask you to kiss me?"

"Didn't you?" He cupped my chin, lifting it.

"I don't know," I whispered. His mouth was right there. Inches from mine.

"I think you did." He lowered his head slightly. Tipped it to one side.

"M-maybe I did."

"Mmmm." His head inched down a little more.

My breath caught in my throat. My eyelids dropped, enclosing me in soothing blackness.

When his lips met mine, I gasped.

He groaned.

His lips were soft, supple. They caressed mine gently at first, the kiss a sweet torment. I lifted my arms, draping them over his shoulders and surrendered. When I parted my lips, his tongue slipped inside.

This was a kiss that made my brain turn to mush. Made me want to give him everything I had, everything I was. It made me wish I was his to kiss and tease and torment forever.

When it ended, I struggled to breathe. My heavy eyelids lifted. I stared into his fiery eyes. He looked dangerous and feral. A man. A beast.

"I'm so fucking weak with you," he said.

"Are you?"

"Yes." The hand that had been holding my chin slid down to my neck. His fingers curled. He didn't choke me, but he held my throat. It was a strangely thrilling sensation, having him grasping my neck like that, looking at me with smoldering eyes.

"Your pupils are so wide, I swear I can see into your soul."

That was a weirdly provocative thing to say. I felt my top teeth bite into my lower lip. I tasted him. I smelled him. I felt him. "What do you see?" I asked.

"A woman who loves too hard."

"Can you do that?"

"You can. If it means you're the only one who is willing to make sacrifices."

"What about you?"

"I can't love." Something flashed in his eyes, and I sensed something, an invisible wall, sliding between us.

"Can't? Or won't?" I challenged, reacting to the strange, uncomfortable separation I felt.

"Maybe both." He leaned back, creating an even greater sense of separation.

A cold chill sliced straight through me. "Why?"

"Because I won't make sacrifices."

"Isn't love worth it?"

He shook his head. "Not from what I've seen, no."

Cold turned to hot again as simmering anger replaced chilly loss. "Maybe what you've seen isn't the whole truth."

"Maybe. But I'm not willing to take the chance."

"I see." I tensed my leg muscles, using them to push myself to my feet.

He let me stand but held onto one of my wrists. His eyes were full of emotion as they tracked my movement. It was as if he wanted to comfort me but was afraid of something.

Crazy. A man like him, afraid.

"Are you leaving?" he asked.

I glanced down at his hand, still holding my wrist, keeping me from leaving. "Am I?"

He tipped his head and studied me. "You should."

"I should," I echoed. "I guess I am, then."

His gaze left my face. His fingers loosened. "Go. Find something to prove your brother's innocence."

"I'm going to do my best." I took a couple of steps away but then turned right around and flung myself into his arms. I clung to him, ear pressed to this chest. His rapid heartbeat pounded in my head. "Thank you," I said. "For helping him, even though you don't believe he's innocent."

"You're welcome." He had tensed up. I could feel it.

With great effort, I managed to back out of his arms. I clenched my hands, fighting the urge to flatten myself against him again. "I'm sorry," I said, my gaze dropping to the floor. "I guess . . . I'm confused. I need a friend, and you've been so great."

He lifted my chin and gazed deeply into my eyes. "Sweet Abigail. There's nothing wrong with needing a friend. There's nothing wrong with needing to be held. I'm the problem. Me. You've done nothing wrong."

"I don't understand you."

"When you get near, I . . . have certain urges." His neck turned an interesting shade of red.

"Okay, that I get."

"We started off on a bad note. My fault. I'm trying to make things right, to treat you as you deserve. But when you come too close . . ." He closed his eyes and sighed. "I've said it before. I'm weak."

"No weaker than me," I confessed. "I feel the same way." My heart started thumping hard in my chest. "I want you to touch me. I crave your kiss."

"But you know what kind of man I am." He shoved his fingers through his hair. "You deserve so much better than me. I'll use you up until there's nothing left."

"Won't you give me a chance to find that out?"

His eyes widened. "Are you saying you aren't afraid?"

"I'm saying I am afraid, but that isn't going to stop me from wanting you."

He scooped me into his arms and gave me a crushing kiss.

My head spun as he carried me across the room, kicked open a bedroom door, and laid me on the bed. The kiss didn't end. Not when he practically tore my clothes off me, or when I did the same with his. Nor when he climbed over me. Within minutes I was burning for him, from head to toe. Writhing and groaning and whimpering. He cupped a breast, kneading its fullness and I arched my back, spine tightening.

Yes, at last I'd told him what I wanted. Finally we'd disposed of the shoulds and should nots. We wanted each other. There was no reason why we had to deny ourselves.

I reached up, raking my fingernails down his chest, and he grabbed my wrists and forced them up, over my head. "You have no idea what you're in for," he growled.

"Is that a promise or a threat?"

"Both?"

I couldn't help smiling. "Mmmm."

Holding my wrists in one fist, he reached and grasped.

"What are you doing?"

"I need something to tie your wrists."

A little shiver of anticipation zigzagged through me. While it did intimidate me somewhat that he seemed to need to tie me up almost every time we had sex, I also enjoyed being powerless and completely under his control. It was a secret thrill, feeling so utterly immobilized.

He found my bra, used it to bind my wrists together. Then he sat up on his knees and looked down at me. My blood burned at the fire I saw in his eyes. He was a beautiful, powerful, slightly dangerous man. And he made me feel things I never thought I'd feel.

"Open your legs for me," he commanded in that voice that sent shivers up and down my spine.

I bent my knees and eased them apart, exposing myself to his dark gaze.

A wave of throbbing heat pulsed there, where his gaze was fixed. I wriggled and tried to catch my breath.

"Your pussy is so sweet. Tight and wet for me."

I whimpered. "Yes. Yes."

"But you're not ready yet. No."

14

Wasn't ready for him? Really?

How much more ready could a girl be? My inner walls clenched. All I could think about was his thick rod stroking in and out, in and out, pounding deep and hard.

He turned his attention back to my breasts. As he weighed the fullness of each one, he tormented the other's nipple, pinching, tugging, pulling it until little blades of pleasure-pain pierced my body. I alternated between arching toward his touch and shrinking away from it. It hurt, but good.

So good.

He crawled off the bed.

"Where are you going?" I asked, desperately hoping he hadn't changed his mind.

"I'll be back in a minute." Standing over me, he flicked the nipple he'd been torturing and smiled. "You look so pretty like this, burning for me. I can barely stand to leave you. Even for just a moment."

So why was he going? What could be so important that he had to leave right now?

I didn't ask. I merely nodded.

He reached into the bedside drawer and pulled out a padded satin sleep mask. "I think you'll enjoy this," he said as he strapped it in place. Now blind, I waited, body trembling, blood pounding, heat pooling between my legs. If I thought the torment would ease with him gone, I was wrong. Dead wrong.

By the time he returned to me, I was almost breathless. Whether it was one minute or an hour, I couldn't say. Time seemed to drag.

He said, "I have a few things for us." The bed's mattress sank under his weight. He was next to me. That side of my body tingled. Still, even though I knew he was right there, I startled when he touched my thigh. "Anxious?"

"Yes."

"Good." He wrapped something around my leg, a strap of some kind. Then he pulled my legs wider apart and fastened another one around the other leg. Right away I could tell I couldn't move them. Now both my hands and legs were bound and I was blindfolded. A wave of nervous anticipation rushed through me.

What would he do next?

"How do you feel when you're bound?" he asked. "Are you afraid?"

"No."

"Perhaps you should be?"

A shiver zipped through me. "Why do you say that?"

"I warned you, you have no idea what you're in for." He was bent over me now. I could feel his breath gusting over my chest. It was like a feather-light caress. Soft. Fleeting. In the next instant a sharp pain pierced me again. My nipple. I jerked, muscles clenched. When it didn't ease up, a little sob slipped out.

"Too much? If it is, say red. If it isn't, trust me. You'll like what comes next."

I held on. My fingers clenched into fists, fingernails digging into my palm.

Finally it stopped. His warm, wet tongue swirled around the hard little nub, soothing the pain, and a strange sensation zoomed through me. Adrenaline. A rush of energy and pleasure. Oh, it was intense.

"Now you see why?" he said, his voice husky.

"Why . . . ?" I echoed, barely able to speak. It was as if my nerves had become supersensitive. I could smell his skin. I could hear his breaths and the slough of fabric as he moved over the cool sheet stretched under us. Everything was amplified. Intensified.

"Can you say red?" he asked.

"Yes."

"Say it for me," he murmured as his teeth grazed my other nipple.

"Red."

"Good." Something cold and hard pinched my other nipple. But I didn't shrink away from the pleasure-pain this time. I tightened all over, gritted my teeth, and waited, knowing there would be a wonderful reward coming soon.

"Your trust is so exquisite," he said softly, his voice reflecting deep emotion. "I am in awe of you."

Ever so gently, he laved that nipple with his tongue, drawing out the pleasure, easing the pain. With each lick, the heat pounding through my body intensified. With each lick, I became more desperate for his next touch.

He licked and kissed and nibbled his way to the cleft between my breasts, then continued lower, down the center of my stomach. As he came closer to my aching center, I tilted my hips up, tightening everywhere, silently pleading for just one touch between my legs.

His little kisses skirted around the area that burned the hottest. He bit my inner thighs, and my legs trembled. I strained against the restraints holding them in place. I wanted to open them wider, to open myself to him fully.

Something brushed across my nether lips, and I jumped.

"Patience, Abigail."

Patience? How could he say that to me? I'd been patient. For a lot longer than he realized. "Take me," I whispered, tipping my hips up.

"Now, that is an intriguing invitation, but I'm not ready yet."

I whimpered. "If you'd untie me—"

"No, what fun would that be? You make a small effort at seduction, but only because I've put you in the position of having to. You prefer it like this, being powerless." A light touch meandered up the inside of my thigh.

My entire being focused on that fingertip or toy or whatever it was as it traveled inch by inch closer to my center. Beneath my skin, my muscles quivered. My heart rate raced. My blood pounded in my veins. He was right. Absolutely. I craved this, how he tormented me, drew out my longing until it was nearly excruciating.

He did that now. His touch strayed up over my mound across my body and back down the other thigh. My skin tingled, goose bumps puckering in the wake of that light, teasing stroke. But I was in agony, and there was no reason to think it would end anytime soon.

Surrendering to it, I absorbed all the sensations fueling the fire burning deep inside. The sound of my own little gasps and moans. The scents of my need and Kam's skin and his minty breath. The sensation of my body quivering and tightening as my need grew and grew.

I didn't beg. I didn't plead. I merely accepted every touch, every stroke, every pinch.

"Ah, yes. You're learning so quickly." Now his voice was smooth and low, the vibration humming through me. I didn't allow myself to think about what might come next. I didn't allow myself to think at all. I just felt.

This time, when that soft touch wandered up my thigh, it

didn't wander off its target; it dipped between my wet folds. I felt them open to him, welcoming his exploration. A pulsing throb vibrated there as his exploration grew more aggressive. A light touch turned to a firm stroke. And that turned to a series of circles over my clit. And that turned into a series of thrusts inside. I couldn't help clenching my inner walls around his invading digit. I wanted to hold him there, keep him there forever.

He stopped, and I bit back a cry of agony. My tissues were twitching, odd little prickles between my legs. Still, I didn't move, didn't plead.

I heard the slough of clothing. Yes, finally! Soon I would feel his skin against mine. I would feel his arms around me. I would feel his thick rod stroke away the ache he'd ignited deep inside.

The sound of lube being squirted cut through the tense silence. At last, there was another touch. Something slick pushing between my buttocks. When that thing pushed at my entrance, I relaxed the muscles, taking it inside. It sank deep, then remained there.

"You are going to like this," he said. He unfastened my legs, pushed them wide apart. The mattress shifted as he lowered himself over me. "Mmmm," he hummed as he dipped down and kissed me. His kiss was a gentle seduction. Lips. Teeth. Tongue.

Oh yes, I liked that very much.

He kissed my cheeks, my eyelids. He swirled his tongue in the whorl of my ear.

I liked that too.

The skin of my shoulders prickled. Goose bumps. I shivered, despite being so hot I thought I might combust.

The tip of his cock nudged at my nether lips, and I shuddered. The heat swirling through me amped up another hundred degrees.

At last, he pushed inside me.

So full. So gloriously full.

Yes, I liked it. Yes, oh yes.

"Nothing like being filled, ass and pussy?" he murmured against my neck. "Am I right?"

"Yes," I somehow managed to say. After only a few thrusts, I was on the brink of orgasm already. Trembling. Burning. Tight. I could barely breathe. Couldn't think.

"You're going to come."

"Yes," I said.

"Tighten that pussy. Hold me like a fist." He thrust harder, faster.

I tightened the muscles deep inside, and a huge blast of heat raged through me. I was burning up. Oh yes. The first pulse of a powerful orgasm shot through my body, and I cried out. My insides rhythmically convulsed around him, and he drove into me, stroking hard and fast.

His voice joined mine as he too found release. His skin was blistering hot, pressed against mine. His hips slammed forward and back, his rod pounding mercilessly inside my quivering depth until we were both breathless and limp.

I made a little mewling sound when he pulled out of me. And another one slipped from my lips when he gently eased the toy out of my ass. After setting the toy aside, and taking off the mask and untying my hands, he lay down and pulled me into his arms.

I nuzzled him, smiling, still gasping, still shaking all over.

I'd never thought sex could be like this. It was so much more than what I'd ever experienced with anyone else.

"Sleep," he murmured as he smoothed my hair back from my face. "We'll stay here tonight. Together."

"Yes, sir," I muttered as I sank into warm darkness.

* * *

I woke up to the sensation of a gentle stroke between my legs, and I realized I was lying on my side, one of my legs thrown over Kam's hip, the other bent at the knee and resting on the mattress. Even though I'd been asleep, my body had been responding to his patient caresses. I was wet. Hot. My insides coiling into little knots.

He entered me from behind. No warning. His invasion took me by surprise and was so deliciously decadent, I couldn't help groaning loudly.

"This is the way to wake up," I mumbled as I arched my spine, taking him as deep as he could go.

He wrapped an arm around my waist, holding me in place with that hand while kneading my breast with the other. "Glad you're enjoying yourself." He nibbled my shoulder, making little goose bumps erupt across my whole back. "I thought you deserved a little bit of pleasure this morning." He slammed harder, and I trembled. "Do you agree?"

"Oh yes."

He rammed into me again. "How's that?"

"Good."

And again. And again. And with each thrust, I said, "Thank you."

Within minutes, I was on the verge of orgasm. I spread my legs as wide as I could and tipped my hips back to allow him to jam that hard cock deep inside. I set one hand on top of the hand that was now tormenting my breast, weaving my fingers between his. My breaths came in little gusting huffs. In, out. Hard, sharp. I could feel the burning heat of an orgasm igniting. Swirling. Building.

Then he pulled out and bit my neck. I cried out, shocked, frustrated.

"I said you deserved a little pleasure," he said as he laved away the sting on my neck. "A *little*."

Through gritted teeth, I snapped, "You're mean."

He chuckled. "I warned you."

Using the hand resting on top of his, I pushed down, forcing pressure onto my aching breast. "You aren't going to leave me like this."

"I am." He pinched my nipple, then rolled it between his finger and thumb. Cruel bastard.

"No, you're not." I glared at him over my shoulder.

"Oh yes." Wearing a wicked grin so deviously sexy I was seeing stars in my eyes, he pinched my nipple again. "I am. Because you are still trying to tell me what I will or won't do." His tongue swept across his lower lip. "Did you read the contract, Abigail?"

"No. You told me to forget it." I hooked a hand around the back of his neck and pulled, trying to coax him into kissing me. "But I didn't throw it away. I will read it. I promise."

He pressed his mouth to mine, and a moan swept up my throat. I curled my fingers in his hair and held him. My lips parted, and I hoped, prayed, his tongue would push inside and do all the naughty, wonderful things it tended to do inside my mouth.

"Hmmm." He angled his head down but not close enough. His breath caressed my face, tickling my lips and making me suck in little gasps of air.

Hmmm, indeed. His front teeth depressed his full lower lip, giving me an almost irresistible impulse to kiss it. I pulled harder on his neck, but he resisted.

His gaze focused on my mouth. "I think you need some training. Lots of training."

I had no doubt I was going to enjoy every minute of that training. Every second. "I think you may be right." I wrapped the other arm around his neck, and this time he didn't fight me as I pulled. "I think we should start now," I whispered against his moist lips. The fleeting contact between our mouths made my lips tickle and tingle. A little giggle bubbled up my throat.

"No," he said against my mouth. "It's time to get moving." He sat up, pulling me with him. And before I knew it, he was carrying me across the room, toward the bathroom. He turned on the water before setting me on my feet, and when I tried to kiss him again, he growled, grumbling, "Would you like to have a cold shower this morning?"

"No, thanks."

"Then you'd better behave." He gave my bottom a sharp smack. The sound was amplified in the tiled room, making me jump. The stinging that followed made my skin warm. And that made me warm everywhere else.

He took a long up-and-down look at me and shook his head. "You're insatiable." Then, much to my disappointment, he left, shouting through the door after he closed it, "If you touch yourself, I swear, you'll be sorry."

I turned the water to steamy hot, grabbed the soap, and smiled.

Sorry? We would just see about that.

15

An hour later I was on my way to work . . . with a big, goofy smile on my face. While I was still extremely worried about my brother's future, the night I'd spent with Kam had put me in a very different frame of mind. I trusted Kam when he said Joss's safety wasn't currently an issue. All I needed to focus on was doing what I could to find the real guilty party.

Determined to do just that, I went into my office with a solid plan. The assumption was whoever had done it knew my brother fairly well. This person also had no qualms about allowing an innocent man to be fingered for the crime. That kind of planning and underhanded deviousness had to have shown itself in other areas of the person's life. In other words, I believed he or she would have a criminal record. Thus, I would start there.

With one conversation with Kam, I had access to someone who could help me find out which of my brother's friends had shady pasts and which did not. This someone turned out to be an old friend of Kam's from school named Dave. Having no criteria by which to eliminate anyone, I gave Dave a fairly lengthy list of names and then went on the Internet to see what I could dig up on my own. Better to do something than to sit around and wait for the phone to ring.

By a little after ten, however, I was in need of some caffeine. My mood was good, but my energy level, not so great. I cracked open my door, catching Kam saying my name in a conversation with someone on the phone. Hoping it was Dave, with information about Joss's friends, I peered through the crack, noted that he didn't see me, and stepped to one side to eavesdrop.

Once, I'd been told it wasn't ever a good idea to eavesdrop on someone else's conversation. Rarely do you hear something you'd like to hear.

Truer words had never been spoken.

But, despite that fact, I'd also learned a long time ago that even though I might not like what I was hearing, there was still a good likelihood that what I heard would be useful in one way or another. In fact, as a kid, eavesdropping had kept me alive.

Considering the situation with my brother, I wasn't going to pass up this opportunity either.

"No, she's never mentioned her parents. Why?" he said.

A prickly chill shimmied up my back. Were they talking about someone who knew Joss, or me? If it was me . . . *Oh no.* I leaned closer and held my breath. I couldn't miss a word. Not one.

"I don't know about that. Are you sure?" Kam asked whomever he was talking to. His voice was laced with doubt. Little did he know what he was probably hearing was true, if they were talking about me. I had a lot more skeletons in my closet than most anyone would guess.

"Okay. I think you're wasting your time. But you're being paid to do a job. I get it." He paused to listen to the voice on the other end. Then he said, "Call me when you get something," and hung up.

I took several slow, deep breaths before opening the door.

His gaze jerked my way. His eyes widened for a split second, then returned to normal.

I forced a smile. "Hey, have you heard back from Dave yet? I'm expecting a call."

"No." Turning his attention back to the computer on his desk, he started poking keys. I didn't like the way he was acting—distant, cold.

"Okay. I hope he gets back to us soon. I thought I'd head down to grab some coffee. Would you like some?"

"Sure. Black. Thanks." He snatched up his phone again but didn't dial.

I felt his gaze on my back as I walked across his office to the door.

Wow.

Crap.

Ugh.

Just last night I'd fallen asleep in that man's arms. I'd felt not only accepted but cherished. And safe. So safe. Now . . . the way he'd watched me made me feel as if last night had never happened.

What had he been told? What did he know?

The instinct to run was almost unbearable. I'd followed that instinct before, when someone had gotten a little too close to the truth. Would I be forced to run again?

Not again, please!

Dammit, Joss. If only you'd been able to stay out of trouble.

This time it isn't his fault, I reminded myself.

My mind raced as I rode the elevator to the lower level. The door rumbled open, and I stepped out, hurried into the café, and poured two cups. As I was about to pay, my cell phone rang. I didn't recognize the number, but something told me to answer.

"Hello?"

"Sis."

Leaving the coffees sitting on the tray, I scurried into a corner, cupped my hand around the phone. "Joss? Are you okay? What's happening?"

"I'm fine. Got myself a nice hotel room. I wanted to call you to tell you not to worry about me. I'm okay. I talked to Sue. She told me you called her."

"I'm trying to find out who is really behind the theft."

"You still believe me, then? You believe I didn't do it?"

"I believe you."

I could hear his sigh of relief. "Do you think it's someone I know?"

Hoping I wasn't being eavesdropped on, I peered over my shoulder, checking to see if anyone was close enough to overhear my conversation. I didn't see anyone within earshot. Stephanie was stuffing coins into a vending machine. And a few other employees I didn't know were sitting, scattered, at tables, eating, drinking, talking. "I don't know what to think, to be honest. I'm not Brenda Leigh Johnson, and this isn't an episode of *The Closer*. But I have to figure it out soon. Kam said the company has hired an investigator. I think he's digging into our past a little too deep for my comfort."

"But you've got nothing to hide."

He had no idea.

"I know. It's just that . . . the more they look at you, the guiltier you appear. We've got to clear your name."

"I don't know. Maybe it's better if you just let it rest and go on with your life."

A cold chill zoomed up my spine. "What are you saying?"

"I'm saying it's about time you start living your own life."

What was he doing? What was he trying to say? "I am living my own life."

"No. Everything you do, you do either because of me or for me."

"That's what older sisters do." My heart started thumping hard against my breastbone. Was my brother going to do something crazy? Would he turn himself in? Or would he disappear? Cut himself off from me? Oh God, I couldn't imagine living my life not knowing where he was, wondering if he was dead or alive.

"No, that isn't what older sisters do," Joss said. "That's what you do. Only you. You go way beyond what you should."

"That's because I love you."

"And I love you too. And that's why I'm telling you to drop it, go on with your life. I'm safe. I'm not going to starve to death or anything. I'll be fine."

I felt my fingers tightening on the phone. My stomach was coiling up into a tight knot. It hurt so bad I could barely breathe. "Joss, don't do anything crazy."

"I'm doing this for you. I'm letting you go."

"No."

"Just for now. For a while."

My heart stopped. "No."

"I love you, sis."

The air left my lungs. "Tell me where you are."

"Take care of yourself for once. If you love me, that's what you'll do. You'll take care of yourself."

I was frozen in place. Dizzy. I leaned to the side, letting the wall prop me up. "Joss."

"I'll be okay. I don't need you anymore."

"Joss!"

Click.

"Joss!"

I hit redial.

There was a beep. Then the call went straight to voice mail. I left a message and hung up.

A sob tore through my chest. I stumbled, knocking into a

chair. I felt a hand on my shoulder and turned. A woman I didn't recognize asked, "Are you okay?"

"I'm fine." Trying to pull it together, I grabbed the coffee cups, paid, and staggered out to the elevator. I caught a few people staring at me. They must've witnessed my breakdown.

Humiliated, and succumbing to the urge to hide, I went for the staircase instead. Climbing two flights gave me some time to pull myself together. I rode the elevator up the rest of the way.

As usual, Stephanie gave me a little wave as I hurried past her. She had beat me upstairs, probably having taken the elevator. Kam was still at his desk. He didn't acknowledge me until I set the cup down. Then, it was a polite nod. No smile.

Something was definitely wrong.

I went into my office and tried to pretend I wasn't petrified and upset. Having things go from happy to this stressful within such a short time was going to kill me. My insides were twisting and turning.

I heard Kam call my name, and my nerves pulled tight. My heart started thumping hard and fast again. I hadn't felt this nervous around him since that very first day when I'd come to beg him not to go to the police.

Smoothing my sweaty palms down my thighs to dry them, I stood and took slow, deliberate steps out of my office and into his.

Kam watched me. His gaze never left my face. Not for an instant. "Please sit." Looking over the rim of his cup, he drank some of the coffee I'd brought up.

"Yes, sir?" My voice vibrated a little. Dammit, I was shaking.

"Why are you looking like a frightened little rabbit, Abigail?" His gaze fixed to mine, he stood, circled the desk, arms crossed over his chest. "Are you nervous?"

"Um, no. Not nervous. I just noticed—"

"Noticed what?" He stepped between the chair I was sitting in and the front of his desk. Leaning forward, he set his hands on the arms of the chair, crowding me. "What did you notice?"

Unable to speak, I stared into his eyes. Just last night those eyes had been full of wanting and need and raw male hunger. Now they were cold and hard. A big lump formed in my throat. I tried to swallow it down, but I couldn't.

"Are you trying to come up with a good lie?" His words sliced through me like razors.

"I—I don't know what you mean."

"You don't know what I mean? How many secrets do you have, Abigail Barnes?"

"Everyone has secrets. Even you," I countered.

"Sure, but my secrets aren't..." He blinked. Wobbled. Shook his head. His brows drew together and his face paled. "What did you do?"

"What do you mean?"

He straightened up but teetered backward. His ass hit the desk and he slumped to one side, catching himself with his arm. "Shit." He blinked. One hand flattened on his forehead. He stared down for a moment, then looked at me again. "Tell me now. What the fuck did you do to me?"

My blood turned to ice. "What's wrong?"

He tried to stand but fell back down.

"Are you sick?" I reached for him, to help him, but he smacked my hands away.

"Get the hell out of here. Get out now." Looking like he might fall over, he reached for the phone, grasped it in his hands. But before he had said a word, he collapsed onto the floor.

I screamed.

A couple of hours later Kam was on his way to the hospital, and I was on my way home. After he'd collapsed, Stephanie had come barreling through the door, reacting to my shriek. She'd called 9-1-1 while I tried to explain what had happened. Before I knew it, the place was swarming with police and rescue personnel. Kam was lifted onto a stretcher while I answered a flurry of questions blasted at me from all sides. Once things had settled down, I left.

No word yet on what was wrong. I hoped it was nothing serious.

As I drove home his words kept echoing in my head.

What did you do?

What the fuck did you do to me?

What had he meant by that? What made him think I would do anything bad to him?

Nothing. Unless . . .

He couldn't have found out the truth. Nobody knew.

Once I was home, I couldn't stop pacing. My phone wasn't ringing. I didn't know whether Kam was seriously ill. I couldn't be sure, after what he'd said, whether my brother was still safe. All I wanted was for someone I cared about to tell me everything was okay.

Joss.

Kam.

Both.

Either.

God help me, they were all I had in this world. And now, it seemed, I'd lost them both.

Trembling so hard I could barely stand, I sank onto my couch and let the tears go. What did I do to deserve this? Hadn't I only acted out of selflessness? Hadn't I always put other people before myself?

It didn't take long for me to grow weary of my pity party. I dried my face, took a shower, and went to bed.

Tomorrow would be a better day.

There was no way it could be worse.

16

My alarm clock woke me the next morning at six-thirty. Hoping I'd hear something about Kam when I got to work, I got dressed, grabbed a protein bar, and ran out to my car. Making one quick stop for some much-needed caffeine (I hadn't slept much last night), I broke more than a couple of traffic laws to get to work before eight. By the time I pulled into the parking lot, I was flying high on a caffeine rush and anxious to see whether Kam had come to work.

I dashed inside, making a beeline for the elevators. While I was waiting, a man wearing a suit approached.

He didn't look very friendly. "Miss Barnes?"

"Y-yes, that's me."

"Would you please follow me?"

Strange.

Was he the investigator? Had to be.

I didn't ask. I merely followed him. We went down the hall to a small conference room.

He shut the door. "I've been asked to escort you out of the building."

"What?" I snapped, unable to comprehend what he'd just said.

"I've been asked to escort you out of the building," he repeated, enunciating a little slower.

It didn't help.

Once again, I blurted, "What?" Yes, I'd heard him, but I didn't understand.

"You've been placed on leave."

"Leave?"

"Yes, ma'am." Evidently feeling our conversation was over, he grabbed the doorknob.

"Why was I placed on 'leave'?"

"I couldn't say." He opened the door and stepped to the side to allow me to pass.

"When should I return?"

"I was told to tell you to wait to be contacted before returning to work."

Wait to be contacted.

If that happened.

Stunned and confused, I shuffled past the man. "Can you tell me if Mr. Maldonado is okay? He was ill yesterday."

"No, I cannot say."

Even more bewildered, I walked outside, the man who'd informed me I was on leave tailing me to make sure I left. He stood at the door and watched me get into my car. And he didn't go back inside until I'd pulled out of my parking spot.

Ohmygod.

Ohmygod!

I'd just been told to leave work. I'd been escorted out by some security guard before I'd even made it up to my office. What the hell was going on?

I tried to remember what Kam had said on the phone yesterday. It seemed that everything had changed after I'd overheard that conversation. What had he said?

He had to have been talking about me, not one of Joss's friends.

There'd been a mention of someone's parents. I clearly remembered that. Otherwise, nothing else had been said that sounded like it warranted my being put on "leave," escorted out the door, and told not to return.

Was it possible someone had found out . . . ? No.

I became lost in my thoughts as I drove home. Before I realized it, I was parked and staring at the front of my apartment building.

Was it time to pack up my stuff and move again?

My head dropped forward, my forehead resting against the steering wheel. When my brother and I had moved into this place, I'd told myself I was done running from the past. We would stick it out here, no matter what.

No. Matter. What.

But now . . . now that I'd lost my brother and I was alone, this didn't feel like home anymore. It felt empty and cold.

Even so, I didn't want to move again, dammit. I dreaded starting over, finding a new job, a new home.

More than that, I dreaded not seeing Kam again.

That's probably more of a reason to leave than the other. You've become too attached. That wasn't what he wanted. It isn't what you wanted either.

Go. Get a fresh start somewhere. Go to a big city. Maybe out west.

I ran inside, pulled out my suitcase, and started tossing all my most treasured belongings in it. My clothes, the pictures of my brother and me, all our important documents—birth certificates and school records.

I hauled the suitcase out to the car, heaved it into the trunk and ran back inside for one final sweep of the place. But when I got into the car and looked up at the building, I couldn't drive away. I just couldn't. Not yet. Not until I'd spoken with Kam. I needed to find out exactly what was going on. And if the need be, I would tell him the truth. The whole truth.

The truth that even Joss didn't know.

Then, if he rejected me, I would leave, knowing there was no chance he could accept me.

Leaving my suitcase in the car, I dug my phone out of my purse as I wearily walked inside. This was going to be hell. No doubt about it. But I could see no other choice.

With my heart thumping in my ears, I dialed his number and waited, breathlessly, for him to answer.

He didn't.

Either he was still in the hospital, and thus couldn't have his cell phone turned on, or he wasn't taking my calls.

I tried again.

It went straight to voice mail. Again.

Dammit. Now I was going to have to try to track him down and meet with him face-to-face. I had no idea, considering I'd been escorted off MalTech's property, whether I'd be allowed to visit him if he was in the hospital. I decided to call and see if he was a registered patient.

Good thing I did. He'd been released already.

I didn't know where he lived. I'd been to his house, but I didn't have a clue how to find it.

I was screwed.

I flopped on the couch, tossed my phone on the coffee table, and dropped my face into my hands.

I felt completely and utterly defeated. And alone. And sick. And scared.

My eyes blurred. My nose burned.

Shit.

Maybe I should just go. Leave. Vanish. Disappear.

He wouldn't miss me. Nobody would.

Screw it.

I grabbed my purse, my phone, stormed toward the door, yanked it open, and ran smack-dab into a broad chest. Hands grabbed my arms, and I was forced back. The door was slammed.

I jerked my head up.

Kam.

"Pack a bag," he growled.

"I . . . what?"

"Pack a bag," he repeated.

"I have one."

"Where?"

"Car."

"Let's go." Releasing only one arm, he half dragged me out of my apartment, down the walk, and out to my car. Next to it was a big, black SUV I'd never seen before. "Get your stuff."

I popped the trunk of my car, dragged my bag out. He snatched it from me, opened the back end of the SUV, and tossed it in.

"Get in," he ordered.

"Where are we—"

"Just get in."

Hands trembling, I strapped myself in the passenger seat.

What the hell was going on?

He said nothing as he belted himself in and started the vehicle. He stomped on the gas, and the SUV zoomed back, out of the parking spot. Then he stomped on the brake, shifted into drive, and within seconds my apartment building was out of sight.

I alternated between watching the scenery whiz by my window and studying his tense face. When it appeared that his jaw wasn't quite so tight, his eyes quite so narrow, I asked, "Kam, where are we going?"

"Somewhere safe."

"Safe?"

"Yes." He glanced in his rearview mirror.

He'd been checking the mirror a lot, more than normal. I peered over my shoulder.

"Is someone following us?" I asked.

"I hope not."

The vehicle's speed increased a bit.

"Please tell me what's going on," I pleaded.

"We're heading to a friend's property for a while. We have a lot to talk about."

We had a lot to talk about. That didn't sound good. "Can't we talk now?"

"No. We'll wait."

"How far away is this friend's house?"

"A few hours."

A few hours? "Okay," I muttered on a sigh. Leaning against the door, I watched trees and buildings and cars zoom by until I was too bored and sleepy to bother. I closed my eyes and tried to doze. I couldn't.

I checked Kam, to see if he looked more relaxed and willing to talk.

He didn't.

This was going to be a long few hours.

"Now?" I asked, almost four hours later, after Kam had pulled the SUV into the garage and shut the door. We were safe. We were alone. We'd driven over two hundred miles and were out in the middle of nowhere, somewhere outside of Muskegon. Tall, spindly trees lined the roads for miles. Those same trees walled in the house we were presently letting ourselves into. It was a vacation house, nicely furnished.

"Not yet." Carrying both our suitcases, Kam lumbered down a hallway. He left my bag in one room, then continued down the hall with his bag. He shut the door, closing himself in.

I dragged my suitcase toward the bed. I didn't bother opening it. Instead, I headed out to the kitchen for something to drink.

The mood I was in, it needed to be something with a lot of alcohol in it.

I didn't find any alcohol. So I settled for a can of diet cola. Sipping, I wandered a little, checking out my new, temporary home while trying to settle my rattled nerves. The house was really nice, with a set of French doors leading out to a huge deck. There was a swimming pool and a killer view of a lake beyond that.

Yes, the sight of the green trees reflected on the lake did soothe the nerves a little. Until I heard footsteps approaching from the house.

I glanced over my shoulder.

Kam looked a little less intense.

"This place is gorgeous," I said, thinking small talk would get things rolling.

"We're not on vacation," he said, his voice chilly.

"I guessed that much. Ready to tell me what's going on?"

His lips thinned a little as he came closer. Leaving a fair amount of distance between us, he stood next to me, arms resting on the railing, facing the pool and the lake. "Things are really fucked up, and I don't know what to believe."

"Tell me what's happened. Are you okay? You were sick."

"I'm fine."

"I'm glad." I smiled. He didn't smile back. "What did you mean when you asked me what I'd done?"

"I was drugged."

"And you thought I'd drugged you." A shiver raced up my spine as I remembered his words, the cruel, cutting tone of his voice. "Why would you think I'd do a thing like that?" I asked as I stared straight ahead. I couldn't look him in the eye now.

"I became sick after you gave me the coffee."

"Was it the coffee?"

"The results of the test aren't back yet."

"Still, didn't you think it unlikely that I would drug you then, when I'd had so many opportunities to in the past? And also, if you recall, I was drugged too. In New York."

"I did recall that. And yes, I did wonder about the timing, too. But because I had discovered some information about you, and I sensed you were aware of what I'd learned, I felt you might have the motivation to do it."

Yes, it was exactly what I'd feared.

"What was the information you learned?" I asked as I tried to hide my growing panic. He was much too close to the truth.

"I learned you were once considered a suspect in your father's death."

Oh God. "His death was ruled a suicide," I pointed out.

"Yes, I learned that too."

"I was never officially charged with any crime," I added.

"I learned that as well."

My heart did a flip. "So, do you still think I'm capable of killing someone?" I held my breath, knowing his response would mean everything—the difference between a possible future together or not.

"I never did think it."

Thank God.

My insides unknotted. I risked looking his way. He was studying me with sharp, probing eyes. "But you thought I might drug you?"

Glancing down at his foot, he kicked the railing we were

leaning against. It wiggled a tiny bit. "I wasn't thinking clearly then. I was under the influence of the drug."

"What about now?"

Straightening up, he turned toward me. He left one arm resting on the railing. "I'm thinking it's highly unlikely you were the culprit."

"Highly unlikely?" I echoed. In other words, he hadn't ruled me out. I was hurt. Truly. Genuinely. And scared. But then again hadn't I done the same thing? Hadn't I jumped to conclusions when I was drugged? "What drug was it? Can I ask that without appearing guilty?"

"Some kind of benzo-something. I don't know. I think they said midazolam."

A tiny quiver raced up my spine. I was scared, yes—still worried about what he thought of me after learning about my father's death. But I was also feeling guilty for having blamed him for my drugging. "That was what I was drugged with too. Do you think the two incidences are related? If they aren't, that's a mighty strange coincidence, don't you think?"

"I agree. Which is why I brought you here."

For the first time in hours, I inhaled fully. So he didn't really believe I might poison him. And he didn't believe I could have killed my father. "Then it wasn't to interrogate me."

"Partially, yes, it was."

"Oh."

His gaze swept across my face. He shoved his fingers through his hair, leaving it a mess of waves. A breeze riffled through it, making it ever messier. "Shit. I'm sorry. You don't deserve to be interrogated. You haven't done anything but put up with me and my crap since the first day you stepped in my office. Do I seem overly paranoid to you?"

"No, not really." I released a long sigh. "Both of us have been drugged recently. I don't know if that kind of thing has happened in the past. Maybe it is a coincidence and maybe not. Perhaps you've made a lot of enemies I don't know about. Maybe there are a lot of people who would like to see you knocked down a rung or two. Maybe you need to be paranoid."

"Actually, it's been a while since something like this has happened. I'd grown a little lazy, I think. Too trusting. I made myself an easy target."

I gazed into his eyes. "It's sad," I said, watching him as he studied me. His gaze was still extremely penetrating. Sharp. "Here you are, a man who has so much, a good man, a generous, kind man. But because of what you have, you have to be on guard at all times. Always aware there might be someone out there waiting to take it all away from you."

"That's just it, I wasn't living like that," he said. He reached for my hand, took it in his. "How about we take a walk?"

"Didn't you just say you'd been too lax? Is it safe to leave the house?"

"There's nobody around. No one knows where we are."

"No one?" I echoed, doubtful. How could he just pick up and leave? He was the owner of a huge corporation. He was important, needed. Someone had to know where he was.

"Nobody." Not particularly gently, but not too roughly either, he tugged me toward the steps that descended to the patio below and the swimming pool. Suddenly more aware of my surroundings than ever before, I followed his lead. We circled the pool and headed toward the lake's shore. At the narrow beach we found a fallen log. It was mossy and damp, but I didn't care. I sat and stared out at the sparkling water.

"I could get used to this," I said as I inhaled deeply. The air smelled so clean and fresh. Like damp earth and water and green plants. The sunshine made me feel energized and alive. And being with Kam right now, silent, both of us absorbing the beauty around us made it that much better. Especially knowing we were closer to setting things right between us again.

"I could get used to this too." He audibly exhaled. "A part of me wishes I could just walk away from it all, the responsibility and the stress, and stay in a place like this. Somewhere where I can just be Kameron Maldonado. A man. Only a man. Not an entrepreneur. Not a business owner. You know?"

"Why don't you?"

"Responsibility. I can't just dump it all into someone else's lap. It wouldn't be fair to him or her. It wouldn't be fair to all the people whose livelihoods rely upon me, either."

"I understand."

"It's crazy. When MalTech was a small company, all I could think about was making it bigger. All my problems would go away if only I could increase sales, increase profits. I would provide people with jobs. With insurance and education and a future. But the bigger the company became, the smaller my personal life became. Until now, I basically live to make the next deal, to find the next opportunity."

Yes, this was the way it should be. He was opening up again, trusting me, sharing with me. Allowing me to glimpse the man nobody else knew. "I never would have imagined that," I said. "Maybe I knew, on some gut level, that a man in your position would live and breathe work. But I guess I assumed men who did that did it because they loved it. Work was their life because it was their choice."

He shook his head. "Not always."

"You should retire."

"There's nobody to replace me. Nobody I trust. That's the key. Trust. I can't just hire someone off the street, lay everything in his hands, and walk away. He could fuck it all up and screw everyone who has trusted me all these years."

"That's a tough one." Turning slightly, I met his gaze. "But doesn't everyone, yourself included, deserve a life? Happiness?"

"I'm happy."

I gave him an oh-really look.

"Sometimes," he admitted.

"Like when you're in the dungeon? When you're playing those games?" I asked.

"No." He raised a hand, cupping my cheek. "More like now, when I'm sitting on a moldy old log, ants crawling up my pants, talking to you."

"Ants?" I giggled. "Who wouldn't be happy with ants in his pants?"

"Exactly." His tongue swept across his lower lip. His gaze locked to mine. He was going to kiss me. Yes, yes, yes! "I'm sorry for being such an asshole."

"It's okay. I understand why you were suspicious. The important thing is we talked it out. You didn't just keep it all inside."

"Good. But I have one question." He angled closer.

"Yes?"

"You had a bag packed when I arrived at your place. Where were you going?"

"I don't know. Just away for a while. Someplace peaceful. Someplace like this."

"I'm sorry I had you placed on leave. They . . . I was convinced you had spiked my coffee." Shaking his head, he smoothed a lock of my hair back and tucked it behind my ear. "You're a better person than me. I wouldn't have been able to forgive so easily."

"Yeah, well, I don't usually forgive so easily either. But with you it's different."

"I'm glad." He moved closer still. His lips were right there, less than an inch from mine. His breath was gently caressing my face. My nerves were tingling, anticipation zinging up and down through my body.

Despite everything, his gruff attitude earlier, and his accusation, his suspicions, my body craved his touch. Craved it so much it almost hurt inside.

I lifted my hands, flattening them on his chest. One fingertip found a hard nipple, poking at soft knit fabric.

He audibly gasped, and so did I.

It was as if his need fueled mine and the other way around. Our bodies were in sync. Nerves sending little jolts of electricity through our skin and into the other's body. Skin warming. Pupils dilating. Faces flushing.

Kiss me.

Shifting forward, I set my mouth on his. He groaned, and the low vibrations pulsated through me, zooming to my center. The first tingles of heat warmed the tissues between my legs. The sensations were so glorious, I wished I could freeze that moment and cherish it forever.

His mouth started moving, sliding across mine. Lips touching, caressing, brushing back and forth. It was a slow, seductive kiss. The kind of kiss I would remember for a long time.

Maybe forever.

Then, it got better.

His hand, the one that had been so sweetly cupping my cheek, made a slow but steady descent. It followed my neck, lingered for a moment at the ticklish spot at my collarbone before dropping farther. When it found my breast, my spine arched. My breath hitched in my throat. And a flare of bright colors exploded behind my closed eyelids.

Oh, what wicked things his hands could do. Wicked, wonderful things. Like now. His fingertip found my nipple through my clothes. It was pure agony, as that fingertip flicked back and forth over the sensitive peak until it was so hard my insides were clenched.

My hands smoothed up his broad chest to his face. I held him there, deepened the kiss, my tongue shyly slipping inside his sweet, warm mouth to tangle with his. We kissed. And moaned. And groaned. And whimpered. All thoughts of employees and poisonings and murdered fathers flying from our minds.

This was our time. Time for us to just live. And share. And be. At last, it was our time.

17

I was in heaven. This moment. It was pure ecstasy.

The gentle, earth-scented breeze was caressing my face as Kam's hands softly worked over my body, igniting every nerve under my skin. His tongue was stroking mine, filling my mouth with his decadent flavor. The sound of our breathing, coupled with the glorious noises of nature, created a magical song that made my heart gallop and my soul sing.

I'd never felt anything like it.

"I want you now. Here," Kam murmured as he flattened his hands on either side of my head. I stared into his eyes. They were dark, full of lust and hunger and desperation. The writhing flames flickering there thrilled me. He needed me. *Needed.*

"Yes," I said.

He took my hands in his and put them on the bulge pressing against the front of his pants. Feeling naughty and sexy, I curled my lips into a smile and rubbed.

He growled.

How I adored that growl. Feeling my smile widening, I unbuckled his belt and unzipped his pants. As I worked, he kissed and nibbled my neck, which made me shiver, goose bumps prickling my arms, neck, chest. My hands pushed under his shirt. His stomach was a glorious thing. Perfectly sculpted. Rigid planes of muscle sheathed in smooth skin. I could touch and stare at his stomach all day long.

But it seemed he had something else in mind.

Making another little growly sound, he fisted my wrists and moved my hands lower. A fingertip brushed against velvety skin, the plump, engorged head of his cock.

"Yes," he murmured. "Stroke it."

I curled my fingers around his rod and slowly ran my hand up and down, up and down.

"Yes," he repeated. "Yes. Take me in your mouth."

Sliding off the log, I knelt in front of him, knees on the moist earth.

I flicked my tongue over the tip, tasting salt and clean skin. Precome. He tangled his fingers in my hair, using it to move me. I loved how he took control. It was like a dark secret, a wicked thrill—serving him like this, submitting to him.

As he eased my head lower, I opened my mouth wider, allowing his length to inch deeper inside. My tongue cushioned his rod as it filled me. The taste of him exciting every taste bud, all the way to the back.

He pulled, and I withdrew until just the plump head remained in my mouth. I swirled my tongue round and round. I let my teeth gently scrape over the flared ridge circling it. And I soaked in all the sounds of his little gasps and groans and moans of appreciation.

Once again, he pushed me down, forcing me to take him deep, deeper. He touched the back of my throat and I fought the urge to gag, inhaling slowly through my nose. Even as I struggled, the tissues between my legs throbbed. Heat swirled round and round through me. Behind my closed eyes, I imaged his face, ecstasy pulling at his features. Face flushed. Eyes hard. Such a beautiful face. Strong and sexy. Masculine but still perfectly formed, almost too perfectly.

When he pulled me off, it was abrupt and a little shocking. I gasped, jerked my eyes up to his face. It was exactly as I'd imagined. Jaw tight. Flames burning in his eyes.

"Take off your pants," he demanded.

I stared into his eyes as I unzipped my pants and pulled them down. I had to do a little wiggle as I pushed them over my hips. The fire in his eyes intensified then, making the blood in my veins burn hotter.

"Turn around," he said just as I was shoving them down toward my ankles.

I shuffled around, peering over my shoulder as I bent.

His gaze locked on my ass, which was currently covered in a thin layer of sodden black satin. I could literally feel the heat of his gaze on my skin, burning it. The sensation made it that much harder to go slow and draw out this torturous game of submission.

When I had my pants off, he commanded, "Now, the rest. I want you nude."

Remaining with my back to him, I pulled off my shirt and bra. I let them drop to the ground before hooking my thumbs under the waistband of my panties and pushing them down, down over my hips, down my thighs, down my shins. My pussy was burning, clenching as I stepped out of them.

"Good, now turn around."

I shuffled back around.

"Come here." He reached, and I stepped closer until his hands were resting on my hips. His tongue swept across his lower lip. His gaze meandered up and down my body. "You are the most beautiful woman I have ever seen. Do you know that?"

"I . . . thank you."

"I tried to fight it. I tried to tell myself this wasn't right. That I was taking advantage of you. That you were taking advantage of me. That it was all wrong, and we needed to stop. But every time I closed my eyes at night, this was what I saw." His eyes met mine. "Those eyes." He traced the line of my lips with the tip of his index finger. "That luscious mouth." His hand slid down, fingers curving around my neck. "This graceful neck." Down it went again, fingertip skimming down the cleft between my breasts before wandering to the right and circling a nipple. "These perfect little nipples." He pinched it, and a sharp blade of pleasure-pain pierced me. I whimpered as a jolt of need zigzagged through my body. "Who could blame me? Who could be strong enough to deny himself this?"

I was speechless. No man had ever looked at me the way he was, like I was the world's most perfect woman, like he was in awe and had to drink in every tiny detail. Like I was the world's most perfect work of art and he couldn't look close or deep enough. My heart felt as if it were expanding in my chest. I was soaring. I was weightless.

I was . . . wanted.

Needed.

Cherished.

"Come here." Hands on my hips again, he pulled me closer until one knee was resting on the log, next to his hip, and the burning tissues between my thighs were inches from his erection. Taking the base of his cock in one hand, he positioned it at my slick opening. "Now."

I eased down, taking him so deep I couldn't help groaning. Ah, he filled me so perfectly. Our bodies fit together. His hard form the perfect complement to my softness. Both trembling and sweating, we writhed and thrust, our bodies working in perfect harmony. Heat building. Need overcoming us. Blood pounding hard and hot. Waves of pleasure crashing through us. Our voices cut through the noises of nature as we cried out our pleasure, as we succumbed to our need and the tight grip of orgasm made our bodies spasm. Our eyes were locked to each other as we rode out the storm of pleasure.

It was an orgasm like no other. It wasn't just a physical experience. It wasn't just nerves blazing and muscles contracting. It was more. It was so much more.

It felt as if our souls had become tangled together. For that one magical moment. That brief time.

And when it was over, a part of me felt empty, as if his soul had been torn away from mine. I wanted to do it again, to feel that strange, glorious sensation once more. I needed to feel it again.

But when I tried to start moving, firm hands stopped me, holding me in place. Strong arms wrapped around me, holding me against his hard, slick body.

"Not now," he whispered, breath caressing the side of my face. "I just want to hold you."

I closed my eyes and grinned. Could this be any more perfect?

Ten minutes later I learned it could be more perfect. Holding me cradled in his arms, Kam stood. Instead of carrying me toward the house, he went to the water's edge.

His eyes were glittering with childlike glee as he stood ankle deep, grinning at me. "How about a swim?"

I couldn't help giggling. "Do I have a choice?"

"No." Running, he splashed into the water, sending crystalline droplets spraying all around. Splash, splash, splash, and one final splash, as we plunged under the surface. My ears filled with water. Sound muffled. I emerged, sucking in air, laughing, clinging to Kam, legs now wrapped around his waist.

He held me tightly with one arm, placed the other hand on the back of my head, and held me as he kissed me until my head was spinning and the water droplets on my shoulders and back were sizzling from the heat. A pounding throb beat between my legs, and I couldn't help rocking my hips back and forth, rubbing against him shamelessly. It had been minutes since that mind-blowing orgasm, and already I was burning for him again.

"Kam," I whispered against his lips. "Oh God."

"You see, that's what you do to me." He pulled my hair, forcing my head back. That was so damn sexy, how he took control of my body.

That was it, that was the key, I realized as I trembled against him. My muscles were knotting. My blood was simmering. My nerves were zapping. And it was all because of how strong and domineering he was. I absolutely loved being dominated. Loved it. Needed it. Craved it.

There was no going back. I would never enjoy a man who didn't know how to take control in the bedroom.

He bit down on the sensitive skin on my neck, and I writhed, little bolts of pleasure-pain zinging up and down my spine. A wave of adrenaline rushed through me in the next instant, leaving me feeling like I was ready to soar to the moon and beyond. Ready to do whatever this man demanded.

I curled my fingers, clawing into the hard flesh of his shoulders. That seemed to spur him on even more. He dropped both his hands to my buttocks, gripped the flesh hard, and parted them.

"If we weren't in water right now, I would fuck this ass," he growled as the head of his cock prodded at my entrance.

I quivered in response to the wild edge I heard in his voice. He sounded like he was half beast, untamed, dangerous.

I loved a dangerous man.

I . . . loved . . . this dangerous man.

Ohmygod.

He slid inside my pussy, stretching me wide, filling me. With my head tipped back, eyes closed, I let a soft moan slip from my mouth. Using my stomach muscles, I tilted my hips back and forth, meeting his thrusts. In and out he drove. The friction against my clit was divine. Despite the chilly water, my skin sizzled. My body tightened, and waves of pleasure rippled out from my center.

Holding my semibuoyant body in the water, he took me slowly, too slowly. His thrusts weren't rough and fast and hard like I'd come to expect. This was a delectable change. I felt him caress me from entrance to the deepest depth. Every nerve inside came to life.

"I can't get enough of you," he grumbled as he nipped my neck. "I don't think I ever will."

The pleasure was almost too much to bear. Hearing his words. Feeling his cock plunging deep inside. The heat of our bodies warming the water and each other. I hooked my ankles together and rode the waves of need washing over me, focused on all the glorious sensations racing through my body. The scent of water and sex and man. The sound of the birds, the splash of the lake water, the rough husk of our breathing. The tightness knotting my muscles.

His finger slipping into my anus.

A flare of erotic heat flashed through me as his finger pushed deeper, invading me.

"Oh God," I said as a tremble quaked through me. "Oh God."

"Squeeze my cock."

I tensed my muscles, and another sharp blade of heat blazed through me. I was so close. A breath away. A shiver away.

"Yessss," he growled.

I felt his cock expand as he orgasmed. That minute sensation pushed me over the edge, and my pussy started spasming. Huge waves of pleasure crashed over me. Heat blasted to my scalp and down to the soles of my feet. I'd never thought I could come so hard. I'd never imagined I could come twice in such a short time.

When the sensations had eased slightly, I kissed every inch of him I could. Neck, shoulder, earlobe, chin. I was wrapped around him, legs and arms. We were still joined. Still twitching.

He smiled into my eyes, and my heart literally skipped a beat.

I hoped he would always smile at me like that. Tomorrow. Next week. Next month. Somehow we would fix the problems that had brought us here. And we would go on. We would make a future together. A real future.

"As much as I'd love to stay out here and do that again, I need to make some calls." Slowly, he withdrew from me, his semiflaccid cock slipping out. As he set me on my feet, he kissed my forehead and studied me for a moment. His mouth opened, as if he were about to say something. But he didn't speak. He just pushed through the water to the shore while I followed him. We gathered our clothes. And I took his hand in mine as we walked back up to the house.

It was crazy to think this way, but a part of me was grateful that things had blown up at MalTech. If they hadn't, we wouldn't have been together.

With a happy bounce in my step I walked up to the house. He went straight to his room, saying he wanted to grab a quick shower. I thought about offering to join him, but the truth was I could only imagine that would lead to another round of love-making, and I was a smidge sore. I needed a little time before round three. I went to my room, showered, put on some comfy clothes. By that time my stomach was howling in protest.

Time to eat.

Barefoot, I padded into the kitchen, listening for Kam's voice, or any sound that might indicate where he was. He'd said he wanted to make some phone calls. I'd expected to hear him talking. I didn't.

Before digging into the refrigerator, I went on a search and recovery mission. I called his name a couple of times. No response.

I checked his room. The door was open. I checked his en suite bathroom. That door was open as well. It was empty. I meandered farther down the hall, checking two more bedrooms before doing a one-eighty and heading back toward the main living space. Finally, I stepped outside onto the back deck.

I spied him standing next to the pool. His back was facing the house. His head was bent, and he was holding the phone to his ear.

Unsure whether I was invading his privacy, I crept closer but didn't go beyond the edge of the deck. From that position I couldn't quite make out what he was saying, but I could see the tension pulling at his shoulders and upper back. At one point he jerked a look over a shoulder, spied me, then snapped back around and took another couple of steps away.

Oh no.

A sick feeling struck me, making me swallow hard.

Not again.

What is it this time?

I glanced down, realizing I was wringing my hands. I hated this. I despised how up and down things were between us right now. If only we could clean up the mess my brother had supposedly started, we could move on. We could be happy.

He shoved his phone into his pocket, turned.

His lips were thin. His face a little pale. He moved stiffly as he approached.

"What's wrong?" I asked when he was close enough to hear.

"They've put out an arrest warrant."

My stomach squeezed in on itself. "For who? My brother?"

"No, for you. And me."

18

Arrest warrant?

Arrest warrant!

Me.

I was wanted by the police.

Why? Why!

"I don't understand," I managed, somehow, to squeak out.

Placing a hand on my back, he steered me into the house. Once we were safely closed up inside, he said, "We're both suspected of embezzlement. You. And me."

This didn't make any sense. Why would they suspect me of stealing anything? Why? And Kam? They thought he had stolen from his own company? Why would he do that? Fear turned my blood cold, my body stiff. My head suddenly spinning, I grabbed the closest piece of furniture, a chair, for support. "But I didn't steal anything. You know that. I don't have anything."

"I know. But evidently, from what I've been told, you've somehow been linked to the theft that your brother was initially suspected of committing."

"Initially?" I echoed. "What does that mean? Is he off the hook now that I'm a suspect . . . now that we're suspects?"

Kam placed his hands on my waist and helped me into the chair. Once I was sitting, he sat in a chair nearby. "That I don't know. What I do know is that you are most definitely on the hook, and because rumors have been spread about you and me . . . about our personal relationship, I've now been dragged into this mess too."

I felt sick. Nauseated. Ready to pass out. Things were going from bad to worse. Now not only had my brother lost his job because of something he hadn't done, but both Kam and I were about to lose everything we had too. "They think you've stolen from your own company?"

He shrugged. "I guess so."

"This makes no sense. Of all the people, you? You'll be able to get it straightened out, right?"

"I don't know. I don't have enough information yet to know what we're up against." He jammed his fingers through his hair.

"But you can find out?"

"I'm doing my best." He was still looking pale. I understood why. He was worried.

I was petrified.

What if he couldn't prove I was innocent? What if I ended up going to jail?

"Will you tell me now what was stolen? Will you tell me what is going on?"

"Some plans were taken, and all the research too, for a new data compression process we were about to patent. They were sold to a competitor. We hadn't applied for a patent yet, so all the work we'd done on it is lost. Gone. But right now I couldn't give a shit about that."

"We need to find out who stole the plans."

"I've been trying to find that out." He stood and started walking away from me again as he dialed another number on his phone. I watched him from my seat. He didn't speak until he was down by the swimming pool again.

While I waited for him to tell me more, I went outside. I went inside. I went outside again; checked to see if he was still talking. He was. So I went back inside and strolled around the living room. I wandered down the hall, went to my room, grabbed my phone, tried the number my brother had last called me from but then hung up.

What if the police were tapping my phone? My calling anyone could lead the police right to our doorstep.

That sounded ridiculous. Had I watched too many detective shows? Or was it really that serious? Would we appear on *the evening news?*

I needed information. I needed to find out what was going on and why anyone thought I had something to do with it. Outside of being the sibling to a man who had been a suspect, I had done nothing to make anyone suspect anything.

This made no sense.

None.

Oh God, what was going on?

Unable to stand still, I went back outside. Kam was still on his phone. I needed him to tell me he had it all figured out. I needed him to tell me it was all a big misunderstanding.

When he clicked off, I didn't walk to him, I ran.

"What did you find out?" I asked, breathless from the sprint.

"Nothing much. I can't trust very many people right now. That's making it difficult to get information."

"I understand." I wanted to cry. I was going to cry.

He pinched my chin, lifted it. "We'll figure this thing out. I promise. I know you had nothing to do with it. Nothing.

"And when it's all done and over," he continued, as his head dipped lower, "you and I will go on vacation. A real vacation. Not like this. We'll go anywhere you want. Anywhere." He brushed his lips across mine, and I shivered, hot and cold at the same time. He wrapped his thick, strong arms around me and held me.

With my ear pressed against his chest, I let his slow, strong heartbeat soothe my rattled nerves. Then his stomach rumbled. I couldn't help giggling.

He chuckled. "I guess my body's telling me it's time to eat." Easing away, he turned toward the house. He left one arm wrapped around my waist as he escorted me back inside. We went to the kitchen. He hesitated at the counter. "I should warn you, I don't know how to cook."

All too happy to embrace this, the normalcy of a conversation about cooking and food, I said, "That's all right. I can cook. A little. I'm no Rachael Ray, but I do okay."

"Excellent. The refrigerator's stocked. Have at it. But I do ask one thing."

"Sure."

"Teach me?"

"Teach you? Sure." Impressed with Mr. Billionaire Bigshot's willingness to learn, I took a peek at what I had to work with. It seemed whoever had stocked the refrigerator and pantry had assumed the resident was not the kind of person to cook from scratch. This relieved me. Immensely.

I took another look, found some frozen skinless chicken breasts, bags of various vegetables, and boxed potatoes in the pantry, and voilà, a menu was planned. I started with the chicken, since it would take the longest.

"First things first. We need to preheat the oven," I announced.

Kam looked at the stove and blinked. "Okay." He stared at the buttons. I did too.

That thing was nothing like my stove at home.

"I'm embarrassed to admit I have no idea how to turn on the oven," he said.

"Neither do I." I leaned lower, studying the digital display. "This stove is so fancy. It has settings to do just about anything. Of course, that means it isn't so simple as just hitting a power button to turn it on." I turned to the nearest drawer and started sifting through its contents. "Maybe there's a manual in here somewhere."

"Hmmm . . ." Kam helped me search. We dug through a dozen drawers, rummaged through at least that many cabinets. And for all our effort, we got nowhere.

"Time for Plan B," I said as I went toward my room to get my phone.

"What's Plan B?"

"Most companies have owner's manuals online." I opened the browser and started typing in the manufacturer's name.

"You're brilliant."

"That's why you promoted me to personal assistant." Beaming, I displayed the results. "Success." I skimmed the manual until I had some understanding of how the stupid stove worked. Then I shut down the browser. "Now, back to the easy part, preparing the food."

As we'd been searching the cupboards for the manual, I'd been placing the things I wanted to use for our meal on the counter. I now had a couple of bowls and some corn flakes and spices ready to go. "This is a recipe I learned when I was a kid. It's super-easy and tasty. Comfort food." I poured some of the flakes into a large plastic baggy and handed a glass to Kam. "Use the glass to crush the flakes."

"Crush them?" he repeated, eyeballing the glass.

I set the bag on the counter and rolled the glass over it.

"I get it now." He set about pulverizing the corn flakes into dust while I prepared the egg and milk mixture and defrosted the chicken in the microwave. Within minutes we had four coated chicken breasts sizzling in the oven.

"That was easier than I thought," Kam said as he washed his

hands. "What's next? Shall we make a crème brûlée for dessert?"

"That's way beyond my capabilities." I took another look in the pantry, spied a no-cook cheesecake mix, a premade graham cracker crust, and a can of cherries. "But this, I can handle."

"I think I love you," Kam said.

I turned to him, eyes wide. Did he mean those words? Or was he just playing around.

His eyes widened and his face paled, and I realized he hadn't meant what I had hoped he meant. "I mean . . . you know . . . it's cheesecake."

"I know." Hiding my disappointment, I opened the ingredients, flipped the cheesecake box over, and started reading the directions.

"I should go make a couple of phone calls." He thumbed over his shoulder. "I want to see if Stephanie found out what the hell is going on."

"Okay."

He took a step away, turned, took a step toward me, cupped my chin. "You really are special."

"Thanks."

He gave me a little kiss. It was too soft and definitely too quick. But it still made me knees get a little wobbly. I decided that kiss was enough of an apology to forgive him for his little slipup. He hadn't meant to say those words yet. But it wouldn't be long. I could see it in his eyes.

He didn't love me yet. But I had a feeling he was falling in love. Falling hard.

Just like me.

Smiling to myself, I made his cheesecake and put it in the refrigerator. As I was turning back toward the stove, my phone rang.

I checked the screen. It was a number I didn't recognize. But something made me answer it.

"Where are you?" my brother practically yelled into the phone.

"You shouldn't be calling me," I said. "Didn't you tell me you were leaving me alone? So I could live my own life?" The last thing I wanted was for him to be dragged back into this hell. If he had been cleared, I wanted him to stay that way.

"Yes, but that was before . . . Where the hell are you? I've been by the apartment. Several times."

"You need to be careful right now—"

"I am. Do you realize you were on the news last night?"

"No."

"You're wanted. By the police."

"I know. What phone are you using?" I asked. My throat was closing up. Stress. Anxiety. I grabbed a water bottle from the refrigerator. "Is there any chance the line is being traced?"

"Not a chance. It's a throwaway."

I pinched my phone between my shoulder and ear so I could open the water. "Okay. Good. But mine's not."

"We'll keep this short. Are you safe?"

"Yes." I guzzled some of the water.

"Are you with *him?*" His sneer was clear, even over the phone.

"Yes."

"Is he taking care of you?"

"Yes," I said, taking another big chug of water.

"I don't trust him."

"I do." I screwed the water's cap back on. "Do you have any idea why they've decided it was me?"

"No clue. I swear. Can't Mr. Billionaire find out?" Joss asked.

"He's trying. But he's not sure whom he can trust."

"I'll see if I can do anything on this end."

"No, don't." I unscrewed the cap, then screwed it again.

"Listen, Abby, since we were kids, you've been the one taking care of me. It's my turn now to help you. Hell, if they want someone to pin the blame on, maybe I should turn myself in. Let them put it on me. At least that'll allow you to be free—"

"Don't. You. Dare!"

"But my life is already fucked—"

"No!" I slammed the water bottle down on the counter.

"But I love you. I owe you. For everything you've done."

"I love you too. I don't care about the sacrifices. We need to find out the truth. Nobody but the real guilty party deserves to go to jail."

"Okay," he acquiesced.

Breathing a little easier, I reiterated, "You won't do anything stupid."

"I won't."

"If you do, I swear, you'll regret it," I warned.

"That much I know."

"Call me if you find out something."

"Okay. You can call me on this number too. I'll let you know when I switch to a new one. In the meantime you can reach me here at any time. Day or night. You understand?"

"Yes." I snatched up the water bottle again.

"I love you."

"I love you too, baby brother." Before I hung up, I whispered, "I'm scared. For both of us."

"Me too, sis. Me too."

He was gone.

And I was alone. Scared. Gripping that stupid plastic bottle as if my life depended upon it. Waiting, once more, for Kam to tell me something that might give me some hope.

Kam's words kept echoing in my ears. *I think I love you.*

"I think I'm falling in love with you too," I whispered.

"What was that?" Kam asked. He was behind me. Close enough to have heard what I'd said.

Heat burned my cheeks. A lump coagulated in my throat. I

opened the bottle again. "Um, I was thinking about my brother," I said as I twisted around. "He called me while you were busy."

"What did he have to say?"

I downed half the bottle before answering, "He's worried. I guess I was on the news. The police are serious about finding me."

"I have some idea why now."

"What is it? What did you find out?"

"Caribbean Commercial Bank," he said, taking the water from my hands and downing it in a series of thirsty chugs.

"What's that?"

"A bank. On Anguilla." He sat on the stool next to mine. He set the empty bottle on the counter in front of us.

"Anguilla?" I echoed.

"The account is in your name."

"But . . . how is that possible? I didn't open a bank account in Anguilla. I've never been to Anguilla. I don't even know where Anguilla is."

He said, "It isn't necessary to travel to a foreign country to open a bank account there. People do it all the time, open foreign bank accounts to hide assets. From spouses. From lawyers. From the government."

"But I didn't do that. I wouldn't even know how." The bottle was empty, but that didn't stop me from grabbing it and squeezing it. I needed to release some of the nervous energy pulsing through my system. The room filled with the loud crackle of the plastic.

"I believe you."

"Can we find out who opened the account?"

Standing, he took the bottle from me and dropped it in the trash. "I doubt it. Whoever it was, she provided whatever documentation required to open the account. That documentation had your name on it." He opened the refrigerator and grabbed a fresh bottle.

"So whoever opened the account had access to my personal information," I said, thinking aloud.

Sitting beside me again, he unscrewed the cap, took a few swallows, and then handed me the semifull bottle. "Which leads me to believe it could have been someone your brother knew. Or someone you know. Most important, someone who was able to secure a copy of your personal identity documents. Social security card, driver's license."

"What about someone at MalTech? The HR department has copies of all those in my file. And wouldn't that make sense, since the theft was probably committed by someone in the company? I'm the patsy, the one they're pinning the blame on."

He took the bottle from me again, lifted it to his mouth, and took several swallows. Then he handed it back to me. "We'll figure out who it is."

"But if the investigator thinks he has the right person, why would he bother to look deeper?"

"We're going to have to give him a reason."

Now I was starting to feel really overwhelmed. Terrified. This was so far out of my league. I didn't know the first thing about solving crimes. "How will we do that, Kam? Will you hire your own investigator?"

"I think it's probably too late for that."

"Why?"

"Because I asked a friend to take some cash out of the bank for me. Within minutes the bank was surrounded by police."

My heart stopped for several painful seconds. If Kam couldn't access money, and he couldn't pay someone to help us, what would we do? "Oh no."

"I can't get to my money. I'm guessing my credit cards are being traced too."

"Oh God. What are we going to do?" The water I had drunk was suddenly trying to come back up. I had to swallow hard, several times.

"Don't worry. I have some cash on me. Just not enough to pay a PI. We are going to find out who really stole the plans. You and me. And we're going to take that information to the police."

His plan sounded so simple. So easy. But it was far—light years—from simple and easy. "But how are we going to find out anything from here?"

"I need a computer. Did you bring yours from work?"

I shook my head. "I couldn't get it. Security wouldn't let me anywhere near my office. Is there a computer here? Or can we use our phones?"

"No. There isn't one. And I'll need a computer, not a phone. The mobile browser isn't great for accessing the parts of the system I need. Not to mention, it would be easier with a keyboard. I'm going to have to buy one." He fingered a strand of my hair. "While we're out, I think it might be time for a makeover. Have you ever considered going blond?"

19

A few hours later, two people I barely recognized walked out of the Lucky Day Salon. I now had long blond Jessica Simpson hair. I was no Jessica Simpson, but even I had to admit I carried the look pretty well. Especially with the new clothes I was wearing. Kam had absolutely no hair now. His head was shaved smooth. And since he hadn't shaved his face, he was now sporting dark stubble that would soon grow into a beard. The new look, coupled with his new clothes, made him appear even more dangerous than before. And sexy. Very sexy.

We headed to the closest electronics store after that, grabbed a laptop, paid cash, and drove back to our safe house, ready to start digging into Kam's employee files. But as we pulled up to the house, Kam slowed the car.

"Do you remember seeing those cars parked on the street before?" He motioned to a couple of black cars with tinted windows.

"No."

"Neither do I." Pushing the accelerator, he said, "Don't look directly at them as we pass."

"Okay." My heart started racing as we drove slowly up the street. It felt like we were crawling. But in reality, we were going the speed limit.

We passed the house.

And I inhaled. "Is someone watching the house?"

"I think so."

"How did they find us?"

"I don't know." He turned the vehicle onto the closest major street and hit the gas, pushing it to fifty-five.

"Where are we going now?"

"I don't know. I'm using a thruway. . . ."

"I'm scared."

He turned to me. "Do you have your cell phone with you?"

"Of course."

"Let me see it."

I dug it out of my bag and handed it to him. He immediately powered it down. "GPS."

I smacked my hands over my face. "Oh God. It was me?"

"It's okay. You didn't know, and I didn't think to tell you to disable it. Mine is always disabled."

"Where are we going now?" I asked as we pulled up to a traffic light.

A police car shot across the road in front of us, turned left, and traveled down the street we'd just come up.

Staring straight ahead at the glowing red light, he said, "We need to get as far away from here as possible." When the light changed, he hit the gas and we were off again. As we drove south, two more police cars raced past us. And as each one zoomed by I breathed a little easier. For the time being it seemed we were safe. The police didn't know what kind of vehicle we were driving.

Kam poked the buttons on the vehicle's built-in GPS unit as he drove. "We need to get off the main streets, take back roads out of the area before they set up a road block."

My hands were trembling horribly as I helped him get the unit to display an area map.

"There. That's the way we need to go." He pointed at the unit. "Tell me when we need to turn."

"Okay."

For the next harrowing half hour, I talked him through a maze of narrow, rutted, wooded roads. As we drove I kept looking back, wondering if someone was following. I looked up every time I heard a plane. It wasn't until we were on the freeway, humming along at eighty miles per hour, that I started to relax a little.

"I am not made for this running from police stuff," I said a short time later. "I need stability. Certainty. This living with the unknown is killing me."

"I'm not that comfortable with it either." Kam slid his hand over mine, and I felt a little better. Yes, this was terrible. Absolutely terrifying. But at least I wasn't alone. Despite those couple of misunderstandings we had had, I knew I could trust Kam in a situation like this. Ironically, it was everything leading me up to this point, including his doubts, and mine as well, that had me believing that.

We stopped to eat twice, buying fast food at drive-through windows, parking in crowded parking lots, and eating in the relative safety of the vehicle. Every now and then we took bathroom breaks, stopping at rest stops when we could and avoiding drawing attention to ourselves as much as possible.

By midnight we were somewhere in Iowa. I was sore and exhausted. It was dark and empty, desolate. Using the GPS, Kam located a dumpy motel just off the freeway. We checked in under fake names, paid for the night with cash, and dragged our weary selves into the dingy room. After washing my face and brushing my teeth with my finger, I climbed into bed. Fully dressed, except for shoes. Kam pulled me into his arms. It felt so good to be held. I cried a little, and he stroked my hair and told me everything would be okay. Finally, a short time later, I tumbled into a dreamless sleep.

Coffee.

Warm croissants, dripping with butter.

Bacon.

I inhaled deeply. No, that was no dream. I smelled food. Groggy headed, I blinked open my eyes and glanced around the dimly lit room.

The first thing I noticed was that I was alone. Kam's side of the bed was empty.

The sound of running water was coming from the bathroom. And I was stiff. A blade of brilliant light was slicing through the small gap between the curtains. It was most definitely daytime. I checked the clock. Almost noon? Could that be right? Had I slept eleven hours?

I spied the bag and foam cups sitting on the dresser. I went for the coffee first. Delicious. And hot but not too scalding. I downed half the cup while I rummaged through the bag of cartons, pulling them out and flipping them open. Bacon. I wanted bacon.

I found it. In the last foam carryout container.

I crunched and slurped until the bathroom door opened. Then I sighed as Kam came strolling out smelling like soap and looking like a Greek god. He wore only a white bath towel, tucked around his hips to hide the parts I admired most. The skin on his stomach, chest, and shoulders was still damp, droplets of water catching the light when he passed through the stream of sunlight cutting through the dim interior. When my gaze made it to his face, I realized he was sporting a wicked grin.

"Good morning," he purred. "Feeling better?"

"Yes. Thanks. I guess I just needed some rest."

"That made two of us. I can't remember the last time I slept so late."

"Clearly you were up before me. You brought breakfast."

"I did. Is it okay?"

"Delicious."

"Good." With a loose-hipped swagger that made my heart pitter and patter, he sauntered over to me, leaned close, reached, and plucked a piece of bacon from the carton. As he lifted it, my eyes followed the movement of his hand, rising higher, higher, then toward me.

I parted my lips as he eased the bacon between them, took a bite. My mouth filled with the smoky, salty flavor. The brittle meat cracked and crunched. He lifted the rest of the slice to his mouth and made it disappear in two bites.

I'd never found eating bacon sexy before now.

"You're right," he said, voice low and rumbly. "It's delicious." He pulled up the chair that had been sitting in the room's corner and sat. "I'd like some more." He opened his mouth.

He wanted me to feed him?

I selected another piece. His gaze locked to mine as he waited. Feeding someone, I hadn't realized until that moment, was a very intimate act. I placed the bacon in his mouth, holding one end as he closed his mouth over the other, severing it into two. His tongue swept across his lower lip as he chewed. It was a sexy sight. When his lips parted again, I placed the remaining portion in his mouth. "Thank you," he said as he crunched. "It's been a long time since I've had bacon. I've forgotten how delicious it is."

"Me too." I snatched a piece and nibbled as he watched. "This stuff is so bad for you."

"It is."

"I shouldn't be eating it."

"It isn't bad to indulge if you do it only occasionally." He reached around me. "Life is all about balance."

"This coming from a guy I suspect works night and day?"

Donning a crooked grin, he shook his head. "You're wrong."

Like I was buying that. "Really?"

"My life isn't normally all work. It's just been that way for oh . . ." He glanced toward the ceiling. "The last ten years or so."

I laughed, and he joined me. It was another one of those amazing moments where I felt we were connecting on a deeper level than I'd ever found with another man. "I'm wrong?"

"Absolutely. Because I don't want to work all the time. I've just never had any reason not to work that much."

Was he trying to say he did now?

I wasn't sure how to respond. Some words popped into my head. Lots of words. But I was terrified those words would scare him or freak him out. They pretty much did me.

I want to be the reason why you don't work so much.

I'm falling in love with you.

Please, please tell me you're falling in love with me too.

I can imagine a future for us. A long, happy future. Can you?

Instead of saying those words, I filled my mouth with more fried pork and smiled.

Kam stood, took my hand. "Come here. I want just a little more time with you before we have to go." He led me to the bed. I stopped directly in front of it. "Before we have to get back to reality, how about a little more fantasy?"

Like I could turn that down?

I nodded.

Leaving me, he went to the chair and pulled it up to the foot of the bed. Then, confusing me, he sat. "When I say that word, fantasy, what images come to your mind?"

"Oh, I don't know." I felt my cheeks warming. No one had ever asked me a question like that.

"You're being shy."

"I guess. Kind of."

"Why?" He draped one arm over the back of the chair. The pose made his abs flex. Could there be a more beautiful man?

"What about you? What comes to your mind?" I asked.

"I asked you first."

"Maybe I wouldn't be so shy if you shared."

"Okay. I imagine I'm a king, ruler of a rich and powerful nation. I have women throwing themselves at my feet."

"Sounds like a typical male's fantasy," I said, half joking.

"Perhaps. But my fantasy is different."

"How's that?"

"There's one woman who doesn't throw herself at me. She stands tall and proud. She sees past my crown, my throne. And she falls to her knees not because of what I am but because of her love for me."

Love.

I wanted to play out his fantasy. He'd shared it with me. Didn't that mean he was hoping I would?

More than a little nervous, I slid off the bed and stood before him. With eyes locked to his, I undressed. It was secretly thrilling to stand before such a beautiful man completely nude, to have his eyes simmering with need as he looked upon me.

When he didn't say anything, I eased down to my knees. "I will serve you. For as long as you like."

He stood, cupped my chin, and lifted it. Bending, he kissed me until I was breathless and aching all over. When the kiss ended, I could think of nothing but kissing him again. My tongue darted out, finding his flavor lingering on my lip. My heart beat a quick staccato as my gaze met his.

He straightened up, took my hands in his, and placed them

at the top of the towel that was still wrapped around his hips. I tugged it off and tossed it aside. His cock was erect, and my mouth watered at the sight, at the memory of how he tasted.

I wrapped my hand around the base, feeling the steady pulse beat beneath my fingertips. Opening my mouth, I pulled the swollen head inside. He tasted clean and fresh, like man and soap and water. I suckled. I whirled my tongue around the flared ridge of the head. I pulled hard, drawing him deeper into my mouth. My tongue cushioned his length as he slid into the back of my throat, and I relaxed the muscles, taking him as deep as I could.

He groaned, tangled his fingers in my hair. "Have you enjoyed being dominated, my sweet girl?"

"Yes." That was no lie. Since those first days of our relationship, like that insanely hot time in my office, every experience with him had been so exciting and erotic. I'd never experienced anything like that before.

"I can see that." He pulled me forward, pushing his cock into my throat. "Oh yes. How I see that."

I took him deep, relishing the sensation of his thickness plunging in and out of my throat. He fucked my mouth. He fucked it harder than any man ever had. And I loved it. Every torturous second. Every incredible sensation.

As he grew harder, hotter, my body responded. My blood warmed. My pussy dampened. I wanted his touch. I ached for his next command. His pleasure was my pleasure. Truly.

When he abruptly jerked away, I whimpered. It was as if he'd stolen my favorite treat. He pulled me to my feet. "The bed."

I crawled into the middle and waited for him to tell me what he wanted next.

He pulled off the top sheet, bit a corner, and tore a strip. The sound of the rending fabric cut through the heavy silence in the room, sending a shiver down my spine. "On your back." He ripped a second strip from the cotton.

I lay down, centering myself on the mattress.

"Hands up."

I raised my hands, making a wide vee with my arms.

He wrapped one strip around my right wrist, then looped it around the post on the headboard. "You remember our word?"

"Red."

"Good. I don't expect you'll need it. But I wanted to make sure." He walked around the foot of the bed and up the other side. Within seconds, both wrists were bound and I couldn't move my arms.

And I was loving it.

"Open your legs," he demanded.

A pulse of heat throbbed in my center.

Bending my knees, I opened my legs, displaying myself to his hungry, dark eyes.

"Wider," he snapped, sounding as if he were on the edge of losing control.

Trembling now, I drew my bent knees out and back. I felt, as I stretched, my folds unfurling, opening for his inspection.

His tongue swept across his lower lip, and I mimicked his action, tasting his kiss still lingering there. He was seated now, in the chair, at the foot of the bed, looking as regal and elegant and powerful as any king. It was easy to step into his fantasy, easy to believe it.

He was a king, a ruler who had complete and utter control over me. And I was at his mercy, under his command. An image flashed in my head, of a sexy scene from *The Tudors*. How I loved that first season. Henry was young and virile with an unquenchable appetite for sex.

My inner muscles clenched as memories of Kam's last touch flooded my mind.

"How you wish to serve me, my sweet girl."

"Yes, yes, I do."

"Your pussy is telling me that." Leaning forward, he ran his hands up the mattress. He audibly inhaled. "Your scent drives me insane. More. Give me more."

I pulsed my inner muscles, willing more dampness to gather there. I writhed, tensed my stomach muscles, tipping my hips up.

He came closer, crawling onto the bed. From my vantage, he looked like a fierce beast, rippling muscles swelling as he crawled on all fours toward my burning body.

My mouth was going dry, my skin tingling as sweat gathered on my brow. I was already aching inside, and he hadn't touched me. Not a finger.

What they said really was true. Sex was in the mind.

"I have to have a taste. Just one," he said as he bent over the juncture of my thighs.

Those tissues throbbed at his words.

Oh yes. Please. My arms, stomach, legs all tightened as I closed my eyes and waited.

A warm tongue tickled the skin of my inner thigh, and one side of my body prickled, goose bumps covering my arm, chest, shoulder.

A tiny whimper slipped between my lips.

He jerked back. "Are you showing impatience?"

"N-no."

"Good." He dipped down again. This time, he laved the inside of my other thigh, adding some little nips and kisses to the torment. As hard as I tried to be still, I couldn't. My hips began rocking back and forth as the thrumming heat pulsing between my legs increased.

Finally, he parted my folds with his fingertips. The tip of his tongue found my clit. With one stabbing stroke, I was defeated.

I moaned. "Please," I begged.

"Please what?" Using his wicked tongue, he tormented my clit again. "Please stop?"

"No. Don't stop."

"Please do this?" He pushed two fingers inside my channel and groaned. "You're wet. My sweet Abigail. Wet for me."

"Yessss." Using every ounce of strength I had, I clamped those inner muscles around his invading digits as he slowly fucked me. Instantly, a wave of pleasure swept through me.

Adding a tongue dancing over my clit with his fingers fucking my pussy, he increased the torment to almost unbearable levels. How I longed for him to thrust deep inside. More than I wanted to take my next breath.

More than anything.

"You may not come until I tell you," he said, voice hoarse but threat clear. "Do not come."

A little choking cry pushed up my throat. I arched my back and curled my fingers into tight fists. My fingernails dug into the flesh of my palms. But the slight burn did nothing to reduce my suffering. No, it increased it.

"I can't." I groaned.

"You will. You must. It is my command." His tongue swirled around my clit. His fingers shoved deep into my wet pussy, fingernails lightly grazing the sensitive walls as they withdrew.

He was cruel. Merciless. And proving how cruel he was, he continued to lick and suck my clit when he knew I was holding onto my self-control by a whisper-thin thread. "Stop. Please."

Fighting my own body, I wriggled and squirmed, trying to move away from his mouth and hands.

"You haven't said the word. Say the word and I will."

Red. All I had to do was say red.

Red.

He plunged his fingers deep inside, and my inner walls clenched them, holding them in, a wave of blazing heat blasted through me.

Oh God, it was so good. I didn't want him to stop. No way. I wanted him to keep going. I wanted to come.

"Red," I muttered.

He yanked his hands away.

I cried out as I teetered on the edge of release.

Just one more touch would have pushed me over. Just one tiny flick of his tongue or thrust of a finger. Only one.

With eyes closed tight, I fought to catch my breath.

"Good girl," he purred. "You please me."

Little tingles fanned out over my back and shoulders. I'd never heard a man say three simple words in such a sexy way. The sound alone made little shockwaves of pleasure pulse through me.

"You deserve a reward for your obedience," he said.

I blinked open my eyes and watched him climb over my body. His eyes glittered with hunger as he looked down at me. His tongue swept across his lower lip.

"I still taste you," he said, angling lower. "You're sweet. So sweet I can't get enough." His lips slanted over mine, and his tongue traced the seam of my lips. As I parted them to release a little sigh that had bubbled up from my chest, it swept into my mouth, filling it with a luscious blend of man and need.

My tongue tangled with his, gliding along the side, exploring the depth of his mouth as his explored mine. His thick rod pressed at my entrance, and I lifted my legs, wrapping them around his waist and took him deep.

We moaned, the sounds of our voices blending, echoing in our joined mouths. He withdrew, then plunged deep, again and again, and I used my legs and hips to maximize every thrust, taking him as deep as I could, rubbing my clit against his body. Within minutes we were both sweating, writhing, our bodies working together in harmony. Soft and hard. Male and female. Opposites, but made to fit together perfectly.

My insides rippled around him as he glided in and out, and with each thrust, I tumbled deeper and deeper into luscious pleasure. My senses narrowed and intensified. He nipped my neck, and little currents of electricity buzzed and zapped through me. I inhaled deeply, drawing in the scents of man and sex. The sounds of our breathing blended, creating a music that was both sensual and harmonious.

This was what sex should be. A meeting of bodies, minds and spirits. A joining.

We reached our climax together. And we cried out in pleasure, our voices echoing in the room as the vibrations of our climax pulsed through our bodies like huge sonic waves. When it was over, he looked down at me with heavy-lidded eyes, lips curved into a hint of a smile. "Abigail," he whispered.

"Yes?"

He shook his head. "Nothing. I was just . . . nothing." His withdrawal from my body was almost unbearable. But he lay next to me, pulled me against him. "Back to reality."

"I wish we didn't have to."

"So do I."

20

"Those bastards!"

Not long after we had made love, I came out of the bathroom, a towel wrapped around my freshly scrubbed body, and jumped at Kam's unexpected outburst. I hadn't heard him sound this angry since the day he was drugged.

A chill charged through my body like an electric current. "What's wrong?"

"I've been locked out of my own fucking company." He was sitting on the bed, wearing jeans, no shirt, the laptop sitting on his thighs, hitting computer keys. Hard. Fingers slamming against his new laptop's keyboard. "I've been fucking locked out!"

I didn't know what to say. We were counting on his ability to access MalTech's computer network to figure out who might be behind the theft. Without that, what did we have?

Nothing.

No clues.

No information.

No hope.

My fingers dug into the scratchy cotton as I tightened my

towel toga. "Maybe I should just go to the police," I offered. I was done running and hiding. Finished. It wouldn't take long for us to run out of money.

More than that, I was very upset about what this mess was doing to Kam. If he was dragged down with me, his life would be ruined as well as mine. He didn't deserve that.

"No," he growled.

"But—"

"I said no!" His glare reinforced the sharp tone in his voice. He'd said no, and he meant it.

But I was more determined than ever to find a way to clear his name. Even if it meant I would take the fall for a crime I didn't commit. I would go to prison. I couldn't imagine how horrible that would be. But if suspicion was lifted off him, he'd be able to investigate. Maybe he'd find out who the real guilty party was before I went to trial.

I needed to convince him it was the best plan.

That wasn't going to be easy. He wasn't in the mood for convincing.

He slammed the computer shut. "Fuck!"

"They need to bring someone in. A suspect," I reasoned. "They're not going to back off until they do."

"I'm not letting you take the fall for a crime you didn't commit."

"It's the smartest thing to do. I won't go to trial for several months. That'll give you plenty of time to find out who the real culprit is. Then, once you show the police the truth, they'll set me free and everything will be okay."

He studied me for a long time. He said nothing. Just stared. Hard.

"We can't hide forever," I added. "What money you have will run out sooner or later. Then what? We can't get decent jobs without reporting our social security numbers. We can't collect paychecks without bank accounts."

He still said nothing.

I hoped that meant he was starting to see things my way.

I took his hands in mine. "I trust you. I know you'll find out who really did it. And I know you'll take it to the authorities once you collect enough evidence to prove they've arrested the wrong person."

"I don't know."

"Once you're no longer a suspect, you'll be able to dig into the backgrounds of all your employees. Nobody else has better access to that information than you. Nobody."

"I know, but to throw you to the wolves? Just to save my own ass?" Shaking his head, he pulled on my hands, tugging me down onto his lap.

I draped one arm over his broad shoulders. "No, it's not like that. You're not throwing me to the wolves. You're letting them have me so that you can save us both."

"It's weak. Letting someone else take the fall."

"No, it's not. Not in this situation. It's going to take a strong man to let someone else take the fall. Because I know you'd rather be the one to go to jail."

"I would."

"But that won't work. I can't save you. I can't figure this out. I don't have access to the information you do. I don't have the relationships you have."

"I get it. But . . ." He cupped my cheek. His front teeth sank into his lower lip. "What if something happens to you in there? In jail? Shit, I can hardly say the words." He jerked his hand back. "I can't protect you there. No. I can't do that. I can't. We'll come up with another plan."

"What plan?"

"I don't know. Maybe . . ." He ran his fingers over his freshly shaven head. "I'll sneak into the building at night. There's no security crew at night, only a small cleaning crew, and they finish up before midnight. The keys aren't tied to any kind of security system. We don't have an alarm. I'll break in as many times as I need to figure out who is doing this."

It was a semiworkable plan. He had keys. If security was that lax, it shouldn't be a problem for him to get into the building. We just had to hope we could find something, some kind of clue somewhere, that would lead us to the culprit.

"Okay. But if your plan doesn't work, promise me we'll go with mine."

"My plan will work. It has to. Because I hate yours." He brushed his lips over mine. "Mmmm," he said against my mouth. "We have a little time before we have to go." His hand skimmed down the front of my body to cup my sex through the towel.

My breath caught in my throat.

The man was insatiable. But then again, so was I.

I whimpered a surrender, and he pushed me down, onto my back. Already burning with need, I watched Kam roughly strip off his pants and underwear. I began peeling the towel away, but he stopped me with a sharp, "No." That left me to watch his beautiful body move as he finished up and angled over me, fire burning in his eyes.

"When this is over, I'm going to take you to a special place and show you what submission is really like. I'll make you burn so hot, you beg for release, and then, when you can't wait another second, I'll sink into you slowly. Deeply. So deeply I won't be able to find my way out."

I loved the sound of that.

Standing over me, he untucked the towel, pulling it out until I was completely exposed to him. The darkness in his eyes made me tremble. Little pulses of pleasure rippled through me. I wanted to tell him how I felt. The words sat on the tip of my tongue. But I swallowed them back down and remained silent, letting my body tell him what he needed to know.

His gaze wandered down my bare torso. "I can imagine you now, these beautiful breasts bound, my rope circling them, making your pretty little nipples hard." He cupped one of my breasts. Immediately, his finger and thumb went to the nipple, pinching it until it was painfully hard. A little moan slipped up my throat. "Have you ever been bound?"

"No. Only by you. Only what you've done."

"That was nothing. Just wait. I think you'll love it." He bent down and grazed my nipple with his teeth. The sensation sent little, sharp blades of pleasure piercing through me. My spine arched in response.

I wasn't sure I would love having my breasts tied, but I sure was loving this. The sexy talk was making my whole body tingle, from my scalp to the soles of my feet.

He licked the other nipple, tongue circling the areola, round and round. Little quivers of need pulsed between my legs with every circle. It was glorious and excruciating all at once. Already, I was aching to feel his hard cock buried inside of me, stroking away the need building so quickly. But another part of me wanted this moment to last. Afterward, I had no idea what might happen. I could be arrested. Or Kam. It might be a long time before we would see each other again.

As he kissed and nibbled his way to the crest between my breasts, I shoved those horrible thoughts out of my head. Right now all that mattered was this moment. Not five minutes from now or thirty or an hour. Right now.

"Do you know what happens when someone fully submits?" Kam asked.

"No."

As he tickled my thigh with a fingertip he murmured, "They come face-to-face with their darkest secrets. Anything that has been holding them back."

I had some dark secrets, but I wasn't hiding from them. I didn't believe they were holding me back in any way. Still, I saw no connection between those kinds of secrets and some rope play during sex. Sex was fun. And adding a little edge to sex would probably make it more fun. Surely it wouldn't make me come face-to-face with anything dark or serious or depressing. He pushed on my knees, forcing them back. That left me wide open to his feasting eyes, and to his wicked mouth.

He took full advantage of my position right away. His tongue delved between my folds to find my throbbing clit. My spine arched as it flicked quickly over my nub, sending piercing sharp blades of need racing through my body. Just as he had earlier, he slid two fingers inside my pussy.

Within seconds, my body was hot and tight, trembling. I was breathless, on the verge of orgasm. Squirming. Writhing. I begged. I pleaded. Still, he tormented me with his mouth and hands.

Knowing he expected me to hold back my release, I fought my body's response. I tried to distract myself. But it didn't work. I couldn't fight it. I just couldn't.

I relinquished as pleasure carried me away.

Just as that first wave blasted over me, he climbed on top of me and shoved his cock into my convulsing channel. The fullness intensified the pleasure, and I screamed. So full. So good.

"Yessss," I said as he took me hard and fast. His cock hammered in and out of my burning tissues, and I was so thankful. Sweaty skin slid against sweaty skin. Our breath mingled. The sound of our rough breathing meshing into a sexy song. My stomach contracted with every inward stroke, tipping my hips so he could push deeper, to the entrance of my womb.

How I adored being possessed by this man. I wished there would be no other. Never again.

I would be his. Only his. For the rest of my life.

As the contractions of my climax eased, I gained more control over my inner muscles. Squeezing them produced enormous waves of heat as my body tightened around his.

He groaned, tossed his head back, and lost control. My body responded, a second orgasm ripping through me. It felt as if it lasted an eternity. I didn't want it to end, this glorious moment. It was like heaven, being in his arms. Paradise.

I felt a cold chill when he eventually pulled out. Empty. I was empty. After he untied my wrists, I reached for him, and he took me in his arms. I closed my eyes and relaxed. The niggling thought that this might be our last moment together for a while kept popping into my head. No matter how many times I tried to shove it out, it just kept coming back.

"I'm scared," I admitted.

"You have nothing to be scared of."

That was a lie.

"How can you say that?" I challenged.

"Because it's true. I won't let anything happen to you."

If he was arrested for breaking into MalTech, that would hurt me as much, if not more, than my being arrested. How could he not realize that? "I'm scared about you going back. What if someone's in the building? What if you're caught?"

"If there's anyone who knows how to get in and out of that building without being discovered, it's me." He pressed a kiss to my forehead. "So please don't worry."

"Easier said than done."

"Just in case something does happen, I'm going to find someone to help you, to take care of you. I have some money hidden away. I'm going to use that, plus the cash I have left with me to set up a trust in your name, and then I'll take the fall for everything. That way you'll be able to go on with your life, reconnect with your brother."

No!

My hold on him tightened. Even the thought of being separated from him hurt. And imagining him in prison . . . ? No. No-no-no. "You can't do that."

"It would be for the best."

I couldn't let this happen. No way. Not a chance. "How will you convince them that you were the one to do it? What possible motive could you present that would be even minutely believable?"

"I don't know." He visibly thought about my question for a while, and I started to hope he might reconsider. There had to be another option. "I suppose I could say I was trying to sell off the assets of the company and drain it before filing bankruptcy. That way I'd keep at least some of the assets and wouldn't have to pay back the creditors I still owe." His fingertips softly stroked up and down my arm as he spoke. Up and down.

"That sounds so shady. So . . . unlike you."

"True. But greed does things to people, even good people. I don't doubt they'd buy it."

"Probably."

He glanced at the clock and audibly sighed. "We should go. We have a long drive ahead of us."

"If there was any other way . . ."

"There isn't." He snuggled me tightly. "I . . ." He visibly swallowed.

I held my breath. Was he about to say . . . ? Was he about to admit he cared about me?

"We need to go," he mumbled.

My heart sank a little.

It was too soon. He couldn't say the words yet.

Maybe later. Maybe tomorrow.

Maybe never?

21

Crime was so not my thing.

It was dark. Quiet. The parking lot was empty. As far as I could tell, there was nobody around. But still I couldn't shake the feeling that I was being watched. I hoped it was just a bad case of guilt.

Standing at my post, hidden in the shadows, not far from the building's entry, I checked my pocket for the tenth time, making sure I had ready the throwaway cell phone Kam had bought me, just in case someone pulled up.

I was Kam's lookout.

If there'd ever been a job I couldn't afford to screw up, this was it. And because the pressure was so high, I was alert to every tiny sound, every little flash of light. The flicker of a firefly made me jump, the rattle of a squirrel digging in the Dumpster. To think I might have to endure this torture for hours . . .

The cell phone buzzed in my pocket, and I practically had a heart attack. I hit the button and whispered, "Yes?"

"Come on in. It's clear."

"Didn't you want me to stay out here and keep an eye out?"

"If we're going to get anywhere, I'm going to need you inside, helping me."

"Okay. I'm heading in. Where are you?"

"My office."

"Got it," I said as I grabbed the door handle.

"Use the stairs."

"Okay." My heart started thumping in my chest as I inched open the door. I said a prayer while I slipped inside and eased the door closed behind me.

Wow, was it dark.

The cell phone's screen served as a convenient flashlight as I quietly crept down the hall toward the stairwell. As I traveled without being wrestled to the ground by any security guards, I gradually became less terrified and more determined to make this trip worthwhile. I didn't walk up the stairs, I ran until I was breathless. By the time I was facing Kam's office door, I was sweaty and breathing heavily, but no longer petrified.

The door was open, so I tiptoed inside. "Where are you?"

"Here." He was directly behind me.

I whirled around. Now I was inches from him. A wave of sensual heat rocketed through me.

Now is definitely not the time.

"It took you a long time. I was getting worried," he said.

"I just don't do well in the dark." A nervous giggle bubbled in my throat. "I wouldn't make a good cat burglar."

"Hopefully you'll never have to do something like this again." He took me in his arms and held me for a moment. As good as it felt to be in his arms, I couldn't help getting antsy. I started wriggling, but he tightened his hold, tipping his head down to whisper, "Listen, if anything happens, if anyone comes in the building, I want you to hide. Here." He shoved something into my hands, a small cloth bag. "Don't lose this. No matter what."

"Okay." I put the cloth bag in my jacket pocket and zipped it shut. "May I ask, what's in it?"

"Money. It could come in handy later. Now, I think we should start down in Human Resources." Taking my hand in his, he pushed through the doorway and led me back toward the stairwell. At the top of the stairs he turned on a small flashlight, training the light on the steps so we wouldn't fall. HR was a few stories below us. I didn't ask why he hadn't asked me to meet him down there.

Once we were safely closed in the Human Resources office, Kam handed me his flashlight and produced a second one from his pocket. He pointed the beam of light at the file cabinets lining the wall. "You start here."

"Okay." I pulled open the top drawer and stared down at the dozens of green folders inside. "This is going to take ages. There are . . . how many employees? What should I look for?"

"Roughly two hundred. Look at their applications and hand over anyone who either indicated they have been convicted of a felony or worked for a competitor before coming here."

"Okay." I started at the back, pulling each file and inspecting their applications. Meanwhile, Kam did the same, working through a cabinet at the opposite end of the wall. It was tedious, frustrating work. Even though I fell into a good pace, it didn't take long before I felt we were wasting time.

When my eyes became too bleary to read, I checked my phone. We'd been there for three hours. I groaned. "This isn't working. Have you found anything?"

"Nothing." Looking as frustrated as I felt, he scratched his smooth scalp. "If I had access to my computer, this would go a lot faster."

"It's too bad you can't log in under someone else's password."

"Yes, it is . . ." Moving swiftly, he grabbed me and planted a hard kiss on my mouth.

"Isn't this a bad time for playing?"

"You're a genius. I'll be right back." He dashed out of the office. Confused, I listened as his footsteps echoed down the hall. The distant sound of a door shutting signaled he'd gone for the stairs.

At a loss what to do, I continued pulling employee files. But rather than focusing on random people, I went for employees who knew me. Julie. Stephanie. The human resources person, Terry Stimpson. I set those files aside and was about to look up my own and my brother's, to see what was in them, when Kam returned, looking like he'd just solved world hunger.

"I knew she wrote down her passwords," he announced proudly.

"Who?"

"Stephanie. She has a memory problem."

"I guess that's good for us."

"It is." He plopped down at the HR department's desk and powered up the computer. "Did you find anything?"

"Not yet. I was just about to look up my own file, to see if anything was missing when you came back."

"Good idea." He was nervously tapping his fingernails on the desktop. "Dammit, this computer is slow. It's time for an upgrade."

"I'm sure Terry will be happy to have a new computer."

"Hmmm," he said. "Looks like she's been doing more than work on this computer."

"Oh?"

"I opened a web browser, and a bunch of online gambling sites popped open. She's set them as her default pages."

"Interesting." My hands full of files, I looked over his shoulder. "Doesn't that give her motive to steal from the company?"

"Only if she's been losing."

"Do you know anyone who wins at gambling?"

"No." He tapped on some keys. "Do me a favor and pull her employee file."

"I have it right here. I haven't looked at it yet." I handed it to him.

"Thanks." He flipped it open.

I went back to the cabinet, leafing through the Bs. Bardon. Barello. Barkel. Baroni. No Barnes. "Our files are gone."

"Whose?" Kam asked as he thumbed through the documents in Terry's file.

"Mine and my brother's. Do you think that's significant?"

"The police probably asked for them."

"Wouldn't they make copies and leave the originals here?"

"I don't know."

A shiver zinged up my spine. "It's kind of creepy, thinking someone might have my file. With it, they have access to everything they need to assume my identity. They could . . . open bank accounts and apply for credit cards, obtain loans . . ."

"Let's hope it's in the hands of someone who wouldn't do such a thing," he said, sounding distracted, as if he didn't really know what he had just said. He sighed. "I'm not liking what I see here."

"What is it?" Abandoning my search, I stepped up behind him.

"Before working for us, Terry Stimpson worked for Axis Tech. Odd coincidence that Axis is the company that just registered the patent for our process."

"Do you think she's the one, then? Is that enough to be suspicious?"

"It's enough for me. Especially with the gambling." He folded the entire file and tucked it into his jacket. He motioned to the computer screen as he hit the button to power it down. "We'd better get going."

"Okay." I jerked my head toward the papers in his jacket. "What are you going to do with that? Aren't you taking a risk by borrowing it? What if she realizes it's gone?"

"I'll bring it back tomorrow night. I need some time to go over everything and make some copies," he said as he led me toward the door. "Do you have the bag I gave you earlier?"

"I do." I patted my pocket.

"Good." He pulled open the door and motioned for me to head out first. "I think we might have found our woman. Now all we need to do is see if we can gather enough evidence so we're not arrested the instant we try to turn it in."

"I hope you're right."

"Me too."

Three hours later we were safe and sound in a seedy motel on the outskirts of town. We hadn't wanted to go too far, since Kam wanted to do some more digging on our new suspect, but we hadn't wanted to stay too close, where we might be picked up by the police. I tried calling my brother with my new phone, but he didn't answer. I hated that we were going through this separated and we didn't have each other for support like we always had.

My brother and me.

It didn't help that Kam was completely focused on digging up dirt on Terry Stimpson—as, I admit, he should be. He was busy, leaving me to think. Still, I realized the sooner we had enough evidence gathered to prove she was a viable suspect, the sooner we would be dropped off the suspect list. I'd offered to help, but I'd been shooed away.

Thus, after failing to find something to distract myself, and also failing to reach my brother after several attempts, I'd resorted to pacing and imagining all sorts of horrible things.

Finally, when Kam had been at it for hours and I was at my wit's end, I went to him and said to the side of his head, "Give me a job. Any job. I need to do something before I go out of my mind."

He was sitting on the bed, head tipped down. Papers were

scattered all over the butt-ugly bedspread. I couldn't tell if his eyes were open or closed. He didn't respond, didn't move.

"Kam? Is something wrong?"

He sighed. Hard. Loud. "I've got nothing."

"But you said she worked for a competitor. And she had a gambling habit. That's something."

"It's not enough." He started stacking the papers. "The police aren't going to arrest her because she plays online poker. I need more. I need real evidence that she was involved."

"How are you going to get that?"

"I need to see what she's been up to lately. I need to find out who she's been talking to. I need to find out how she set up the Anguilla bank account. Someone helped her." He shoved the papers into the file and raised his head. "I need to go to her house."

Immediately my insides started twisting and turning. I'd hoped, prayed, he would find something that we could take to the police. Things weren't going the way I'd hoped. Not at all.

I picked up the file and flipped it open. "You want to go to her house and what? Ask her about the bank account?" I knew, in my gut, that wasn't what he intended. Why I'd asked such a stupid question, I couldn't say. Maybe I hoped he wasn't thinking what I knew he was.

"I'm going to have to break in. Check her records. Check her cell phone."

Exactly what I'd feared. "That's too risky."

"I don't know how else we can get the information we need."

"I don't like this idea."

He tossed his hands up. "Give me an alternative, Abigail."

I tried to come up with one. I couldn't. But that didn't mean I wasn't going to try to stop him. "We're the innocent ones in this thing. If we start running around breaking the law, then we'll end up looking even guiltier. I think you should try taking what you have to the police. We can call in an anonymous tip."

"Hmmm."

He hadn't tossed my suggestion out yet. I took that as a good sign.

I continued, "We'll tell the police our side, but do it anonymously. We can use the throwaway cell phone. It can't hurt to try."

"Fine. But I'm still going to watch her. If we don't see the police following up on the tip within forty-eight hours, I'm going with my plan." He motioned to me. "Better pack up, just in case. If they are able to trace the call, they'll be on our doorstep in no time."

"Okay." I prayed the police would take our tip seriously as we gathered our things and headed out to the SUV. He handed his throwaway phone to me after we'd strapped ourselves into the vehicle. "Go ahead. Dial." Then he stomped on the gas, and we zoomed out of the parking lot.

My hands shook as I made the call. And my heart raced as I waited for someone to pick up. It rang six times before I got an answer.

I almost hung up.

"Canton Public Safety, how may I help you?" someone finally said.

"I need to speak with a detective regarding the MalTech case."

"Hold please."

I glanced at Kam. He'd pulled into a convenience store parking lot. He was watching me with sharp eyes.

"Detective Norford."

I cleared my throat. It was clogged. I felt like I was being strangled by an invisible rope. The stress of this situation was tearing me up inside. "Hello. I am an employee of MalTech. I wish to remain anonymous. But I have some information regarding the case. There is an individual named Terry—Teresa Stimpson. She is the manager of the Human Resources department. This individual has an online gambling habit and access to the personal information of all the employees in the company. I believe she may have used information gained from her position to open a bank account in another individual's name, to hide the proceeds of some illegal acts committed recently."

"What did you say your name was?" the detective asked.

"I didn't. Please check it out." Before I said something I regretted, I cut off the call. "Okay. It's done. Now it's up to the police."

Kam extended a hand. "The phone."

I gave it to him, and he got out of the car, strolled to the trash can in front of the store, and tossed it in. Minutes later we were zooming down the road.

"Where are we going now?" I asked, my heart still thumping in my chest.

"There's only one way to know if they've taken our tip seriously. We need to watch Stimpson."

"She'd be . . ." I checked the vehicle's clock.

"At work now. Yeah. I know." He turned to me. "You wanted to do something, rather than sit around and wait. We're doing something."

A wave of panic shot through me. What was he thinking? Of going back to MalTech? During the day? That was crazy.

I had to stop him. "Okay, yes, I did say that. And I meant it, but showing our faces anywhere near MalTech is dangerous, don't you agree?"

"Dangerous, yes. If we're recognized." He scratched his stubble-covered face. Since we'd been on the run, not only had he gotten his head shaved but he'd quit shaving his face. Now he was sporting a short, dark beard. He looked a little different from his smooth-shaven, full-head-of-hair self. Darker. More dangerous. Edgier. But he wasn't completely unrecognizable.

I shook my head, giving him an I'm-sorry look. "I don't think we're going to fool anyone."

"As long as I stay off the executive floors, I'll be fine. Not too many of the employees have met me. And you . . . you look different enough, I think, to walk in without being recognized."

I combed my fingers through my bleached and extended hair. "You're serious? I look that different?"

"Serious."

I wasn't so sure about that. When I looked in the mirror I still saw me, Abigail Barnes. Bordering on terrified, I asked, "What are we going to do if we get inside without being hauled off to jail?"

"We're going to watch the HR department, of course." Pulling up to a red light, he flipped on the turn signal. "I might keep an eye on my office too, see if anyone's going in there and what they're doing."

"You said you need to avoid the executive floors."

"Good point." The light changed, and he stomped on the gas and turned the corner. We weren't far from the office. Not far at all. I didn't have much time to talk him out of this ridiculous plan. "I'll let you watch my office. I'll watch HR."

"You're serious?" I asked, having a hard time believing he wasn't pulling my leg. He had to be joking. We were wanted by the police. This was the last thing we should be doing.

"Yes, I'm serious."

"This is crazy."

"You're talking to a guy who took bigger risks to grow this company."

"I hadn't realized."

As he pulled up to yet another red light, he glanced my way. "There's plenty about me you don't know."

He said that as though I didn't realize we were still more or less strangers. "Of course. There's plenty you don't know about me too." *Beyond the obvious—like how to make me scream with pleasure.*

Looking curious, he nodded. "I hope to change that. Soon. After all of this is behind us."

"Me too."

He placed his hand on my leg and squeezed my thigh, and my heart did a flip-flop in my chest. Again, he glanced my way. I could see something dark flickering in his eyes. That darkness was so intense, I couldn't hold his gaze. My eyes dropped to my leg, to his hand on my leg, so close to the juncture of my thighs. Images of the last time he'd touched me flashed through my mind, and my skin warmed. My face heated.

There was nothing I wanted more than to have all of this awful trouble behind us. I longed to understand this man, to learn all his secrets, to take time to just be together.

As we drove the rest of the way to MalTech, we generated a plan. Kam came up with a story that we worked for a company that provided technical service for computers. We came up with a fictitious company name, and he made a quick call to Stephanie, told her to put our company in the system so that security would let us through if we ran into them. We were hoping to avoid that, because there would be some risk that he would be recognized, but it was better to be prepared just in case.

Before going in we made a stop at a nearby office supply store and picked up two computer bags and some more throw-away cell phones. Kam slid his recently purchased laptop into one and handed it to me. He carried the empty one.

"What about ID? We don't have ID," I pointed out.

"Nothing we can do about that right now. We're just going to have to come up with an excuse if we're asked for it."

It would be a miracle if we actually pulled this off.

But in the back of my mind I had a plan. If things got crazy,

I would turn myself in, just like I'd planned earlier. And I would claim to not know where Kam was. That would leave him free to keep digging for the information that would prove my innocence.

I hoped.

Oh God, I was petrified this was going to blow up in our faces.

As the SUV turned into the parking lot, I had a mini panic attack. My heart raced. My lungs imploded. I couldn't breathe. I had chills, but felt hot at the same time.

Kam shifted the vehicle out of gear and pocketed the keys. He took one look at me and asked, "Can you do this?"

"I think we're making a mistake. Why can't we just trust that the police will follow up on our tip?"

Kam cupped my cheek and gazed deeply into my eyes. My fears didn't evaporate, but they did ease a tiny bit. "Because I learned a long time ago that if the police have one suspect in mind, they'll focus on that suspect and shove any evidence that points to someone else under a rock. We can't sit around and watch them do that."

I had kind of learned that too. But in my case it had worked to my advantage. Would the opposite happen now? Instead of being found innocent of a crime I had committed, would I be found guilty of one I hadn't?

22

As we approached the employee entrance of MalTech, I fought wave after wave of nausea. It was the hope that this crap would soon be over, one way or the other, that propelled me forward, toward the door. I was still fairly sure we were making a mistake going into the building and risking being recognized. But at this point I was almost desperate enough to have it over not to care whether it ended poorly.

After this stunt I figured I would either have more information to take to the police or be conferring with a court-appointed attorney about my case. Once, a long time ago, I'd taken a chance with the system and walked. There was always the hope that my luck hadn't run out.

Kam stopped when we reached the door. He pivoted to face me. "Okay. You'll be clear upstairs. Stephanie knows we're coming in. She'll give you a signal if anyone comes. Go to your office and stay out of sight. Let me know if anyone uses my computer or searches my office. Got it?"

"Got it."

He pointed at my computer case. "Do you have the phone I gave you?"

"Yes."

"Meet me at the car at six-thirty. Not a minute earlier. If I don't show, take the SUV and go home. I left the keys in the console. The vehicle's yours, and you'll be free and clear. If I'm arrested I'll be confessing to everything. You won't be a suspect any longer."

A chill burned through my body, hot and cold. "Six-thirty? We're staying that long?" With every minute that we spent in that building, our chances of being caught increased. It was insanity spending hours in there.

"Like I said, you'll be safe." Once again, he cupped my cheek. His thumb grazed my lower lip. "I won't let anything happen to you. Trust me."

Trust him?

I did. Yes.

But I still hated this plan. Absolutely despised it.

Unfortunately, as my gaze found his, I knew there was no changing his mind. He was going in there. And I wasn't going to stop him.

I found out a very short time later what a horrible, terrible plan this had been. No sooner did I get to my office than Stephanie came to tell me Kam was being escorted out. In handcuffs.

I couldn't help wondering if that hadn't been his plan from the start.

Horrified, I ran to the window in his office and looked down. There were three police cars angled up to the front of the building, their lights flashing. Kam was standing next to one of them, his hands behind his back. From my position I couldn't tell if they were handcuffed. I assumed they were.

Tears burning in my eyes, I flattened my hands against the glass and swallowed a sob.

"You did this on purpose," I muttered. "You wanted to be caught."

As if he could hear me, which was impossible, he tipped his head up. He saw me.

Our gazes tangled.

"No!" I mouthed.

He said something back, but I couldn't tell what it was.

A flare of anger burned through me. "No, dammit!" I smacked my hands against the glass. The sob I had swallowed surged back up my throat, and this time there was no pushing it back down. Up it came, out of my mouth. Tears obscured my vision. I blinked, trying to clear them.

He'd intentionally arranged this. I had no doubt. This was his way of protecting me. It was the most selfless, giving thing anyone had ever done for me.

I hated him for it. Hated.

His office door opened, and I spun around, my heart jerking in my chest. Had his plan failed? Were they coming for me next?

Stephanie shut the door, closing us in his office. "It's okay, Abby," she said, voice soothing as she hurried toward me.

"No, it's not. He's innocent. You know that, right? You know he didn't steal from his own company—"

"Innocent or not, he's made a choice," she said, cutting me off. "He's decided he would rather go to jail than let you or anyone else pay the consequences."

The way she spoke for him . . . "Did you know what he was planning?"

"I did."

Her admission was like a knife being plunged into my chest. She'd known. Not me. He'd spoken to her about it. Not me. "How could you let him do it? How?"

"You know Kameron Maldonado. You know there's no stopping him once he gets an idea in his head."

I did, but still, I hated her too. They'd planned this together. Behind my back.

I felt deceived.

I felt betrayed.

Yes, he'd done it to protect me. But why wouldn't he tell me what he was planning? Why? Didn't he trust me?

I sank to the floor, my legs giving out. My hands trembled as I cupped them over my mouth.

Stephanie squatted beside me. "Abigail, we don't know each other very well, but trust me, Kam was going to do this whether I helped him or not."

That wasn't the point. Not really. It wasn't just about Kam going to jail. It was about him deceiving me. It was about his lack of trust.

And it was about his sacrifice.

No one, not my mother, not my father, not my brother, had ever done anything like that for me before. I wasn't sure how to react, how to feel.

"Go home," Stephanie said, placing her hand on my shoulder. "You have a job, I'm sure. No one has said anything about you being fired. But there isn't anything for you to do right now. You look like you could use a day or two to yourself."

Time to myself? Maybe that would be a good thing.

Then again, maybe it wouldn't.

23

By six o'clock the next morning I gave up trying to go to bed. There was absolutely no way I was going to sleep. Gritty-eyed and foggy-headed, I stumbled into the shower, steamed myself into semiconsciousness, dressed, caffeinated myself into further consciousness, and headed to work. I couldn't sit around my apartment anymore. I needed to be busy. I needed something other than memories and what-ifs to occupy my mind. As I was dragging down the front walk, I caught the flash of movement out of the corner of my eye.

I jerked my head.

Joss.

A sob ripped up my throat.

I sprinted toward him while he headed my way, arms outstretched. We crashed into each other in the middle of the front yard.

I cried in his arms. Hard. All the pent-up confusion and anger and sadness surged out like huge tidal waves. As much as it physically hurt to cry that hard, I couldn't stop it. My brother held me the whole time, a hand smoothing down my back.

When I'd finally managed to gain control over myself he asked, "Are you okay now?"

"I was so worried about you."

"I told you I was fine. Perfectly fine." He stepped back, extended his arms out to both sides. "See? Not a scratch."

He looked fine, all right. Hair wasn't mussed. Clothes were clean. And new. Actually, he looked better than fine. Clearly Kam had given him a generous amount of money to live on while he was in hiding.

"Where have you been?" I asked as we headed up the front walk.

"Staying in a hotel in Northville."

"You were that close all this time?"

Joss pulled open our building's front door and stepped aside to let me in first. "I wanted to be near enough to keep track of what was happening at MalTech, and with you. You scared the shit out of me when you took off with Maldonado."

"Now you know how I've felt all these years."

"Yeah, I do. I can tell you one thing, I won't do anything like that to you again. I swear this whole thing has knocked a few years off my life."

I shoved the key to our apartment in the lock and twisted it. "I think it's knocked a few years off everyone's life."

"Glad it's over now."

"It's not over," I said as I pushed open the door.

"What do you mean? On the news this morning, they said they arrested Maldonado for embezzlement."

"Yes, he turned himself in."

Catching our nosy neighbor across the hall poking her head out of her door, I took my brother's hand in mine and pulled him inside. "Let's go inside to talk."

Once we were safely inside, and away from any curious stares, I motioned to the kitchen. "There's coffee if you want."

"No, thanks." His gaze meandered through the space. He smiled, visibly inhaled and exhaled. "It's good to be home again."

"It's good to have you home again." I gave him another hug, closed my eyes, and tried to push back another torrent of tears. This whole mess had really torn me up inside. Having spent so long not knowing what was happening to my brother, having been suspected of a crime, having watched the man I was falling in love with be carried away in handcuffs.

"You're a mess," my brother said, holding me at arm's length. "Where were you going?"

"To work."

His gaze wandered up and down my trembling, shaky body. "Like this?"

"Yeah. I figured that now that I'm not a suspect anymore, I will be expected to return to work." I dragged my thumbs under my soggy eyelashes. "I'm tired. Really tired."

"You should get some sleep."

"I couldn't. I tried. Lying in bed thinking wasn't working. It was only making things worse."

"You should take something to sleep, then." He jerked his head toward the door. "I can run up to the store and buy something."

"No, I don't like drugs."

"A little over-the-counter sleep aid won't hurt you if you take it only once."

"I know, but a part of me needs to go to work. They've got the wrong person—" Another sob cut off my words.

"You aren't going to be any good to anyone like this." Using his bulk, Joss more or less pushed me down the hall toward my bedroom. "You need sleep first." Once I was in my room, he stood at the door, using his body to block my exit. "Change your clothes and get in bed. I'll run up to the drugstore and pick up something to help you sleep."

"But I have to help Kam. He's been arrested, and he didn't do anything wrong. He confessed so I would be cleared."

"Okay, I get it, but you still aren't going to do him any good like this. You're too tired to think straight. You can't stop crying. Really, what are you going to do when you get to work? What can you do?"

Dammit, he had a point. I couldn't stop crying, thanks to my exhaustion. My head was still foggy. An obvious clue could probably smack me in the face and I wouldn't see it.

Smearing my tears with the back of my hand, I nodded. "Fine. I'll sleep."

Joss shouldered the doorframe. "You can call in today and report to work tomorrow, or even the next day. When you're ready. You've been living a fucking nightmare, and were unfairly suspected of a crime. Your boss has been arrested. And you were kidnapped—"

"He did not kidnap me! He was helping me."

Joss shook his head. His expression was sympathetic. No, it was pitying. "Nobody is going to see that but you."

"Not until I prove he's innocent." I poked an index finger at him. "You see now? That's why I need to go in to work. I need to find out who really stole the plans."

"Nothing is going to happen to your hero Maldonado for a few days. Take it from someone who's been in his shoes once or twice. He's in jail. He'll be arraigned in a day or two. Who knows, if the police didn't do their job, and gather enough evidence, maybe he'll be set free for lack of evidence anyway."

He had a point there too, but I didn't like his tone, the sarcasm.

I said, "What he did was honorable."

"Sure, it was." My brother pushed away from the door. Set a hand on my shoulder and leveled a pleading look at me. "Please get some rest. Who will you be helping if you collapse from stress and get hurt?"

"Fine. But I'm not going to collapse."

"I'll be back in a few minutes." He stopped once again at the door. "Can I get you anything before I go? Some water? Something to eat?"

"No, thanks."

"Okay."

I reluctantly went to my drawer, pulled out a fresh pair of sweats and a T-shirt. And, wishing I had something of Kam's, even an old, ratty shirt, I flopped onto the bed and closed my eyes.

Images flashed.

Memories played out in my head.

It would be a miracle if I slept.

I woke up not knowing where I was for a moment. One second I was with Kam, lying in bed, writhing beneath him as he stroked my body from head to toe, and the next I was in my bed alone. Horribly alone.

Kam was in jail.

Oh God.

The minute my eyes were functioning, I checked the clock. It was three o'clock. In the morning. I'd slept for . . . fifteen hours. I was thirsty and needed to use the bathroom.

I took care of the most pressing issue first, then wandered down the hall toward the kitchen. As I passed my brother's room I heard voices. His voice. And a female's. She was giggling.

Clearly, this whole mess hadn't affected his love life at all. He was right back to his old games.

Shaking my head, I kept going toward the kitchen. In there, I grabbed a water bottle and sat at the breakfast bar to unscrew the cap. I heard my brother's door swing open. Voices grew louder as he and his houseguest continued to talk in hushed voices. They were coming my way.

"You're sure you can hold her off for a little longer?" the woman asked.

Who was she talking about?

"Yeah. It won't be a problem. Just do what I said."

"Okay." There was the sound of kissing, sighing. Then, "You are so sexy. I can't wait until we're out of here, in our own place, far away from everyone."

"Soon, babe. It'll happen soon," Joss said.

What were they talking about?

He was planning on moving away with some woman? Where was he going? Who was the *she* they were talking about?"

Something made me slide off the stool and circle around the back of the counter where I would be hidden in deep shadow. Ducking behind a row of cabinets, I focused on breathing slowly, shallowly so I could listen.

They kissed again. The woman moaned. "I can't get enough of you. I missed you so much."

"Just do what I said. We need that bastard to stay in jail. I'm tired of hiding."

Bastard?

Was he talking about Kam?

"At least they only found the smaller account," the woman said. "The second one is still safe."

"Good. We're going to need every penny."

What the hell? Money? Account?

What account was he talking about? What the hell was going on?

My brain started making connections.

Kam. They wanted him to stay in jail.

Bank accounts.

Me.

Was Joss somehow connected to the theft after all? Was

there another bank account somewhere? Under whose name? And who was he working with? Who was the woman?

My brother? My freaking brother was involved?

No.

Couldn't be.

My brother was troubled. He made some stupid mistakes, some really crappy decisions. But he wasn't a bad person. He wouldn't steal from his employer and then let the owner of the company go to prison for the crime he had committed.

I'd raised him to be better than that.

"See you later. Babe, remember. Be smart," my brother said. He was in the living room, somewhere close to the door.

"I will," the woman said. "I love you."

"Yeah."

My heart slammed against my rib cage as I heard the front door click shut.

I heard him walking toward me, toward the kitchen. I didn't need him to know I'd been listening. Crouched low, I skittered around the end of the counter, ducking into the living room. The couch provided cover as I made my way around to the exit at the opposite end, where the bedroom hallway connected. As I rounded the corner, stepping into the hallway, I heard the refrigerator door open and close. I was in my bedroom a handful of seconds later.

In my bedroom.

And in shock.

There were so many questions whirling around in my head, I could barely keep track of where I was. But the biggest, most pressing question was why. If he'd done what I was beginning to suspect he had, I needed to understand why he would do something so underhanded.

Why?

There was the money. I got that. We weren't rich. We lived a pretty simple life. But we'd made it through tough times, and we'd done it together.

Why?

Why would he turn his back on me now? By using my name on the bank account, he'd pretty much set it up to make me look guilty. My brother. The man I had bailed out. Over and over and over.

Why?

I paced my room for what felt like hours, until sunlight was leaking in my room through the slit between the curtains. I poked my head out into the hall and heard Joss's faint snoring from his room.

He was sleeping.

Now was my chance.

I needed to go to the police and tell them what I heard.

But that wouldn't give them much to go on. Would they even believe me? I had nothing to prove what I'd heard. No other witnesses.

If I could locate the second bank account, that would clinch it. If.

How?

Dammit, I was no detective.

There had to be a record of the bank account somewhere. Right?

My brother's bedroom door was open. I peered inside. He was lying on his back, snoring.

Should I go in there and take a look around?

No. It was too risky. Better to do that when he wasn't at home. I closed his door and scurried back to my room to think.

The problem was, I was too confused to figure anything out. I showered, dressed for work, put on some makeup, fixed my hair, and headed out to the kitchen to grab some coffee and something quick to eat. I found a cell phone sitting on the kitchen counter.

I swiped the darkened screen and, with one ear listening for any sign that he was awake, I started checking his phone records. The phone log contained calls dating as far back as two months ago.

Two months.

This wasn't the phone he'd acquired recently, while he was in hiding. He'd had it for much longer.

I checked the phone number.

He'd never called me from that number before. It was a phone line he'd kept secret from me.

I wondered how many other secrets he'd kept.

Scrolling through the phone log, I saw that he'd made most of his calls to one phone number. That number was saved in his phone, but the only information he'd saved was one initial. T. That was it. No name. No address. Nothing else.

T.

One name popped into my head.

I was willing to bet this person, T—especially after seeing the last call he'd received had been from her—was the woman my brother had been with tonight.

Could it be her? Could it be Terry. Human Resources Terry?

I needed to find out.

Maybe I could do a reverse lookup on the number?

I needed something to write with.

I circled around the counter and started digging in the junk drawer for a pen and a piece of paper. As I was searching, I heard footsteps. I jerked my head up.

Joss. "Good morning, sis. You look better."

I almost jumped out of my skin. After catching my breath, I somehow said, "I feel better. Thanks."

"Good." His brows furrowed. "What are you doing?"

"I was just looking for a pen and a piece of paper. To . . ." My gaze jumped to the phone and then back to my brother.

The phone's screen had blacked out, but I knew, having used touch screen phones before, that when my brother swiped the screen, he'd see the screen I had just been looking at. Would he remember what had displayed when he'd last used his phone? Would he realize I had been snooping? ". . . make a shopping list," I finished. "Since we've been away, some of our food is expired."

"Oh. Okay." His gaze wandered from me to the counter, settling on his phone.

"Was there anything in particular you wanted me to buy?" I asked, trying to distract him.

"No. Not that I can think of," he responded. He slowly moved toward the counter. "I think I'll go take a shower." He leaned against the counter and, kind of hiding his movement, grabbed his phone and pocketed it. "Are you heading into work today?"

"Yes."

"Okay. I'll see you later." He waved over his shoulder as he retreated.

"Call me if you think of anything you want me to buy," I shouted to his back.

"Will do."

His door shut.

Oh God, he was going to figure out I'd been messing with his phone.

Abandoning my search for a writing implement, now that I'd totally forgotten T's phone number, I went back to my room, grabbed my purse and car keys, and headed for the front door. In the distance I could hear water running. The sound was coming from my brother's bathroom.

Had he checked his phone already? Was he suspicious?

I locked the front door on the way out and hurried to my car. Within minutes I was zooming down Ford Street, heading to work. I had no idea what to expect when I got there. Would

I be welcomed back? Would I be scrutinized? Now that Kam was in jail, did I even have a position?

Really nervous, I drove to work, parked in the huge lot, and tried to hide my anxiety as I strolled inside. I took the elevator up to the tenth floor and exited.

Stephanie was sitting at her desk. She saw me and smiled. "Abigail! You're back!"

"I'm back."

"I'm sorry about your loss. Was it . . . your grandmother?" She winked.

What?

"I heard you were out of work because of a death in the family," she said, giving me a strange go-with-me look.

Why was she trying to get me to lie?

She jerked her head toward Kam's office. Someone was in there. Someone who didn't know I had been there the day Kam was arrested.

"Oh." I schooled my expression to what I hoped would reflect grief. It wasn't difficult. I was an emotional wreck. "Yes. My grandmother. I hadn't seen her in a long time. She lives— lived—in . . . Omaha. I used to visit her every summer when I was a kid."

Stephanie's expression of commiseration was completely believable. "I'm so sorry. You missed a lot of crazy stuff going on."

"Oh, really?" My gaze flicked to the closed door.

"Yes. Have you been out of the state the whole time? Have you heard anything?"

"Nothing."

"Mr. Maldonado's in jail. For embezzlement," she said, doing one hell of a good job at pretending to be telling me for the first time.

My stomach churned. Hearing it . . . hearing it spoken aloud made me feel sick. "What? No way. Really?"

"Yes. Could you imagine? The guy was stealing from his own company."

"I don't understand. Why would he do that?"

"I don't know. It doesn't make a lot of sense to me either. But what do I know about how rich people think? I'm not rich. Maybe he was trying to hide income from someone? Maybe he owes somebody money?"

"Maybe."

Kam's doorknob rattled.

"Anyway," Stephanie continued, her gaze hopping to the door before returning to me, "I was told you need to report to HR when you came in."

"Okay. I guess I'll do that then." I eyed the shut door, wondering who was in Kam's office. "Do you think they are going to assign me to a new position? I'd like to get some things out of my office."

"Um . . . hang on." She picked up her phone, dialed. In hushed tones, she asked whoever was in Kam's office if I could go in and clear my desk. A few seconds later, she nodded. "You can go in and grab your personal belongings."

"Thanks." I opened Kam's office door and slipped inside. His office looked pretty much as it always had. With the exception of the laptop computer that was usually sitting on the desk. I guessed the police had confiscated it as evidence. And the man I didn't recognize sitting in his chair, using his phone.

He didn't acknowledge me, so I scurried to my office and closed myself in. Within seconds a strange sensation overcame me as memories of the times Kam and I had shared in that tiny space shot through my mind. Like when I'd been tied to that chair and brought to the verge of ecstasy. How long ago had that been? Not long at all. And yet, so much had happened. So much had changed.

Now he was in jail, awaiting trial for a crime he hadn't committed. And I had just learned that my brother, who I'd protected and cared for all my life, was somehow tied to the theft that had started this whole investigation.

Not since the day our father had died had my life been so turbulent and confusing.

I had hoped and prayed it would never be as crazy as it had been then. Until now I'd been able to keep things relatively calm, relatively normal.

I checked my desk. I couldn't remember where I'd put everything, exactly, so I couldn't say for sure whether anyone had searched through my things. My computer was gone.

I emptied a paper box, stacking the reams on a shelf, and loaded the few personal items I had brought to work in it. Then I headed out, box in hand.

Stephanie gave me a little wave as I headed for the elevator. "I hope you like your new position."

"Thanks."

My heart thumped hard in my chest as I rode the elevator down to the third floor. The fast, hard thudding didn't ease when the car stopped. In fact, as the door rolled open, it amped up a notch.

Especially when I read the placard next to the HR manager's door.

Terry Stimpson.

Terry Stimpson. Yes, she *could* be the mysterious T. Hoping I would recognize T's voice when I heard it, I gripped the box with my sweaty hands and pushed open the door.

Terry was sitting at her desk—the one Kam had been sitting at not so long ago, as we'd searched employee records for clues. Her brown hair was scraped back in a low ponytail, and she was wearing a dark gray suit and white blouse, pearl earrings. It was hard to imagine I might be staring into the eyes of a thief, that this uptight, conservative-looking woman might be capable of committing such a crime.

"Hello. I'm glad to see you're back," she said, not sounding particularly glad about anything.

Hmmm. Did that sound like Joss's little sex partner? I couldn't be sure.

Maybe yes.

Maybe no.

She was speaking in a very clipped, professional tone now. Nothing like how the woman had been talking to Joss.

I tried to look happy. "It's good to be back."

She motioned to the chair facing her desk. "Won't you sit?"

"Thanks." I set the box on the floor.

I couldn't say one way or the other if Terry was T. I needed to listen closely, really concentrate.

She rested her elbows on her desk and leveled a serious look at me. "As you may have heard, we've made some sudden changes in the structure of the company. Your position as personal assistant to Mr. Maldonado no longer exists."

Oh God. Was I going to be fired?

24

My heart had fallen down, down, down. It was somewhere in my ankles. As if things hadn't been horrible already, they were about to get worse. How would I figure out what was going on if I was fired and couldn't get into this building? How would I help Kam get out of jail?

I needed time. I needed access to the company's computer system. I needed a fricking miracle. And I needed to find out who my brother was working with. I still couldn't say whether the woman sitting on the other side of the desk was the woman who had been in my apartment.

I muttered, "Please—"

"I'm not through yet," Terry interrupted, slanting her eyes at me. She cleared her throat. "I've found another position for you in the company."

"Oh, thank God."

Her stern expression softened somewhat. Slightly. Very slightly. "It isn't at the same level, so you won't be receiving the same salary." She flipped open the folder sitting in front of her—my file, the one that had been missing—and extracted a piece of paper. "I hope you find this satisfactory." She pushed the piece of paper toward me.

I glanced down.

Position: Maintenance Department Administrator.

Pay scale: $32,000 salary per year, paid weekly.

Wow, it was lower, less than I'd earned even before being bumped up to executive assistant. My heart slid to my toes. After payroll taxes and health insurance premiums, I was going to have to try to live on less than four hundred dollars a week.

A big, hard lump formed in my throat. I had always lived paycheck to paycheck. Things were rough before. They were about to get much worse. Even after the raise, I had tried to keep my expenses down. I didn't spend money frivolously.

Thank God I'd been smart enough to sock away a fair amount of money in the bank when I was collecting those big paychecks. But that cash, coupled with the money Kam had given me while we were on the run, would only last so long. Then what? What would I give up? Utilities? Food? Rent? Insurance?

Hoping the downgrade would be temporary, and I would be going back to executive assistant when Kam was released from jail, I nodded. "Okay. I'll take it."

"Very well. You can head down now and start your training. The person who has been in that position is being promoted. She starts her new position next week. If you have any problems, please feel free to come to me."

"Thanks." I stood, turned toward the door.

"Don't forget your box."

"Oh. Yes." I squatted slightly and scooped it up. "Thanks." Arms full, I headed for the door again.

"Incidentally, I'm sure I don't need to tell you this, but if you wish to continue your employ with MalTech, you must abstain from any contact with Kameron Maldonado."

I pivoted around to face her. "O-okay."

"It's for your benefit as well as the company's. Because of certain rumors, your reputation has been tarnished. If word were to get out that you were still communicating with the individual who stole from us, you might find yourself out of a job."

Shit. "I understand."

"Good." She flipped the folder shut. "Have a good day."

Feeling a little like I had been thrashed, and still unsure whether I had found the mysterious T, I rode the elevator to the lower level and followed the narrow corridor to the door at the end. A small sign was affixed to the wall next to the doorway.

Maintenance.

I had gone from being on top to the very bottom.

Hopefully there was nowhere to go but up again.

I pushed open the door. The reception area was tiny and cramped. The furniture was old and slightly battered. A young woman who looked like she might be old enough to drive—maybe—gave me a big grin as I entered and jumped up from behind the crappy desk.

She was wearing jeans and a V-neck T-shirt that said RED-NECK PRINCESS.

"You must be my replacement. I'm Baylee." She extended a hand, and I accepted it.

"Abigail Barnes."

She eyed my clothes. "Did you just interview? You're awfully dressed up."

"Um . . . yes."

"Ah, okay. For the future, jeans are just fine. Nobody sees you down here but the guys, and they don't care what you're wearing. Though they are nicer if you wear something a little low-cut." She tugged down the front of her shirt, exposing more cleavage. "You get my drift?"

A little bit of vomit surged up my throat.

Oh God, what depths I'd sunk to.

"Anyway." Baylee plopped in her chair and spun toward the

desk. "It's really quiet down here most days. There isn't much to do. You have to handle requisitions. You know, for toilet paper and paper towels for the bathrooms. And lightbulbs. This place goes through truckloads of that stuff every month. Occasionally you have to get quotes on jobs from outside contractors for repairs. And, of course, you have to answer the phone." She jerked her head toward the one beat-up filing cabinet in the room. "We keep files on all expenses and vendors in there. They're alphabetized by vendor name. I organized that mess." Her chest puffed up with pride. "When I got here, all the receipts and invoices were being stuffed into cardboard boxes, one for each year. It was a huge mess."

"I bet."

She glanced at her watch. "Well, that took about ten minutes. Um . . ." Her gaze swept the room. "I suppose you'd like to sit down."

"It might be nice."

"Let me see if I can find a chair for you." She hopped up again and scampered off somewhere.

I dropped my box in a corner, took her seat, and wiggled her mouse to wake up her computer. I needed to check the company's employee directory, to see how many women had a name that started with a T.

Lots of men.

Only five women.

Five.

And of course one of them was Terry, my *friendly* HR representative.

I could do this. Five was doable. I could figure out which one it was, assuming it was someone from the company.

If it wasn't Terry it had to be one of the others, right?

"Okay, here you are." Baylee came flouncing in the door, carting an old metal and wood chair that had probably been in someone's barn during the Civil War. She plunked it down in front of her desk, and, giving me a get-out-of-my-seat look, circled around to her chair.

I stood.

Her gaze jerked to the computer's screen. "I see you know your way around the company's computer system."

"Yes. I've been working here for . . . a couple of years."

"Oh, really?" She looked extremely surprised. I didn't blame her.

"Yes. My former position was eliminated."

"Oh. That sucks." She flopped into her chair and stuck out her lower lip in an exaggerated faux pout.

"Yes, it does suck."

"But I'm sure you'll work your way into something better in no time. It only took me three years, and now look at me. I'm going to be the Sales Department administrator, starting Monday."

She'd hit the big time.

Okay, not really. But a little niggling bite of jealousy stung me. Here I was, a former executive assistant, and before that an employee with a good performance record, and because of someone else's greed, I was now working in the castoff job of someone who had maybe an eighth-grade education.

The compulsion to cry nearly overtook me.

I must have made a strange face, because her proud look-at-me grin faded.

"Are you okay?" she asked.

"I'm fine."

"It's not so bad. Really." Leaning over the desk she added, softly, "They'll keep their hands to themselves if you tell them you're married." She lifted her left hand and wiggled her fingers. "See?" she said, showing off a gaudy ring with a cloudy faux diamond. "It's a total fake. I bought it from QVC."

If it wasn't for Kam, and the fact that I had to find a way to get him out of jail for both our sakes, I would have walked out then and there.

Seven hours had never dragged so slowly.

When the minute hand hit the twelve, I rocketed out of there as fast as my legs could carry me. With Baylee there, hogging the computer all day—playing stupid online games—I hadn't been able to get any further information about my suspects. Tomorrow I was planning on telling her she could take an extra-long lunch break and I would cover for her, just so I could spend some quality time on that computer.

I needed phone numbers, addresses, drivers' license numbers. After spending seven hours in that closet of an office, and dealing with three perverts with leering eyes, sailor tongues, and wandering hands, I knew I wouldn't last long in that job. I would either hurt someone or walk out. It was only a matter of time.

As I was driving home, my cell phone rang.

Wayne County Jail.

I couldn't click that button fast enough.

"Please tell me you're getting out," I said, assuming it was Kam.

"Um. Hello to you too." Kam. Oh God, it was great hearing his voice!

I steered off the road, parking in front of a gas station. My fingers tightened on the phone, as if by holding it firmer I might keep him there with me longer. "How are you?"

"Shitty. This place is worse than I ever imagined. You?"

"I feel like I'm in prison with you. They reassigned me. I'm the Maintenance Department's admin."

"Bad?"

"Horrid."

"Why?" he asked.

"I'd rather not talk about it now. There's nothing either of us can do about it, and I need to keep a job at MalTech so I can keep digging into who stole the plans."

"Speaking of that, my attorney said I should confess and take a plea."

Confess? My insides twisted. The air left my lungs. "No, don't do that."

"If I plea, I could get as little as three years. Take in good behavior, and I might be out in just over twelve months."

"No! I can't let you do that," I snapped, my eyes watering. "I can't let you lose even a month of your life because of what he did."

"Who, he?"

"My . . . brother." My heart started pounding hard against my ribs. I'd just done it, told someone about my suspicion.

"Your brother? Do you know something?"

"Not really." I squeezed the steering wheel and sucked in a deep breath. God, it was hard to say this, hard to admit what my brother had done. "Last night, in our apartment, I overheard Joss talking to someone, a woman. They were discussing a bank account that hasn't been found yet. He doesn't realize I heard them."

"Who was the woman? Did you know her?"

"I didn't see her. I only heard her. And her voice wasn't particularly unique. But I did get a hold of my brother's cell phone—a phone he's had for months but never used to call me—and looked at his contacts. He calls the woman T."

"T. As in . . . Terry?"

"As in . . . maybe Terry. I got the impression my brother's accomplice works for MalTech. But I don't know whether it was her. I was able to search the company's directory. There are only four other female employees whose names start with a T."

"Wow, you've done great! I'm going to—dammit, give me five more minutes."

"Of course you can have more than five minutes," I said. A twinge of unease flashed through me. "Why? What's wrong?"

"No, I wasn't talking to you." I could hear his sigh. My gut twisted at the sound. "My time's up."

"Okay. I'm glad you called. I . . ." *Click.* "Love you," I said to the dial tone.

If only he'd had three more seconds.

Just three more.

Feeling slightly less nervous than I would have if I were about to face a firing squad, I headed inside my apartment. My brother's car was parked in the lot. I knew he was home. Having probably been caught snooping on his phone (I couldn't say for sure whether he had realized I had snooped), I wasn't certain what to expect. I hadn't ever probed into his personal life before. And, making matters worse, he had a lot to hide at the moment.

There was a huge lump stuck in the middle of my throat. I couldn't swallow it down.

Struggling to clear my clogged throat, I let myself into our apartment. Right away I knew something wasn't normal.

I smelled food.

Joss didn't cook.

Could the mysterious Miss T be in our home? Was I about to find out who his co-conspirator was?

"Hello?" I called out as I shut the door behind my back. I set my purse on the entry table, like I always did.

"Back here!" Joss shouted. "In the kitchen."

I followed the sound and the delicious aroma to the kitchen. My brother was alone. He was standing at the stove, stirring something in a pot. "I cooked dinner."

"*You* cooked dinner?" I echoed, surprise and confusion overcoming my fear.

"Yeah. I learned to make a few simple meals for myself when

274 / *Tawny Taylor*

I was in hiding. It got real old eating frozen dinners all the time."

"I imagine it would." I peered into the pot. It was some kind of red sauce. "It smells incredible."

"Sit down. It's almost ready."

"Okay." I checked the table. It was set for two. There was an open bottle of wine sitting in the table's center. Wine sounded nice. Relaxing. As long as I didn't drink too much. Relieved, since it seemed he hadn't realized I had been checking his phone, I nodded toward the hall. "I think I'll go change my clothes before I eat."

"Sounds good. Everything will be on the table by the time you're done."

And it was. Spaghetti with meat sauce and salad and baked breadsticks—still warm.

Wearing yoga pants and a T-shirt, I sat down and inhaled deeply, drawing in the scents of the bread and tangy sauce. My mouth filled with saliva. "This smells incredible," I said as I filled my bowl with salad.

"Thanks." My brother's chest puffed up with pride. "I kind of like cooking. And I'm pretty good at it. I was thinking I might like to go to cooking school."

"Cooking school?" This was a surprise. A pleasant one. For the first time ever my brother was talking about getting an education. But hearing him talk like that made me feel a little sad. He might have come to the realization that education wasn't a four-letter word too late.

Or it could have been a big, fat lie—to maybe throw me off.

"Yeah. I might like to work in one of those fancy restaurants someday. You know, the kind that doesn't have a printed menu?"

The kind we didn't go to.

The kind rich people went to.

As we ate, my brother chattered on and on about food and

cooking and his dream of someday being a famous chef. He didn't say a word about his phone. Not one. As we finished up our meals, and he was acting like the brother I'd known and loved for most of my life, my anxiety eased even more. He hadn't realized I'd checked his phone. He didn't know what I'd heard.

I was safe.

Safe for now.

Roughly a half hour later I was stuffed full of pasta and salad and bread, and I was feeling very relaxed, thanks to the wine. I stretched and yawned and pushed up from my chair. "After that meal, I'd say you have a promising future as a chef."

"Thank you. I thought you'd say that."

I waddled to the couch. "Ohmygod, I'm so full."

"Glad you enjoyed the dinner." Standing next to the table, a dirty plate in each hand, he motioned to the hallway with his elbow. "By the way, I bought a new phone when I was in hiding. I wrote down the number and put it on your dresser in your room. I didn't call you with the phone because I thought it wouldn't be safe."

That was a semireasonable excuse, and I might have bought it if I hadn't seen that he'd been using the phone since long before he'd gone into hiding.

He was lying.

My brother was lying.

Because he'd done something terrible.

My baby brother. The kid I would have died for. The kid I would have done anything to protect. Anything.

Now I couldn't protect him. Not without letting an innocent man pay the price for his crime. An innocent man I loved.

Oh God, this was going to kill me.

My mood did a swift nosedive as I sank into the sofa's welcoming softness. Ahhh, so cozy. I was feeling so sleepy. So very sleepy. Probably the stress.

"How are you doing?" my brother called from the kitchen. I could hear the clanking of dishes, the rattle of silverware. I should be helping clean up. But I was too tired.

"I'm tired," I said. My voice was rough and scratchy. And I felt a little like I was drifting, floating. I swung around, lying down on my back.

"You've had a lot going on. You need to sleep. Don't fight it."

I couldn't fight it. The darkness fell upon me like a thick, heavy blanket. I let myself tumble into sleep. Vivid dreams, strange and scary, played out in my mind as I slept. But then I woke a little. I jerked. I screamed. But my brother was there, soothing me, telling me everything was going to be okay.

"Thank you for protecting me," he said as he stroked my hair out of my face. "I know what you did. I . . . I saw it. I'll never forget. Not ever."

He saw what?

He said, "I saw. Dad."

He saw *that*?

He couldn't have. No.

"I don't know what you mean," I mumbled. My lips and tongue felt funny. Swollen.

"Shhh. I'll keep your secret for the rest of my life. You don't have to hide anything from me anymore. I'm grown. I can handle the truth. You can tell me everything." I can tell him everything.

My eyelids were heavy. They fell closed. "Everything about what?" I asked.

"About the missing money. What do you know about the missing money?"

"What money?"

My brother leaned closer. His breath warmed my cheek and ear. "Why were you looking at my phone? What were you searching for?"

"Her name," I blurted.

Why had I just told him that? My eyelids snapped open. My gaze met Joss's.

"Whose name?" he asked, brows scrunched together.

"The name of the woman who was with you last night," I answered.

Why was I saying these things? Why was I answering his questions?

"Why did you want to know who I was with?" he asked.

"She talked about another bank account," I said.

"She's nobody. Not important." He stroked my face, gently, slowly. It felt good, soothing.

"Nobody?" I echoed.

"Forget about her."

"But the bank account—"

He grabbed my shoulders and shook me. "It's not what you think, Abby. Do you hear me? Open your eyes." I forced my heavy eyelids up. "It's. Not. What. You. Think." He punctuated each word with a little nudge.

"It's not? Then what money is it?"

"My money. My money for school."

"You didn't steal from MalTech?"

"No! I didn't steal anything from them or anyone else. I borrowed the money for school. I swear to you." His lips thinned, and a dark, terrifying expression pulled at his features. "Your boyfriend stole the money. You know that, right? He was the one who did it, and he's trying to get you to help him pin it on someone else. On me."

My head was foggy, and I couldn't follow what he was saying. What did it mean? "I . . . I . . . don't know."

"You love me, right?"

That was a stupid question. "Yes. Or course, I love you."

"Then you have to believe me, Abby."

"Yes . . ." Some stray thought popped into my head. But just as quickly it popped out. "I . . ."

"You believe me, right? I didn't steal anything. That rich bastard just wants you to believe it was me. He's rich. He has everything. He has more money than he can ever spend in his lifetime. You and me, we have nothing. Don't we deserve to be happy too?"

"Y-yes, but . . ."

"Shhh. Go back to sleep." Releasing my shoulders, he stroked my forehead. "Go back to sleep, but remember, Kameron Maldonado is the guilty one. It wasn't enough for the rich bastard to have everything he already had. He needed more."

I felt the darkness falling over me again. My brother's last words echoed in my head as I let it carry me away again.

He needed more.

He needed more.

He needed more . . .

25

Someone tried to split open my head with a sledgehammer. That was what it felt like.

Knowing it was going to be excruciating, I forced my eyelids to lift a tiny bit, allowing as little light in as possible.

None came in.

It was still dark.

I felt like death. I felt like I'd mainlined a gallon of tequila. Since when did a little wine do that to me?

Oh crap, I had to pee too. That meant I had to get up. And walk. All the way to the bathroom.

Groaning to myself, I pushed to my feet. My head almost exploded. The pain took my breath away and made my stomach twist.

That was it, I would never, *never,* drink wine again.

Using the wall to support myself, I lumbered to the bathroom, one heavy-footed step at a time. My muscles didn't want to respond. My limbs felt as if they'd been tied to blocks of cement. I hadn't felt this bad since . . . since that day in New York.

That day. When I'd been drugged.

Had I been drugged again?

By my brother?

No.

Had I?

No!

Somehow, by a miracle, I made it to the bathroom without falling over. When I was done I decided I needed my bed. My soft, warm, cozy bed. Unable to stand fully erect, I shouldered the wall as I lifted one foot at a time. Left. Right. Left. Right. As I was passing my brother's shut door, I heard muffled voices again. My brother's low rumble. A higher pitched giggle. He had a houseguest.

Was it her? Was it T?

I tried to press my ear to the door to listen, but I couldn't make out what they were saying. And it was extremely difficult standing up. I was so dizzy, any sudden movement made the whole world spin.

Quickly, I abandoned the idea of trying to listen and pushed on, dragging my heavy body to my bedroom. I had never been so grateful for my bed than I was at that moment, as I basically crashed onto it. I closed my eyes and willed myself to stay awake. I didn't have the strength to stand outside his door for an hour, but if I could stay awake long enough to get a tiny peek of the woman as she left, it would be worth it.

All I needed was one small glance. Just one. Preferably of her face. I lay in bed and fought to stay awake. Every minute was a struggle. Every second. My eyes felt like they'd been rolled across the Mohave Desert. My head was very foggy, like it was full of thick goo. And my body felt so heavy, I could swear it had been encased in concrete.

Worse yet, this strange, nagging doubt plagued me as I lay there, odd bits of last night's dreams playing through my head.

In my dream my brother had told me he'd taken out a loan for school, that the bank account was for that, not for any money he'd stolen. He was innocent, and Kam was guilty. Kam was greedy, trying to convince me that he was actually the victim instead of the thief.

What a weird dream that had been.

Weird, but also vivid enough to give birth to the smallest doubt that I might have jumped to the wrong conclusion. After all, the police had to have evidence in order to keep Kam in jail. Evidence I didn't know about, but convincing enough to make them believe they could bring him to trial.

How I wished I knew what it was.

How I wished what my brother had told me was true, that he was innocent and I had taken their conversation out of context.

And yet Kam had been so convincing. And he'd been so kind, helping protect me and my brother. Why would he do that if he was the one who had committed the crime? Why would he hide the person he intended to blame? And why would he protect me if by doing so he would draw the police's attention to himself?

So many pieces didn't seem to fit.

And I was tired. So tired. Too tired. A part of me just wanted to sleep. For hours, days, weeks, until it was all over.

Starting now.

Sleep was right there, seducing me. Tendrils curling around my body, pulling me down, down into the darkness again.

I didn't want to fight anymore. I couldn't.

As I drifted, sounds became distant and sensations dulled. I was floating. Drifting on a gentle current. Until a loud thump yanked me back up, and my eyelids snapped open. My heart jumped in my chest.

My brother's door opened with a squeak. Someone was

whispering, but the tone was harsh, syllables emphasized. They were arguing.

I tiptoed to my closed door and, holding my breath, curled my fingers around the doorknob and twisted. Praying the hinges wouldn't squeak, I stood behind the door and gently pulled until there was a small gap between the door and the frame.

Then, holding the door in place, I moved into position so I could peer through the crack.

The woman was tall, slender. Like Terry Stimpson. Her back was to me.

"That's the stupidest thing I ever heard," she said, voice mocking. "Brainwashing?"

Did she sound like Terry Stimpson? Maybe. Maybe not. I leaned closer.

"Yes, brainwashing," my brother answered. "I read about it on the Internet. According to the site I found, that's what the military does to prisoners of war. They give them drugs and then make them talk. And then they make suggestions, tell them what to believe."

Brainwashing? My brother had tried to brainwash someone? Me? Was that what he'd done? Had those not been dreams?

The woman laughed. She had a strange laugh. Unique. High pitched. I would probably recognize *that* if I heard it again. "Ridiculous."

"Let me at least see if it worked," Joss said. "She's my sister, for Christ's sake. You have no idea what she's done for me."

So he still felt some sense of obligation to me. Very little, considering what he had done. My eyes started burning once more. How could he drug me? Was money that important to him?

"What about *me*, Joss? What about what I've done for you? Drugging Maldonado. Twice. So you could access his computer remotely without him noticing what you were doing. You couldn't have planted that evidence without my help." Drugging Maldonado! My brother and his accomplice had drugged him? And planted evidence by hacking his computer? Was that the day Kam had collapsed in his office?

"Once," my brother corrected. "You drugged him once. The first time you got my sister."

"Yeah, well, that wasn't my fault. I didn't know she would drink the damn water. Plus I set up the accounts and handled the transactions."

"I'll always remember what you've done for me. Baby, you're making too much out of this. All we need is another week or so until our passports come in. Just another week or so. I can't kill my sister for that."

"Yes, you can. And you must, if she learns anything else."

The longer I listened, the more I doubted it was Terry. But if it wasn't her, who was it? Whoever this T woman was, she was dangerous. Ruthless. A shiver swept through me.

I had to find out who she was. I had to find a way to stop her.

"Fine. If she does any more snooping, I'll take care of it. I promise."

"You'd better, Joss. There's too much at stake here for both of us."

"I know." He pulled her to him and kissed her roughly. Watching him made me uncomfortable, but because I hadn't gotten a decent look at the woman yet, I didn't shut my door and walk away. I needed her to glance my way. But I didn't dare make a sound to force her to do it.

One little glance. That was all I needed.

I watched my brother and his lover paw at each other for a while. The longer it went on, the more convinced I became that she wasn't going to turn my direction. I swallowed more than one sigh of frustration.

At least there was her laugh. And I also knew roughly how tall she was and what color hair she had. Average height. Brown hair.

It wasn't much to go on.

"Come on, back to bed. We have plenty of time yet," my brother said, tugging on his lover's hand as he moved toward his room.

I inched back to stay out of sight but kept watching. If he took a few more steps, she'd have to turn toward me.

Keep going. Please.

I held my breath and waited.

"No, baby. You know I can't." The woman jerked her hand away before she had turned my way. "I need to go to work."

He took one step. Another. "You don't have to be there until nine. It's five."

"I realize that. But I don't want to risk your sister waking up and seeing me. Especially with you being unwilling to take care of things." The edge in her voice made my blood run cold with fear.

"I promise, she's out cold. Nobody could wake up after what I gave her." He took another step.

The woman twisted. "Well . . ."

Yes, that's it. Turn this way.

"Give me another thirty minutes," my brother pleaded. "I'll make sure you enjoy every single second if it."

"Well . . ." She pivoted the opposite direction. "Where is she?"

"On the couch. In the living room."

"Go check on her first," the woman demanded. "I want to make sure she's still sleeping."

Oh shit! Ohshit, ohshit, ohshit!

I couldn't get to the living room without going down the hallway. They were about to find out I had woken up.

What to do?

"No reason to waste any precious time checking on her. I dosed her good. Come on," my brother said, tugging on the woman's arm again and forcing her to turn toward me at last.

A gasp tore up my throat.

That wasn't Terry Stimpson from HR. Or Tracy Fenner. Or Tina Rooney. Or any of the other employees at MalTech with first names starting with T.

Of all the people, I hadn't even considered *her*.

This was it.

I had all the proof I needed. My brother and his lover were the real thieves. They were hiding some unknown sum of money in a bank account. And they had drugged Kam and planted evidence to make him look guilty.

If that bitch had it her way, I would be dead before the end of the week.

Hands trembling, I shut the door, staggered to my dresser, and dug out a pair of jeans and a shirt. I had to go to the police. Now. This minute. Before my brother and his lover realized I was awake.

God, I hoped I could drive there without killing myself.

An hour later I was in the emergency room. After staggering into the police department and pleading for help, an ambulance was dispatched to take me to the ER for tests to confirm I had been drugged. I couldn't tell by the officer's stony mien whether he'd believed a single word I had said, but I was hopeful the drug test would prove that part of my story. The rest, I realized, was sketchy and lacked specifics, but I didn't dare risk waiting any longer to tell someone what I had learned. If I had waited and something happened to me, then I might die without having the chance to tell the truth.

They probably didn't have enough yet to free Kam from suspicion, but I hoped it wouldn't take long for them to gather more evidence, now that they knew who to look at.

Several hours later I was several tubes short of blood. And I was free to go.

Free to go where? Free to go how? My car was still sitting in the parking lot outside of the police department. I checked the clock. It was almost nine. I was due in to work any minute now. I briefly considered calling in, but I decided even that was too risky. I was afraid to walk out in public where I might be seen. So I requested a cab and sat in the back corner of the emergency room waiting area until it arrived. Every time I heard the whoosh of the automatic doors open, my body tensed. What if my brother somehow found out where I was?

Maybe it was unlikely, but having been through so many shocks lately, I was at the point of pure paranoia. My own brother had lied to me, drugged me, and tried to brainwash me. I didn't have actual medical proof that he'd done those things yet—the blood test results took some time to come back—that he'd more or less confessed. And someone I thought was trustworthy was his accomplice. Another horrific shock. Was it no wonder I was trembling uncontrollably? Was it no wonder I was afraid to show my face in public until I received a call that my brother was in jail?

I checked my cell phone. The battery was at roughly fifty percent. It rang as I was checking it. My brother. I let it click to voice mail.

It rang three more times as I was riding in the cab to a nearby hotel. I had hoped those calls would be from the police. They weren't. They were all from my brother.

I had four new messages. Also from my brother.

And three texts.

Where are you?

Are you at work? Want to grab some lunch during your break?

I'm getting worried. I've called. I've texted. Why aren't you answering?

I decided, after the last one, that responding might be a good idea. It would maybe throw him off track. He didn't have his passport yet. He couldn't leave the country. But that didn't mean he couldn't run.

I'm fine. Just busy. And tired. That wine made me sick last night. Yes, at work. I'll call you later. Love you.

Hoping that would throw him off for a while, I checked into the hotel and parked myself in my room to wait for a call from the police. While I had initially thought going to work would be a good idea, I'd decided, after those calls and texts, that I had to lie low. I wasn't going to risk being found by my brother before he'd been arrested. Period. End of story. I just hoped I wasn't going to have long to wait. Living in limbo like this was horrible.

The first bit of good news came about ten hours later. Those ten hours had been dull, boring, and yet horrifically trying. I'd paced most of the time. The rest I tried to occupy my mind by watching old movies on cable.

But that call was so worth all those hours of hell.

"Abigail. You did it! You did it!" Kam practically shouted into my ear. "When I get my hands on you I am going to kiss you until you can't breathe."

Tears of happiness welled in my eyes.

There was a lot to be sad about—particularly finding out my

brother was truly a hardened criminal, willing to drug me in order to cover his tracks. But at least I had been able to save Kam from serving time in prison for a crime Joss had committed.

"Abigail? Are you there?" Kam asked.

I sniffled. And sputtered. "I'm here."

"You're crying."

"I am." Sitting up, I wrapped myself in the blanket and dragged my hand across my face.

"Are you okay? What happened?"

"I'll tell you when I see you."

"I'll come as soon as I'm through here."

"Okay. How much longer will that be?" I checked the clock on the nightstand. It was a little after seven.

"I have no idea. They're processing me now."

"Do you need a ride?"

"No, I'll call Stephanie and have her send a car."

A wave of chilly hatred swept through me at the mention of her name. "Oh. Um, you probably can't do that. Even if you could, you don't want to."

"Why?" he asked.

"She's in on it."

Silence. "No." It was a shocked whisper.

"She is. She was at my apartment this morning. I heard her talking to my brother about everything. There's no doubt she's been part of this thing since the beginning."

"Damn."

Silence.

Clearly, he was devastated by this news. I was sorry I was the one who had to deliver it to him. After all, she was the one he had trusted when he'd arranged to be arrested.

"I'm sorry," I said, softly.

"I trusted her."

"Yes, I know." When he didn't speak again, I asked, "Do you need me to come and pick you up?"

"I . . . I don't need you to. But if you want to . . ."

"Call me when you're ready, and I'll be there," I told him.

"Okay. See you soon."

I opened my mouth to say the words I'd been trying to say since he was arrested, but he cut me off. "Abigail?"

"Yes?"

"I owe you my life."

The tiniest ripple of happiness swept through me. "No, you don't."

"Yes. Yes I do."

"I'll see you soon."

"Okay." After a beat, he said, "Bye." And that was the end of the conversation.

Figuring I had at least an hour, I scurried into the shower to freshen up. I wasn't sure what Kam would have in mind once we were alone. But I was willing to bet he was going to want to make up for lost time. With all that had happened I wasn't exactly in the mood to play his tie-me-up-and-make-me-beg games, but the thought of having his arms around me sure sounded great.

I had just finished up showering when my cell phone rang. I recognized the phone number. It was Kam's cell phone. It was in his possession again. That had to be a good sign.

"You can come and pick me up at your convenience," he said by way of a greeting.

Dabbing my face with a towel, I said, "I'll be there in about twenty."

"I can't wait to see you."

I smiled. My gaze caught my reflection in the mirror. "I can't wait to see you too."

"It's pouring, so call me when you get close and I'll come outside."

"Will do." I grabbed a second towel with my free hand and used it to squeeze some of the water from my hair.

"Abigail?"

"Yes."

"I . . . I want to say something, but I don't want to take it wrong."

"Okay." A niggle of unease swept through me, replacing the fleeting giddiness that had lifted my mood slightly. "What is it, Kam?"

"I . . . I . . . I think I need to wait and tell you later."

"All right then. I'll be there soon."

"Thank you."

"You're welcome." When he didn't say anything else, I added a quick good-bye and clicked off.

What was wrong now? I'd never heard that man sound so unsure. Not even when he was facing prison.

A little uncertain whether I was mentally or emotionally prepared for another jarring shock, I quickly dressed, hurried out to my car, started it up, and zoomed toward the jail. My palms sweated so badly as I drove that I had to keep dragging them down my legs. They were shaking too hard to dial his number while I was driving, so I set my phone in the cup holder and decided to put off trying to call him until I was parked. By the time I had pulled into the crowded parking area by the jail's main entrance, my heart was thumping so hard in my chest, my breastbone was getting sore. And I was breathing so quickly I felt a little lightheaded. I was nervous. I was excited. I was a mixed up bundle of joy and sorrow, confusion and happiness, relief and anxiety.

Sitting in the parking lot, my engine turned off, the view out my windshield distorted because of the heavy rain, I dialed his number. He didn't answer after six rings. I tried a second time, and when the call cut to voice mail, I began to wonder what was going on.

I tossed my phone into my purse, powered down the window, and peered at the entry, looking to see if he was waiting somewhere close by.

I didn't see any sign of him.

People scrambled out the building, heads ducked to shield their faces. But none of those people were Kam. I checked my clock, sighed, and shoved open the door.

Swiveling to lock my car, I jumped when he tapped my shoulder. I hid my fright by chuckling and twisted around.

I said, "I thought I'd find you here—"

That wasn't Kam.

Pure terror rocketed through my body, chilling me from head to toe. I jerked back, slamming my butt against my car. "Stephanie. What are you doing here?" I asked, trying to pretend I didn't know anything.

"Taking care of some urgent business." Her back to the building, she flipped open the flap of her coat, showing me, only me, the gun she was holding. That gun was pointed at my stomach. And I couldn't breathe.

"I knew the moronic brainwashing crap wouldn't work." She shoved the gun into my belly. "Get back in the car."

"W-where are we going?" I stuttered, my gaze locked on that gun.

"Somewhere quiet where we can have a little talk."

I'd watched enough of those real crime shows to know that if I got into the car, I would probably end up in a ditch somewhere with a bullet in my head. But that gun was poking into my stomach, and I could see the muscles in her hand tense as her trigger finger curled ever so slowly around the trigger. Was she going shoot me? Right here? In the parking lot? Despite the fact that we were outside of a police station and the minute shots were heard there'd be a flood of officers pouring through those doors?

She'd be a fool if she did.

"I'm too scared to drive," I said, lifting my hands in a sign of surrender. My gaze flicked to the doors. There had to be cameras out here, recording what was going on. Wasn't anyone watching?

"Put your fucking hands down," she spat. "And smile. You're glad to see me."

"No, I'm not." I lifted my hands higher and prayed someone was monitoring the parking lot cameras. If not, I was in trouble. "Tell me, Stephanie, why did you drug Kameron? Why?"

26

"Put. Your. Fucking. Hands. Down," Stephanie enunciated through gritted teeth.

Feeling slightly empowered by the fear I saw flashing in her eyes, I jerked up my chin. Rainwater was running down the sides of my face, dripping off my chin. "Why should I put my hands down? Are you afraid someone is going to see what you're doing? You'd better leave. Right now. You know there are cameras out here. You know there is probably a horde of police officers rushing toward the door at this moment. They're going to arrest you for attempted murder. That'll make your other charge look like a cakewalk."

"Shut the hell up."

"Or what? You'll shoot me?"

The muscle in her jaw clenched. Her gaze jerked to her hand. So did mine. For a handful of terrifying seconds I watched the muscles in her forearm tense.

Images—of my childhood, my parents, my brother—flashed through my head as time ticked by, one fraction of a second at a time. Despite time slowing, I couldn't move. I was frozen in place, unable to stop what I knew was coming next.

"Throw down the gun!" someone shouted.

"Put down the gun, now!" yelled another.

My gaze jerked up to her face. My gaze locked on eyes void of emotion. Her soul was empty. Why hadn't I noticed that before?

"Put down the gun and raise your hands!" said someone else.

Stephanie's eyes narrowed. She wasn't ready to give up. She might never be ready to give up. Would she shoot, despite the consequences?

A second passed. Another. She didn't move a muscle outside of her eyes. They were snapping back and forth, from me to something or someone behind me. Right, then left. Right, then left. Her lips started moving, but I heard no words. Was she praying?

Her face flinched.

Her eyes went cold.

And then I heard a pop. Her empty eyes met mine. Now there was something in them. Pain. She fell before I realized what had happened. As I whirled around to see where the sound had come from, someone tackled me from behind, hauling me away from her. Things started happening too fast. I became confused, lost.

"Are you hurt?" someone asked as I was rushed toward the building's entrance

I looked up. It was Kam. Kam was holding me. We were in the vestibule, closed between two sets of doors.

He jerked me against him. "This was my fault. Mine." His voice echoed sharply in the closed space. "Dammit, if I'd known she would have a chance at coming after you before they picked her up, I wouldn't have asked you to come."

"I'm okay," I said, suddenly feeling like all the bones in my body had turned to mush. My legs trembled. My hands. I struggled to stay upright. Wrapping my arms around Kam's waist, I let him support me as he hurried me away from the mêlée. "It was Stephanie. She was the one who drugged you that day."

"We'll talk about that later. As soon as they get her away from your car, I'll take you home."

My head bobbed. "Okay."

Had I really almost been shot? Had that really happened? It seemed like a bad dream, a nightmare. I had to see for myself. I had to know if it was real. I pushed through the doors, stepping outside. The overhang shielded us from the rain.

Then I heard that awful laugh. The sound sent another wave of horror through me.

I stared at the wall of police officers standing around my car. I watched as it parted and Stephanie was escorted past me, her arms pinned behind her back, handcuffs securing them.

She was laughing. Hysterically. The sound was haunting. Bone-chilling.

When our gazes met again, all I saw was dead blackness. "You know why I drugged him?" she sneered. "I did it because I could. That's why. He was an easy target. And it was fun."

"She's crazy," I said, more to myself than Kam as I snuggled into his warmth. If it weren't for him holding me up, I would have fallen. I was so glad to have him back. So, so glad. My teeth chattered as I spoke.

"She is." Kam's hold on me tightened. He smoothed a hand down my back. "I found out she's been stealing from the company for years. Falsifying invoices for services that were never performed and then pocketing all the money. She's stolen millions from MalTech. And that's not the worst of it."

"You found out all of that today?"

"Not exactly. I hired a detective before I was arrested. He discovered the fake invoices a couple of days ago and took those to the police. It was your call, though, that let us know who she was working with. I'd already made plans to replace her, but I was waiting for her to slip up and reveal her accomplice before I made it official. I was thinking about promoting a certain friend of yours. . . ."

"Julie!"

"Julie."

"She'll be great. I know it. Thank you, Kam." I squeezed him as hard as I could. "So if you knew about Stephanie, were you just released from jail today? Or have you been free to leave for a while? Were you waiting for them to catch her?"

"No, I was still being held, which infuriated me. I was afraid for your safety. The damn police wouldn't listen." He jerked his head toward the car, which was no longer surrounded by armed policemen. "Looks like we can go now."

"Good." My teeth were still chattering, and I couldn't stop shaking. "I've had enough of police and guns for a lifetime."

"So have I." He walked me toward the car, stopping next to the passenger door. "Before you get in, there's something I've been wanting to do." He palmed my face and kissed me. It was the kind of kiss you read about in fairy tales. Magical. Wonderful. Beautiful. I looped my arms around his neck and kissed him back, letting my mouth and body tell him how desperately I had missed him. By the time the kiss ended, we were both a little wobbly and breathless.

But I wasn't quaking from fear anymore.

And I wasn't cold.

"Wow," I said, fanning my face. "I've been waiting for that for a long time too."

He chuckled. How I had missed the sound of his laughter. "Actually, that wasn't what I was talking about."

"It wasn't?"

"No, but the kiss was nice. Really nice." His thumb dragged

across my lower lip, which was still overly sensitive. A tingle swept through my body as the nerves fired beneath the skin. "What I wanted to do was tell you I . . . I love you."

"What?" The word flew from my mouth before I realized I'd said it. I had heard him. It was just such a shock.

His eyes widened. "Did I say something wrong?"

"No!" I flattened my hands on either side of his darling, handsome, traffic-stopping face. "No. You didn't say anything wrong. You just caught me by surprise."

"Yeah, I suppose my timing's a little weird."

"I'm not complaining. You can say those words any time you want."

His lips curved into a stunning smile. "Good."

"Like now. You could say them again," I suggested, thinking this time I would provide a more appropriate response.

"Very well." His smile brightening, he said, "I love you, Abigail."

"I love you too, Kam." I pulled on his head, bringing his mouth down within range so I could kiss him again.

This kiss was even better. It made me wish we weren't standing in the middle of a public parking lot.

I had a sneaking suspicion it had the same effect on Kam. He growled. Then he groaned and cut off the kiss. His cheeks were a little red as he stared down at me, looking as if he might gobble me up.

"We need to go. Now," he said.

"Yes. Now."

Kam insisted, as we drove to his house, that I sit with my legs wide open so he could stroke me the entire way. I had never had a man ask me to do that.

Ohmygod, what a wicked thrill.

I spent the entire ride with my eyes clamped shut, with his

hand down my pants, squirming and moaning as his right hand explored my folds, fingers dipping between my labia. I was barely aware of the car stopping.

Kam cut off the engine, then cupped my chin with the hand he had been using to steer. The other one was still between my legs, tormenting me. "Abigail." His mouth crushed mine. The kiss was electrifying. It made me breathless, dizzy, desperate for more. I clawed at his chest. I whimpered. His tongue shoved its way into my mouth, and I lost all ability to think. All I could do was ride the waves of pleasure crashing through me.

When he broke the kiss, I sucked in a huge lungful of air.

"Let's go inside," he said.

It wasn't until he'd removed that wicked hand from between my legs that I could function at all. I blinked open my eyes. We were parked in his driveway, all right. Trembling from head to toe, I managed to get out of the car and into the house without my legs buckling. Kam's strong arm wrapped around my waist helped keep me steady. But his nearness, his heat and scent, made me all the more shaky. My shoes *click-clacked* on the polished wood floor as we made our way through the foyer with the soaring ceiling and down the hallway, toward his bedroom. But this time, instead of going to his room, we turned down another hall and stopped outside a set of black double doors.

"What's this?" I asked. In the back of my mind, I knew what it was.

His dungeon.

Instead of telling me, he opened the doors.

Yes, that was what it was.

Since the very first time Kam had talked to me about domination, I had tried to imagine him in a dungeon. My mind had conjured up all kinds of images. None of them, however, bore any resemblance to this room.

It was hard to describe. Elegant was a word that came to mind. And yet I never would have thought a sex bondage dungeon could be elegant. I had imagined a dark place, dank and dreary and frightening. This room was none of those things. Three of the walls were papered with a damask in shades of gray. The fourth was spanned by a series of gray silk–swathed French doors. Soft light shone from the gorgeous multitiered crystal chandelier hanging at the apex of the angled ceiling, reflecting on the gleaming wood floors and the wood furnishings. Directly beneath that chandelier stood a table that was roughly at bed height, the top padded.

I was speechless as I took in the details. My heart thumped heavily in my chest. And the tissues that had been burning from Kam's touch began tingling once again when Kam, using hands on my shoulders, coaxed me to face him.

"I have been waiting for this moment for so long. I almost don't want it to end." He flattened a hand against the side of my head and stared into my eyes. His thumb grazed my jaw. "You're not afraid."

I shook my head. "I trust you." Wrapping my fingers around his wrist, I pulled that hand down. It followed the column of my neck, glided over my collarbone, and finally settled over my breast. My eyelids fluttered as the pressure against my nipple made it tingle and harden. "I'm yours, Kam. All yours."

His fingers curled, squeezing my right breast, and my spine arched. I wanted so much more. I wanted his thick cock buried deep inside. I wanted his weight pressing me into a thick, soft mattress. I wanted to hear him say my name on a sigh as he found release. And yet, I too feared having this magical, special moment pass too quickly.

Finally, the suspicions were gone. The worries were behind us. We could relax. Enjoy. Explore.

This place, this lifestyle, was a part of Kam that I had only glimpsed. I was eager now to experience it more fully. To see how I might fit into Kam's world, his life. And how he would fit into mine.

"Teach me," I said as I swayed against him.

He pinched my nipple through my clothes, and I shuddered. "Look at me," he demanded. I met his gaze. In his eyes I could see the heat of his need. It burned like a searing blue flame. "Take off your clothes."

Unable to speak, I pulled off my shirt first. My pants were next, but I was too shaky to stand. I wobbled over to the table and leaned against it for support. His gaze never left mine. He watched, silent, jaw tight, expression dark. His mien reminded me of a wild animal, tracking its prey, waiting patiently for the right time to strike.

He didn't move, didn't speak until I had everything off, including my panties and bra. I stood before him completely nude, his gaze caressing my flesh, his menacing, sexy expression making me long for his touch.

What would he do next? What sort of wicked pleasures would he show me in this strange and wonderful place? My whole body shuddered. Would he lick and nip me from head to toe until I couldn't take any more? Or would he just put me out of my misery and shove that big cock into my pussy and pound away the ache throbbing deep in my center?

I couldn't wait to find out. I was breathless with anticipation.

He stepped up to me and stared deeply into my eyes. His fingers curled around my waist. I thought he would pull me to him, flatten my body against his, but instead he lifted me and set me on top of the table. My butt rested on the cushioned tabletop, my legs dangling over the edge.

I felt my lips curling up. I loved this, how he built anticipation in every moment, every touch, every glance.

"Open your legs," he commanded, his gaze flicking to my knees, which were clamped together.

Watching his face for a reaction, I slowly dragged them

apart, wide, wider, as wide as I could. My folds unfurled, and I was exposed. Deliciously open to his feasting eyes.

"Pretty, Abigail. You're going to enjoy this."

I had no doubt I would.

As if to illustrate, he scraped his fingernail down my slit. My insides quivered, heated. Oh yes, I was going to enjoy this. A lot.

He caught up the bottom of his shirt and pulled it off. I drank in the sight of him. Muscles flexing, smooth skin gleaming in the soft light. I still couldn't believe I was here with him at last. In this place, his most secret, private place.

"Now that I have you here, I'm not sure what I should do with you first." The metal of his belt rattled softly as he unbuckled it.

He could . . . take off those pants and shove that thick cock inside me. That would most definitely work.

Hoping to inspire him, I pulled my legs wider yet, stretching my inner thigh muscles until they burned. I lifted my hands to my breasts. My thumbs flicked over my nipples, sending tiny tremors of need zinging through my body. I liked this table. I liked this room. In it I felt sexy, and beautiful. I felt like I could do or say anything.

His eyes darkened. He wanted me. Badly. I felt so incredibly powerful, having a man so strong look at me with obvious wanting. He knelt, which put him at just the right height to eat my pussy, parted my swollen pussy lips, and audibly inhaled. "You're so wet already. I love that smell. The scent of your need. It's intoxicating."

I clenched the muscles inside, wishing he would end the torment. I'd had enough. The anticipation, that had been so thrilling in the beginning, was now more of an aching, throbbing desperation.

"Lie back." Angling closer, he blew a cool stream across my burning flesh.

I fell onto my back and shivered.

But then I felt nothing. I heard footsteps, retreating. He was . . . leaving?

I angled up on my elbows, and he gave me a stern look. "You said you trust me."

I immediately dropped down again.

What was he doing?

"I know you like this," he murmured a few moments later as he wrapped some kind of cuff around my wrist and buckled it. As he did the same with the other one, my heart pounded hard against my breastbone.

Oh, how well he knew me.

With great care he pulled my arms up and out in a wide vee and attached chains to each cuff so I couldn't move my arms.

"Are you ready to receive your reward, Abigail?" His voice was smooth and mellow, seductive.

A reward? Wasn't just being there with him a reward? "Yes."

He parted my nether lips, and his tongue flicked up and down over my clit. In response, my empty pussy tightened, amplifying the need simmering in my veins. He suckled on it, and a wave of heat crashed through me. My whole body tightened as I soared toward release. I could feel it building inside, gathering strength, swirling deep in my center. The pleasure was almost unbearable. I writhed, arms tugging against the restraints. My stomach clenched, rocking my hips forward and back in time to the pounding ache building inside of me. A moan slipped from my lips.

"Are you losing control, Abigail?"

"Yessss."

His tongue circled over my clit now, round and round. I heard the sound of lube being squirted from a tube. A second later something cool and slick was sliding between my ass cheeks, probing at my anus.

My heart caught in my throat. What was he pushing in *there?* The ring of muscles clamped tightly.

"Trust me," he murmured. "This is your reward, Abigail. Accept it. Take the pleasure that is yours to have."

Eager to please him, and equally eager to experience every decadent pleasure he offered, I concentrated on relaxing my bottom. The toy was big—larger than his cock. It pushed against my body's resistance for one burning moment, and then my muscles opened and it slid inside.

A head-to-toe shiver quaked through my body.

As Kam licked my clit and fucked my anus with the toy, I tumbled head over heels into a torrent of aching sensual need. I was lost, powerless, on the verge of ecstasy.

"Look at me, Abigail."

Somehow, I found the strength to open my eyes. Despite the overwhelming sensations blasting through my system. Despite the toy that was buried deep in my ass.

He was nude. I wasn't even sure when he'd undressed. His thick, hard cock was ready. A droplet of precome glistened on the tip. He curled a fist around the base, gave it a couple of pumps, then tore open a condom wrapper.

Finally the sheathed tip of his cock was easing inside me, and I just about cried with gratitude. Ah, to be filled so perfectly, ass and pussy. He entered me a fraction of an inch at a time. His slow, deliberate invasion was glorious torment. I clamped my inside muscles around him as he pushed deeper, deeper until his cock nudged my cervix.

"Ohhhh," I said on a groan. I was burning up. My blood simmering. My muscles so tight I could barely stand it. Air was sawing in and out of my lungs. My heartbeat was thundering through every cell in my body. I was teetering on the brink of release. It was there. Within reach. Just another second or two.

Kam eased out of me just as slowly as he'd entered, and I quivered at the sensation of his thick rod stroking along my sensitive nerves. A huge wave of heat slammed me, and I sank my teeth into my upper lip. A couple more slow thrusts. That was all I needed. My stomach clenched. My thighs quivered.

"You are so perfect." I felt his cock swell even more, and another wave of heat blasted me. He growled. The deep rumble vibrated through my whole body. "Can't wait another second."

He pulled out, then slammed deep. One hard, sharp thrust. Then a second. And a third. Yes, oh yes. He was fucking me hard and fast. My body responded immediately. Every muscle spasmed as a powerful orgasm rocketed through me. The heat blasted from my center, out. To my chest. My face. My feet.

I screamed as I was overcome by the raw pleasure ripping through me. His movements grew even rougher as he rammed in and out, pounding away his need. His domineering possession pushed me into the maelstrom of a second orgasm that was nearly as powerful as the first. My insides blazed and convulsed, twitched and thrummed. I was exhilarated, soaring, swooping, spinning. Until gradually, all the pounding, throbbing pleasure eased, leaving me gasping for breath.

Wow, was that some reward.

But it was more than that.

This experience went beyond anything I'd ever shared with a man before. Beyond a physical act. Beyond sex. Beyond domination.

In that moment, when we'd both been swept up in rapture, I'd felt like we were one. Joined in body and mind and spirit. Complete and whole. Perfect.

When I opened my eyes I found Kam still standing with his cock buried deep inside of me. His head was thrown back, he was breathing heavily, and his chest covered in a sheen of sweat. He looked so beautiful.

He lifted his head, looked at me. "I've never lost control like that." He grimaced as he pulled out of me, tugged off the used condom and discarded it. Next he removed the toy from my anus, leaving me feel empty but also twitchy and contented. Then he walked around the side of the table, stopping at the head to free my wrists from the cuffs. I was grinning like a goon as I pushed upright. He returned to his position at the end of the table, wedged his hips between my legs, and stared into my eyes. His thumb grazed my lower lip. "I owe you a thank you."

A tiny chill buzzed up my spine.

No, he wasn't . . . no . . . "Please, please don't tell me that's what this was all about tonight, thanking me for helping you get out of jail."

With his hands at my waist, he helped me off the table. Then he took my hand in his and led me out of the dungeon, down the hall. "It has nothing to do with that, though I do owe you a thank you for that as well. Without your help I don't know if we would have gotten enough to get Stephanie. At one point, I almost took the prosecutor's deal, just to put an end to it all."

I breathed a little easier at that response. For a moment I was doubting what I'd felt just now, questioning the connection I'd thought we'd shared. "I'm glad you held off."

"Time was running out." Stopping in the middle of the hallway, he smoothed his hand up and down my arm. "But that's not what I'm talking about. I'm talking about something else entirely, about showing me what an idiot I had been." He started walking again, out toward the main living space.

"An idiot? You?"

"Yes, me. Thanks to what I saw as a kid, I told myself I would never fall in love with a woman. Because falling in love would make me weak, like it did my father."

At last he was talking about his family, his parents. "Oh, I'm so sorry. Your parents' marriage wasn't happy?"

He continued into the living room, sat on the couch. I sat next to him.

"No," he said. "As long as I could remember, it was pure hell. They said 'I love you' to each other all the time. But those were just words. Their actions said something else entirely. Still, I grew up expecting my marriage to be like theirs. Public bliss and private hell. But, thanks to you, I learned that love isn't like what I saw when I was a kid. True love, genuine love, doesn't make a man weak, it makes him stronger. And a good woman doesn't use a man's vulnerabilities against him, she builds upon his strengths. That's what you've done for me. To think I almost let you go."

"You did? You almost let me go?" My head was spinning now, and my heart was practically leaping out of my chest. He loved me. A lot. And I loved him just as much. We had just shared the best sex of my life, and I had learned that receiving a reward in Kam's dungeon was absolutely incredible. Trusting Kam was a good thing. A very good thing. I couldn't wait until the next time we went in that room. And now, in this quiet moment, he was opening up to me more than he ever had.

"That whole thing with the drugging? I knew it wasn't you. But I reacted that way because I could see I was falling in love. I was . . . afraid. But no sooner did I shove you away than I was craving having you back in my life. I couldn't live without you."

"You know I've had some problems trusting too, thanks to my parents," I admitted. "My mom and dad didn't have the best relationship either. My father . . . he wasn't a nice man. Certainly not trustworthy. He abused my mother. My brother. And . . . me. So, I think I've always gone into relationships expecting to be hurt, and feeling I needed to protect myself. But something was different with you. Even in the beginning. I never would have let another man tie my hands. I never would have trusted a man that much."

He pulled me into his arms and held me tightly. I had never felt so cherished, so loved and protected. "I promise I will always strive to deserve your trust. It's the most precious gift anyone has ever given me." His embrace loosened, and he leaned back slightly and gazed into my eyes. "I need to go get something. Wait here."

27

Kam was holding a large envelope in his hand again. When he pulled the contents out, I recognized them.

The contract.

So he wanted to make it official? I would be his *submissive*? All this talk about love and trust had led us back to that?

"I've never . . . felt this way about a woman before," he said. "When we were . . . making love . . . all I could think about was having you, taking you." Something flashed in his eyes. "*Keeping* you. Will you, Abigail? Will you be mine?"

What was he trying to say? My gaze flicked to the contract in his hands. "Be your what?"

He slid the papers back in the envelope and handed it to me. "This whole thing has opened my eyes. I hadn't realized until now how little I have in life."

"I'm not following you," I said as I flipped open the top flap.

"I have more money than I could spend in a lifetime. I have cars. I have buildings and land. But what I don't have is a true legacy, the kind that will carry on after I'm gone."

"Again, I'm not following you." I pulled the contract out. What did a legacy have to do with this domination and submission stuff? "What are you talking about?"

"I'm talking about a family. About a future. About children. About . . . a wife."

"What?" My eyes dropped to the paper in my hands. The top line read "Contract of Marriage." *Marriage?* "What is this?" My heart couldn't have pounded any harder if I'd run a marathon.

Laughing, he yanked the paper and envelope out of my hand. "It's nothing. Trash." He lowered himself onto one knee. "This wasn't the way I wanted to do this, but it seems you've given me no choice." He took my hands in his and gaze into my eyes. "I don't need you to sign a damn thing. I just need you to say yes, that you love me, that you'll marry me. I want you to be my partner in life. My lover. My future. The mother of my children. And behind closed doors . . . my submissive."

I couldn't speak. I was beyond happy. Overjoyed. And yet I was petrified. There was something he didn't know about me yet. I couldn't marry him. Not without telling him.

Would he change his mind once he knew?

Kam's brilliant smile faded. "You haven't answered, Abigail. Tell me, is it because you're overcome with happiness?"

I nodded.

"Good. Then I'll take your silence as a yes." He stood, gathered me into his arms, and a wave of heartache blazed through me.

I was a murderer. There was no other way to describe what I had done. And this man was looking toward the future. How could he do that by marrying a woman who had spent years running from her past?

He couldn't.

Up until now, it had been easy to push this whole issue aside. As much as I wanted to believe he loved me, and as much as I wanted to believe he wanted something more than sex, I hadn't let myself actually think about what that meant.

I should just refuse him.

No. It's been this long. The case was closed. By now it's been forgotten.

It would be kinder, easier on him if I left. I need a fresh start. This place has been too full of pain.

No. He cares for you. Genuinely cares.

Tears were welling in my eyes, and I couldn't hold them back. I was afraid that if he saw I was crying he would ask me why. He didn't want to know why.

Holding him, I blinked a bunch of times, trying to clear my eyes.

You should pack up and leave. Just in case.

"What do you think about maybe moving?" Kam asked. "I was thinking . . . I've had this dream since I was a kid. To live out west. Buy a ranch and slow down. What do you think? Would you like to get away from all this crap?" He cupped my chin and gently lifted it. His brows furrowed. "You're crying."

"I'm . . ."

I couldn't lie to him. The words sat on my tongue and I couldn't spit them out. Here was this honorable, kind, generous man planning his future with me, pursuing his dreams. If I ran away it might destroy him.

No, running would be the cowardly thing to do, not the brave.

But you're trying to protect him.

That wasn't the way to do it.

I inhaled deeply, exhaled. How could I tell him? How would I find the words? Terrified, I forced the first sentence out of my mouth. "I need to tell you something." It got easier after that. "And I need you to listen, really listen. Because I think when I'm finished you might have some different ideas about what your future should look like."

One brow lifted. His mouth twisted. "Okay."

My heart was pounding so hard I was getting dizzy. I stared down at the floor. I couldn't look at him when I told him. I couldn't bear seeing the shock and disgust on his face.

I opened my mouth, but no words came out. A huge lump of something was clogging my throat. It wouldn't let the sound past. I coughed to clear it.

"Whatever it is, I can tell you with certainty that I love you. Nothing is going to change that," he said.

"I . . . I haven't told this to anyone. Ever."

Kam placed his hand on top of mine. My hand was shaking. His wasn't. "You can trust me."

"I . . . I don't know how to say it." How could I talk about this? How? Once I started all the memories would surge to the surface. The terror. The desperation. It had taken me many years of pushing them down to even begin to move forward with my life.

Until now.

This was different.

I had to talk about it, no matter how bad it hurt.

The fact was, I couldn't marry Kam without knowing for sure I wouldn't have to run away again, to hide from the terrors of those years and the fallout of my actions. All this time I'd feared I might end up being arrested for that crime. Tried. Imprisoned. My life completely turned upside down. I couldn't let Kam live with that risk.

Or our children, if we had any.

Until I put this behind me, there was only so much life I could allow myself to live. Marriage. Children. Those were out. I couldn't risk hurting them, upsetting their lives because of something I had done years ago.

I had to find the strength. I had to face the horror. Now.

He said, "If you can't tell me now, that's okay. Whatever it is, I can wait. Nothing is going to change how I feel about you." Wrapping his arm around my shoulder, he stroked my face. "I can't wait to make you mine. For always."

That sounded so wonderful. Too wonderful to be real. Like a dream, but better. A dream I'd never had the courage to dream.

I cleared my throat again. "You know about how I was a suspect in my father's death? We talked about it." I pulled in a deep lungful of air and blurted, "I killed him. I murdered my father."

Ohmygod, I'd said it.

The world started spinning, and I clenched my fists, wishing it would stop.

Gently, Kam cupped my chin and forced me to look at him. He blinked. He tipped his head and blinked again. I waited for him to speak with my heart in my throat. When he didn't say anything, I added, "He was going to kill my brother. It was only a matter of time. . . ." Words flowed from my mouth then, all my darkest secrets and fears, the horror of those awful days and nights, as if the dam holding them back came crashing down and I simply couldn't stop them. "I was so scared. I was just watching him torture my brother almost every day. Joss was getting weaker and weaker. The beating was taking its toll. And the mental abuse, it was killing his soul." My gaze slid once again to the floor. "Maybe it was already too late? It seems I didn't save Joss after all. I thought all his mistakes had been because he didn't have a mother and a father to help him through his teens. Maybe it wasn't that."

"Where was your mother?" Kam asked, his voice barely above a whisper.

"We didn't know. I remember one night, maybe three years before my father died. We heard shouting and banging. The next morning, when we got up, Father told us she'd run off with another man. She was starting a new family and didn't want any part of us."

He cringed. "Damn, what a thing to say to your kid."

"That was one of the nicer things he said. We never saw her again."

"What about the police? Did you go to them for help or a teacher? A friend? A neighbor? Anyone?"

"The one time I told someone what was happening we were both beat. There was nobody I could trust. No one."

Studying me, he shook his head. "Abigail, I know you didn't kill your father. You weren't arrested. There was no trial."

"That's true. But I made it look like a suicide. I'd read books, true crime, thrillers. I learned how to fake a suicide, and that's what I did." I blinked as tears obscured my vision. After all this time wondering, I had to ask, "Does the fact that I took months to carefully plan out each step make me a murderer?"

"No. You planned it out because you were afraid of the consequences if you failed, but—"

A sob surged up my throat, and I swallowed it down. "I would have taken Joss and run away, but we had nowhere to go. And once he found us . . . He would have killed my brother first. He would have made me watch."

"Shit. He was that evil?"

"He was. He wasn't human." I sniffled. "But does that matter? Maybe it wouldn't to a judge? I might feel better if you talked to someone about it. The police. Or an attorney. A judge. Do you know someone? Someone you could trust to tell you the truth?"

"That's not necessary." Kam lifted my chin again, forced me to look at him. His eyes weren't hard. I didn't see any sign of contempt or judgment in them. "I hate what this has done to you. I had no idea."

"Please, Kam. I'm begging."

He sighed and added, "Yes, I know someone. He used to work for the county prosecutor's office. He'd be able to give me an objective viewpoint." My insides twisted. Was I really ready to face the truth? Yes? No. Yes. "But there is no real issue here." He kissed one of my hands, then stared at it, cradled in his. "This is important, Abigail. I want to help you, to free you from the chains of your past. Will you trust me? Me, not an attorney? Not the police? Not an ex-DA? Me?"

I couldn't hold back the sob that surged up my throat this time. I clapped my hands over my mouth.

He said, "I know you trust me. You've shown me again and again. This is no different. Abigail. Trust *me*. Not just with your body. But with your heart. With your soul. With your guilt and regret."

My heart exploded into a million pieces.

Tears came. Hard. Fast. I couldn't hold them back. After a few seconds I didn't bother trying. I let them fall. At last someone knew. My terrible secret was out. I couldn't take it back. *Oh God.*

Once the tears had eased, I slid my hands aside, using them to frame my face. "I want to believe you. . . ."

He gathered me into his arms and smoothed a hand down my back. "I hate what that bastard did to you. Hate it. And I'm pretty sure you haven't told me the worst of it."

That much was true. I dragged a thumb under my lashes. "Please call your friend. I'm done running. I want a future. I can't live in the past and have a future. It doesn't work."

"You're right, you can't." Easing back, he looked me in the eye. "I can call him. But all the answers you need are right here." He placed a hand on his chest and then on mine. "You don't need an attorney or a judge or a jury to tell you the truth. You already know it. Just like I do. If you were a murderer, you wouldn't feel guilt. You wouldn't feel empathy. You wouldn't feel anything. Please, Abigail. Listen."

He was asking me to trust him.

He was telling me to believe him.

I was listening, but could I hear him?

"Kam, he's dead. I did it. Maybe I don't belong in prison, but I don't deserve to be happy either."

He pulled me against him, enclosing me in a warm embrace again. "Somehow I am going to help you see the truth. If it takes me the rest of my life, I don't care. You're not a cold-blooded killer. You are a loving, giving woman who is willing to sacrifice everything for the people she loves. If anyone doesn't deserve to be happy, it's me. I don't deserve you. The way I've treated you . . . Oh God. I've been such a bastard. I have no right to ask this." Holding my hand, he lowered himself onto one knee. "Please, please, Abigail, take me. I submit to you now as I hand you my heart and ask if you'll be my wife. My lover. My partner. I am a better man, a complete man, because of you. I must have the chance to show you how much you mean to me."

I was stunned. "But I just told you—"

"You protected your brother. And that brave and terrifying act has haunted you every day since then. You were not arrested because you did nothing wrong. Let me help you leave the past behind you now. Let me be your present and future. I will help you heal from that hell. I will help you put all that pain behind you. And the fear. And the guilt. There's no reason to run anymore, Abigail Barnes. There never was."

"You . . . really believe that?" I asked.

"Of course. Because I know you."

He wanted *me*. He loved me?

Despite the terrible thing I had done.

Despite my brother and his girlfriend having stolen from him, and costing him millions of dollars.

Despite everything.

I was free?

To live? To love? To look forward, not back?

"I . . . I . . ."

"Abigail, stop. Stop it now!" Jumping to his feet again, Kam grabbed my face and looked me in the eye. His eyes were full of fire, anger, frustration . . . desperation. "Dammit, I didn't want to tell you this. I didn't want you to know, because I know it's going to hurt. But if I have to stand by and watch you punish yourself for a crime you didn't commit, I am going to go crazy. Do you hear me? It will destroy me."

Ohmygod.

His words echoed in my head.

If I have to stand by and watch you punish yourself.

Punish yourself.

That was what I'd been doing. I'd been punishing myself. All this time. Yes, that was what I'd been doing—telling myself I didn't deserve to be happy, to be free, to be loved.

I didn't have to do that?

But I'd killed my father. I'd planned it out.

Kam stood. "Abigail, you didn't kill your father. Someone else did."

"What?" My heart stopped. "Someone else? How could someone else have killed him? Who? And how would you know?"

Kam paced in front of me, back and forth, fingers raking over his shaved head. "I didn't want to tell you. I wasn't sure it would help." He stopped and gazed down at me. "But seeing you like this . . . It has to be better than letting you believe you did it."

My mind was spinning. Round and round, thoughts whipping and whirling, too fast to grasp. "Who? How?"

He knelt again, this time on both knees. "I got a message. On the way here. It was from Stephanie's attorney. Your brother confessed. To several crimes. Your father's murder was only one of them."

My brother? He killed my father?

Could it be true?

"My brother?" I echoed. "How? He was just a boy."

"I don't have all the details. But I was told his statement is completely believable. And he was able to back it up with some kind of evidence."

"Maybe he's confessing to protect me?" I reasoned, trying to sort things out. "What evidence could he have?" Joss had been so young at the time. Could a boy his age be capable of killing? And if he had done such a thing, could he have hidden his guilt from everyone all this time?

No. He couldn't.

Unless . . .

Maybe?

Yes. He could if he was . . . if he was the kind of man I hadn't wanted to believe he might be. A man like our father. A man who felt no guilt.

Suddenly images flashed through my mind, and all the pieces fell into place. I'd been blind to the truth. I had blinded myself.

I clapped my hands over my mouth again. "Ohmygod," I said through my splayed fingers. "I didn't want to believe he . . . I wanted him to change, to become the man I thought he could be. But I was just fooling myself, wasn't I?"

"You love him." Kam stood, placed his hands on my shoulders. It was a good thing he did that. I wasn't feeling very sturdy. His touch steadied me, gave me strength. "When you love someone, you want to believe the best."

"Yes, you do, you want to believe the best. But if you truly love someone, you can see them for what they are, not what you want them to be. No matter how painful it is. My brother is a liar, a thief, an addict, and . . . a murderer. How many other crimes has he confessed to, Kam?"

"I don't know. It doesn't matter. All that matters is you are innocent. You're free."

"Free?" I whispered, barely able to comprehend it.

Free of regret?

Of fear?

Of guilt?

I looked into Kam's eyes.

Happiness was right here, within my reach. All I had to do was accept it. All I had to do was find the courage to say yes.

I could do that!

Who would have ever imagined that sorrow and blackmail would lead to this?

It was a miracle. For both of us.

Out of the ashes of our tragic pasts had bloomed a perfect love, a love that would heal us and make us whole again. And all I had to do was say one word and it was ours. A lifetime of love. A lifetime of giving. And a lifetime of surrender. "Yes, Kameron Maldonado," I said, with my heart in my throat. "I will marry you."

Turn the page
for a sizzling preview
of Tawny Taylor's

DARKEST ECSTASY

An Aphrodisia trade paperback
on sale September 2014.

He had his quarry.

There. That one. The lush blonde in the black dress. She was perfect. Just the right combination of sweet temptation and seductive siren. Long legs. Full tits that made his mouth water. A hundred carnal promises glittering in her eyes.

Another man stepped up to her and set a hand on her shoulder. Her gaze flicked to the man, then back to Talen. Her lips curled in a sultry half smile.

His cock hardened. *Let the games begin.* Energized by the challenge, he waved the waitress over.

"A bottle of champagne. To that woman. In the black dress." Then he leaned back in his seat and waited, watching her every move as the bottle was delivered and as the waitress told her who had purchased it.

She smiled in his direction, then excused herself from the man who had thought he'd be fucking her tonight. Her glass in one hand, the bottle in the other, she crossed the crowded bar, collecting stares from admiring men and glares from women along the way. She moved with the smooth fluidity of a dancer.

Her hips swayed seductively. Her shoulders were back, her full breasts pushed out.

Stunning.

"Hello," she said, smiling down at him as she approached his table. "Thank you for the champagne." She set the bottle on his table. "I couldn't possibly drink this whole thing by myself, so I thought I'd come over and share some with you."

"Thanks. Please, sit." Pushing his full glass aside, he motioned to the waitress. "May I have an empty champagne glass, please?" he asked her.

"Sure. Can I get you anything else?"

Talen looked at his new companion. She shook her head. "No, thank you."

"I'll be right back."

He turned his attention back to Blondie.

"I'm Angela."

"Angela." He extended a hand, and she placed hers in it. Her grip was neither too tight nor too loose. "Tage Garner."

"It's good to meet you, Tage Garner. Thank you again for the champagne. It's delicious."

"I'm glad you're enjoying it." Lips. She had very nice lips. He could imagine them circling his cock while he fucked her mouth.

Peering over the rim of her glass, she sipped. "Have you been to this club before?"

"No. I just joined."

"You'll love it. I've been a member for about a year. I'm here at least twice a week."

"Dom or submissive?"

"Oh, submissive. Most definitely."

He felt himself smiling. "I was hoping you would say that."

"Were you?" She tipped her head. "You know, I haven't had very much of this champagne yet, only a few sips. We could take this party somewhere private if you like."

That sounded like a great idea.

When the waitress stepped up, he accepted the glass and the bill. After signing for it, he escorted his quarry to his newly leased private suite upstairs. As they climbed the steps, he admired her fine ass as it swayed back and forth in front of him. He couldn't wait to get his hands on it. On the rest of her, too.

Upstairs, she allowed him to steer her toward his suite with a hand on the small of her back. Beneath his fingertips, he felt her muscles flex as she responded to his touch.

This was going to be fun.

Inside, she walked straight to the center of the room, turned so her back was to him, reached around, and dragged the zipper of her dress down, exposing a deep vee of smooth skin.

"Are you sure you haven't had anything else to drink?" he asked. He hadn't noticed any signs of intoxication, but he wasn't so lost in need yet that he'd be willing to ignore the first rule of D/s. Safe. Sane. Consensual.

"Nothing else. Just a few sips of champagne." She pulled the garment down to her waist. She wasn't wearing a bra.

"Limits?"

"None." The dress slid to the floor. She wasn't wearing panties either.

His cock twitched at the sight of her beautiful body. "None?"

Slowly, she turned to face him. Her lips were curved into a semi-smile once again. Her eyes were downcast, as a submissive's eyes should be. "I have been a submissive for a long time, trained by some of the most demanding, sadistic doms around. I can handle *anything*."

His balls tightened.

He had found his dream sub. But was she wife material?

To hell with that. I just want to fuck her.

Smiling to himself, he decided he would put her to the test.

He knew exactly how he wanted to test her first. He unzipped his pants.

Her little pink tongue darted out, swiped across her lower lip. Yes, that was exactly what he was thinking. He stepped up to her, close enough to reach, grabbed a handful of silky blond hair, and said, "Suck my cock. Hard."

"Yes, master," she murmured, then eagerly opened her mouth for him.

"Oh damn," he growled as he rammed his cock deep into her mouth, then withdrew, only to thrust deep again. Over and over. She took him easily, greedily. Her little tongue cushioned the bottom of his rod as he glided in and out. The head of his cock hit the back of her throat, but she didn't gag, she didn't pull away. No, she opened to him, taking him to the hilt, slurping and sucking until he was seeing stars and on the verge of coming.

Mere seconds before losing control, he jerked out of her mouth. There was so much more to do yet, pleasures to explore, limits to test. He couldn't let it end so soon.

"You've been well trained," he said as he tucked his still-erect cock back inside his pants and zipped up.

She placed her hands at her sides and kept her eyes downturned. "Thank you, master. It's my pleasure to serve you."

"Hmmm." His body thrummed as possibilities whirled around in his head. A submissive with no limits could be rather useful to him. His gaze meandered around the room. Having just leased the room, he hadn't set up some of the bigger pieces yet. The St. Andrew's cross was waiting to be assembled. Same with the large table he liked to keep in the center of the room. For now, he would have to make do with the bench. There was plenty of fun to be had with that.

He positioned her as he wanted, kneeling, legs spread, chest and stomach resting on the upper support. Ah, perfect. Now he had full access to that ass he'd admired earlier. "Safe word?" he asked as he cuffed her wrists and ankles in place.

"Red is fine."

"Red, it is." He stepped back to admire the view. How he wanted to bury his rod deep inside her. She was clean shaven everywhere. Her folds glistened with her juices. She was wet. Wet and ready. He went to his storage cabinet and gathered a few things—dildo, condoms, lube. He wasn't in the mood for discipline. Just fucking. Lots of fucking. His eye went to her puckered anus.

There. He would take her there.

"Anal?" he asked.

"Love it."

His whole body tightened. Could this woman be more perfect for him?

He unwrapped a condom and rolled it onto the dildo. Then, without warning, he shoved it into her cunt.

She shuddered with pleasure. "Thank you, master," she whispered, hips rocking forward to take the toy deeper. It plunged to the entry of her womb. He left it there and switched it on. "Ohhhhhh," she mumbled. "Thank you."

Damn that was a pretty sight. Once again he stepped back to admire her. Her legs were long and lean, her stomach flat, breasts full and natural, ass round and firm. Her smooth skin was starting to shimmer with sweat as the toy buried in her pussy made her insides burn for him.

He was burning for her, too.

Working quickly, he rolled on a rubber. Then he squirted out some lube onto his fingers to test her anus.

Two fingers in. Oh, she was tight but willing, giving just enough resistance. As he plunged his fingers deeper, the ring of muscles tightened around them. Damn.

He couldn't wait.

At his withdrawal, she whimpered. The sound sent a wave of heat blazing through him. It was sweetly seductive. He had to hear it again.

He smoothed some more lube around her anus. Slowly. He entered her slowly, inch by inch. Oh, it was hell. And heaven. Both. As he drove deeper, his body tensed more. By the time his stomach was resting against the pillow of her ass cheeks, he was sure his hair was singed, he was so hot. "Damn."

Her muscles tightened, and a pulse of carnal heat blasted through his center. Just as slowly, he withdrew, letting her body caress him as he pulled out. She was perfect. Completely and utterly perfect. This once wouldn't be enough. He had to have her again. In the ass. In the pussy. In the mouth. Anywhere and everywhere.

"Meet me again," he said. To his own ears, he sounded breathless.

"When?"

"Soon." The tip of his cock still remained inside. This time, he thrust quickly inside, driving deep.

She cried out. "Yes!"

"Yes," he echoed as he jerked back to thrust deep. "Yes," he repeated as he buried himself in her ass. "Damn. Damn."

"Master," she said. She whimpered. The sound nearly sent him over the edge. "Please. May I come? Please."

"Not yet." He pounded into her with no mercy, and she took him, rocking back to meet his forward thrusts. His fingers dug into her hips. The soft flesh of her ass rippled with each impact. The sound of skin striking skin and husky, fast breathing was like a symphony. This was fucking at its finest. This was what he couldn't live without, would not live without. Faster, he fucked her. Harder. Each stroke amped up his temperature higher, raised his heart rate. He was spiking a fever, hot and tight everywhere, balls ready to explode.

Her cry as she lost control echoed through the room and sent him careening over the edge. His orgasm blasted through his body like a nuclear explosion. His voice joined hers as he shouted in ecstasy, pounded away the last pulse of carnal pleasure. When he was spent, he withdrew, removed the condom and the toy from her pussy.

"Thank you, master." Her whole body trembled, he noticed, as he unbuckled her wrist and ankle cuffs. Once he had her completely free of the bindings, he helped her turn around and sit. For the first time since they'd entered the room, she lifted her eyes to his and smiled. "I look forward to serving you again soon?" she asked.

"Yes, very soon." And often, he hoped.